USA Today, and *Wall Street Journal* bestselling author, Nina Levine, lives in Brisbane, Australia, and is the author of more than thirty romantic suspense and contemporary romance novels, including the international bestselling Escape With a Billionaire and Storm MC series.

CONNECT ONLINE

ninalevineromance.com

authorninalevine

AuthorNinaLevine

ISBN 978-1-923013-18-6

Cover Design by Nina Levine using artwork from Creative Fabrica

Proofreading provided by Read by Rose

YOURS
UNTIL FOREVER

USA TODAY BESTSELLING AUTHOR
NINA LEVINE

Dear Reader,

I love Gage & Amelia like no other. I hope you do too!

Nina
Levine

xx

To the girlies who want their
billionaires obsessed & filthy.
We see you.
Gage Black sees you.
We're all in trouble.

PLAYLIST

"Stupid Boy" by Keith Urban

"Ordinary" by Alex Warren

"My Heart is Open" by Keith Urban

"Beneath Your Beautiful" by Labrinth, Emeli Sande

"Leave Her Wild" by Tyler Rich

"Never Stop" by SafetySuit

"Stargazing" by Myles Smith

"Landslide" by The Chicks

"When Something Is Wrong With My Baby" by Jimmy
Barnes

"Can't Teach That" by The Roads Below

"King Of My Heart" by Taylor Swift

"Until My Heart Stops Beating" by Sam Riggs

"Obsessed" by Sam Riggs

"When You're Down" by Sam Riggs

"Call It What You Want" by Taylor Swift

"Naked" by Jake Scott

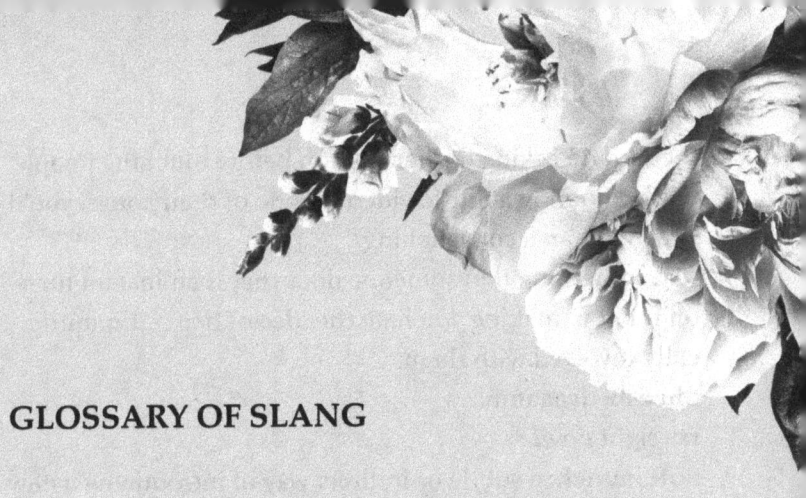

GLOSSARY OF SLANG

BMS: broke my scale i.e. in reference to someone's attractiveness where on a scale of 1-10, they broke the scale, and their attractiveness is off the charts.

BSE: Big Suit Energy

MFW: my face when, used to indicate someone's reaction in a scenario.

TFW: that feeling when, references a particular feeling in a specific situation.

It's giving: used to reference something giving off a certain vibe.

Main character energy: you're acting as if you're the star of your own show. Used in a positive light.

Unalive: used as an alternative for kill.

Credit card slam: used in the same context as "shut up and take my money".

Say sike rn: translates to "please tell me you're joking right now".

We stan a ___ queen/king: it means you're a fan of that person and support them i.e. if a certain singer was focused on asking for permission before touching people while shooting a music video for one of their songs, you'd say, "We stan a consent king."

Ick: something that someone does that is an instant turn-off for you, making you hate the idea of being romantically involved with them.

Sheesh: daaaamn!

rn: right now.

Soft launch: a subtle or indirect way of introducing a new relationship to social media

Hard launch: a sudden and public announcement of a relationship

Low key: used to express something in a subtle way, often to avoid being overly enthusiastic

Rizz: someone's ability to attract others, especially in romantic or sexual context

Snack: someone attractive

Meal: someone who looks good enough to eat

Canon event: significant event that shapes a person's life or who they are

Do it for the plot: said to encourage oneself to take a chance on something ie even if it doesn't work out, I'll do it for the plot

Left no crumbs: you did something perfectly

Just hit the TL: just hit the timeline; it's blowing up

Unwell: Not sick. Just overwhelmed by vibes. Emotionally devastated in the most delicious way.

CHAPTER 1

AMELIA

SOME DAYS you're fighting to keep your composure while your ex plays mind games with you, and other days you're hiding in a hotel bathroom at Nashville's wedding of the year, praying no one saw the period stain on your dress. Today, I'm doing both.

And because my life is a complete mess right now, I don't have a tampon.

"Shit," I mutter as I give up on searching in my purse while also contemplating walking out of here with a stained dress. I should have worn the black dress I'd planned on rather than allowing my mother to get inside my head, *again*, and convince me pale pink was more appropriate.

I'm in the middle of spiraling into a full-blown round of *I Should Have* when my phone buzzes with a text from my brother.

TIM:

How's the wedding, sis? Have you slept
with anyone yet? It's a wedding. You're
legally allowed.

I relish the distraction from Periodgate and tap out a
reply.

ME:

It was a beautiful wedding. Fun and
down-to-earth. Not a single pretentious
toast. James's friends would have had a
coronary. I'm ignoring the sex
interrogation.

COLIN:

Is Sarah having a great time?

ME:

She hasn't stopped smiling. I'm really
glad I brought her.

COLIN:

Why haven't we seen any photos? I
imagine Mom is hanging for one of you in
that pink dress.

ME:

I'm about to send her a photo of the
massive period stain on said pink dress.

TIM:

OH MY GOD. I need this photo for the
group chat.

ME:

I am never taking her advice again.

COLIN:

Promise?

I sigh. This is a recurring conversation with my brothers. Me trying to extricate myself from my mother's expectations; them encouraging me to finally do it.

ME:

> Change of subject before I set my dress on fire.

TIM:

> No pics of Period Barbie. Got it. Send one of the bride. She's hot as fuck.

God, I love my brother.

While Colin can be too laser-focused on trying to help me fix problems and make changes to my life, Tim always knows how to lighten the mood and make me smile.

I send them a photo of Sarah grinning like a maniac at the reception.

TIM:

> Is that the bride photobombing in the background? ZOOM IN. ENHANCE. I need to know if this woman is worth the emotional investment I've already made in this wedding I wasn't invited to.

I grin.

ME:

> I love you, big brother, but not enough to send a photo of Madeline. Besides, I haven't taken any of her. She deserves privacy.

ME:

> And now I must go and figure out how to walk through a ballroom with no one seeing the back of my dress.

TIM:

> Ninja moves along all the walls. It's a pity you didn't choose the black dress to do those ninja moves in. No one would see you.

ME:

> Very funny. Also, if I'd worn the black dress, Periodgate wouldn't be as bad.

TIM:

> Is James dead after this? Please tell me this ends in a funeral.

I release another sigh.

I should have been watching my daughter Sarah bounce with excitement today as her best friend Luna got ready to be a flower girl in her uncle's wedding. For months, Sarah has been thrilled about us flying to Nashville with Luna and her father to see country superstar Madeline Montana (who she idolizes) marry Luna's uncle. After a year of watching my little girl struggle through my divorce, her joy over this wedding meant everything to me. But yesterday, my ex-husband shattered those plans when he failed to bring Sarah home in time for our flight to Nashville. This meant we flew here today to make the wedding, but she missed out on spending yesterday and this morning with her bestie.

Colin and Tim are convinced James orchestrated this on purpose as a way of controlling me and Sarah in much the same way he's been trying to for years now. When he brought her home, he made out like his lateness was unavoidable and that he'd arrange a private flight for the three of us to bring Sarah to the wedding. My brothers are sure he's doing everything he can to reunite with me, but I'm not convinced. I just think he craves control. He got a rude shock when I refused his private plane and instead allowed Luna's father to arrange his jet for us.

ME:

He's the father of my daughter, Tim. You know I won't do anything to ruin her relationship with him.

ME:

I have to go deal with my dress. I'll send you guys more pics later xx

I slide my phone into my purse and steel myself. Of all things to happen today. Period accidents haven't been an issue since high school, yet here I am. Though I shouldn't be surprised—it's perfectly on-brand for the chaos my life has become over the past year. Just one more item on the ever-growing list of disasters.

I slip out of the bathroom without encountering anyone and am halfway along the corridor that leads into the hotel ballroom where the reception is taking place when I spot Luna's father striding toward the corridor.

Seriously.

Why must *he* be the person I run into now?

Gage Black, the man who makes billionaire look dangerous instead of privileged, who sees everything whether you want him to or not, and who's been silently assessing me with those dark eyes since the day we met a year ago.

That was the same day I met his ex-wife, Shayla, who slowly became my friend, and who has shared stories of their relationship that make me want as little to do with him as possible. Though a year of playground pickups, sleepover parties, and birthday parties has shown me another side of him too. The father who knows every one of Luna's elaborate stories about her stuffed animals by heart, who never misses a single one of her "very important" art shows in their living room. The man who remembered, without being reminded, that Sarah is allergic to strawberries and had a second birthday cake without strawberries made for Luna's party so her best friend wasn't left out of the celebration. But those glimpses of warmth make his usual intensity jarring, like a sudden key change in the middle of a familiar song.

He's wearing one of his trademark black suits that probably cost more than most people's monthly rent. His eyes lock onto mine with that penetrating stare that makes me feel exposed, certain he's noting my weaknesses. Which, given what I know about him as the head of a global intelligence firm, he probably is.

I paste on my perfect society smile, the one my mother spent years helping me perfect, and try to sidle past him while keeping my back to the wall. "Beautiful wedding, wasn't it?"

He stops walking. "Interesting technique you've got there." His voice holds a note of amusement that makes my cheeks heat. "Is this some new kind of walking meditation?"

"I'm just"—I gesture vaguely with one hand while pressing myself closer to the wall—"appreciating the wallpaper."

One dark eyebrow lifts. "The wallpaper."

"Mm-hmm." I'm not even sure there is wallpaper. For all I know, the wall's painted. "It's very . . . architectural."

"Right." He takes a step closer, and I automatically try to retreat, only to remember I'm already against the wall. "You know, in my line of work, when someone's acting this suspicious, it usually means they're hiding something."

I resist the urge to touch my hair, a nervous tell I've been trying to break for years. "I'm not hiding anything. I'm simply examining the hotel's design choices. For future reference."

"Future reference," he repeats, in that maddeningly calm way of his.

"Yes. I might . . ." I frantically search for a plausible reason. ". . . need to upgrade my studio's soundproofing."

His lips twitch. "With wallpaper."

"It's very thick wallpaper," I say with all the dignity I can muster while plastered against a wall.

He takes another step closer, and I catch a whiff of his cologne, something expensive and masculine that I try to tell myself I absolutely do not like. "Sarah seemed to have fun today, despite the late arrival."

The mention of Sarah momentarily distracts me from Operation Wall Fusion. "She did. Thank you for helping arrange the last-minute flight changes."

"Luna would have been devastated if Sarah missed it entirely." His eyes do that thing where they seem to see straight through me. "Though I'm curious about the last-minute change." His tone is casual, but his eyes miss nothing. "Seems unlike you to alter plans where Luna and Sarah are concerned."

I lift my chin slightly. "Sometimes co-parenting involves schedule adjustments."

"True," he agrees, and the quietly assessing look on his face makes me wonder if he's filing this information away in that mental catalog I'm sure he keeps of everyone's behavior.

"I should really . . ." I try to slide sideways, but he doesn't move.

"You should really what?"

"Go check on Sarah."

"Sarah's currently teaching Luna and three other kids how to do the Macarena. They're fine."

Of course, he knows exactly where our daughters are. He probably has the room mapped out with threat assessments and escape routes. It's what he does, keeps tabs on everyone and everything. Luna once told Sarah that her daddy has "special codes" for every situation, from Starbucks runs to playground visits. Every outing has its own security protocol, complete with check-in requirements and pre-approved safe zones. The man treats a trip to Central Park like it's a military operation, though Luna's found ways to turn her father's security obsession into her own private game.

"Well, then I should . . ." I take a step, trying to keep my back against the wall.

His eyes narrow slightly. "Amelia."

"Yes?"

"Why are you walking like you're in a heist movie?"

"I'm not," I start to protest, then catch his expression. He's not buying any of it, and I'm running out of wall. I close my eyes briefly and whisper, "I had an accident."

"What kind of accident?" His voice sharpens with concern.

"A wardrobe malfunction. Of the feminine variety." My face burns. "On my dress. My pink dress. That my mother insisted I wear instead of the perfectly good black one I had planned."

Understanding dawns in his eyes, followed by something that looks suspiciously like a suppressed smile.

"It's not funny," I hiss.

"I didn't say anything."

"You were thinking it very loudly."

Now he's definitely fighting a smile. "What do you need?"

"To disappear into the void?" I suggest hopefully.

"Second choice?"

I bite my lip, then decide things literally cannot get more mortifying. "I need someone to go to my room and get my backup dress. And . . . other necessities."

"Other necessities?"

The human body is seventy percent water, but I'm pretty sure mine is currently seventy percent embarrassment. "You know. Some new . . ." I wave my hands in what I hope translates to "underwear" but probably looks more like I'm conducting an invisible orchestra while having a nervous breakdown.

His eyebrows arch. "Are you trying to mime the word 'underwear' in charades right now?"

"Oh my god." I press my hands to my face. "Yes. Fine. I need new underwear."

"Key card?"

I peek through my fingers. "What?"

"To your room," he says patiently. "I'll need your key card."

I slowly lower my hands. "You're going to help me?"

"Unless you'd prefer to continue your wallpaper appreciation session."

I fumble in my purse for the key card, then realize something else. "I also need . . . um. Someone to go to a store to buy supplies."

I swear his lips twitch right before he says, "I'm fascinated to see the charade for this."

"You could at least pretend this isn't the highlight of your day," I mutter, handing him my key card.

Amusement is clear in his eyes as he takes the card. "Where will I find the dress?"

"It's in the garment bag in the closet. And the underwear is in my suitcase."

"Any specific preferences for the store run?"

This is definitely what hell feels like. "Just regular. Not super." I close my eyes briefly. "And if you smirk right now, I swear I'll tell Luna what really happened to Mr. Bunny's bow tie."

A ghost of a smile touches his lips. "Consider it handled. Wait here."

"Where else would I go?" I grumble.

"Fair point. Try not to get into any other accidents while I'm gone."

"You're enjoying this far too much."

"I have no idea what you're talking about." But his eyes are definitely laughing as he turns and strides away, leaving me to contemplate how exactly this became my life.

I press my forehead against the wall. "I should have worn the black dress."

My phone buzzes in my purse.

TIM:

How's the ninja mission going?

ME:

It got worse. Gage Black is now buying me tampons.

TIM:

I don't know what to do with that information.

ME:

Join the club.

CHAPTER 2
GAGE

AMELIA SINCLAIR MAY BE the most quietly chaotic woman I've ever met and that's not something I've picked up on until this weekend. It's not what she presents to the world, but surveying her hotel suite is giving me a glimpse of her that I've not been treated to before. One that completely contradicts everything I thought I knew about her.

Clothes are strewn across the bed, the floor, and over the sofa. Makeup and various beauty bottles clutter the bathroom vanity. Three paperbacks are stacked on the nightstand while two lie on the bed in between the clothes. Coffee-stained sheet music is spread across the floor at the foot of the bed with a pencil placed on top like she was working before she left the room.

It's an assault to my senses. And to my professional pride.

How the fuck someone can function in a mess like this is beyond me. But what really intrigues me is how I missed this side of her entirely.

My first impression of Amelia a year ago was that she had her shit handled. She was always on time for playdates, school drop off, birthday parties, and sleepovers. Her appearance was always immaculate. Not a hair out of place or a wrinkle in her clothes. She never appeared flustered, confused, unsure. And she always approached me with quiet confidence, keeping our interactions politely distant, sometimes bordering on cold. Nothing like the woman who just bared herself to me outside that bathroom. Flailing. Uncertain. *Real.*

I did my due diligence on Amelia when Luna became friends with Sarah. The facts were all there: Twenty-eight. Successful music composer. Divorced James Kensington, lawyer, a year ago. Irreconcilable differences. Comes from old money. Banker father. Socialite mother. Yale education. One child.

But facts don't tell the whole story. And while reading people is my expertise—hell, my reputation depends on it—Amelia's managed to control exactly what I see of her, and for the first time in years, I'm questioning my read on someone. Because, fuck, I would never have imagined the perfectly composed woman I know would exist in this kind of disorder.

Small cracks have started revealing themselves over the last month. Late arrivals for sleepovers. Messy buns and longer bangs than normal. A forgotten playdate last week. Nothing major, but all out of character for Amelia. Signs I should have picked up on sooner.

I locate the black dress in the closet and retrieve underwear from her suitcase, pausing at the unexpectedly large collection of delicate lace and silk for what's supposed to be a one-night trip. Like everything else I'm discovering about Amelia Sinclair today, her lingerie drawer apparently has hidden depths. I try to push that thought aside while cataloging more details that don't align with the Amelia I thought I knew.

A worn copy of "The Art of War" mixed in with romance novels, sticky tabs of various colors marking pages like she's dissecting them for a thesis. Post-it notes on various surfaces around the room, the scribbled messages indecipherable to me. Her laptop open on the bathroom counter amid scattered makeup products, music production software visible on the screen with expensive headphones plugged in like she'd been desperately trying to compose right up until she had to get ready for the wedding.

Being in her private space sends my mind places it definitely shouldn't go. Especially not about a woman who's made it clear she wants nothing to do with me. And who's also the mother of my daughter's best friend.

The quick store run gives me time to process what I've learned. Every detail I've noticed is a piece of a puzzle I've been trying to solve.

Amelia has held my attention without realizing it since the very first day we met. It was during last year's Spring Music Enrichment Week at Luna's school, the day that Amelia was invited as a guest musician to take part in a Q & A with the children and then do a short performance. I was captivated by the way she drew the kids in with her quiet intensity and passion. She started off shyly, but it wasn't long before she commanded the room, and when she played? Fuck. Her talent is incredible. That was the day Luna fell in love with Amelia and begged to learn an instrument because she wanted to be like Sarah's mom who "plays music like magic."

Even her brilliance is something she hides. The latest hit movie she scored wasn't just successful, but rather it started a trend for how action scenes are scored in new films. The critics called it revolutionary, "fusing volatility and precision like no one before." But when one of the other school parents mentioned it to her at pickup last week, Amelia brushed it off and redirected the conversation to the class's art project like it was nothing. I've seen her do that countless times at school events and birthday parties. She has a way of making herself invisible even while standing directly in front of you. It's a skill that would be admirable in my line of work, but I've found it damn frustrating while trying to figure her out.

Back at the hotel, I find her in the ladies' bathroom, leaning against the counter, engrossed in reading something on her phone. Her eyes lift to mine, and for a moment, there's no mask. Just softness. Like I've caught her mid-thought, walls lowered, and all I see is quiet hope and exhaustion tangled together. It's the kind of unguarded expression that makes me want to lock the door behind us and ask every question I've been swallowing down since the day I met her.

"Here." I hand her the bags, watching as relief replaces the tension in her shoulders. "I hope my selection at the store is suitable."

She slows for a moment, like she's trying to reconcile this gesture with whatever preconceptions she has about me. Because, if there's one thing I *am* certain of, she does have an opinion of me, and it isn't favorable. Not with the way she does her best to avoid me. "Thank you."

I could leave, give her space to change in private. Instead, I find myself resting my ass against the bathroom counter next to her, crossing my arms and one foot over the other, and saying, "I'll wait and make sure you have everything you need."

"You don't have to—"

"I know." I pause before adding, "I'd hate for you to be without something crucial that would force you back to wallpaper research."

She stares at me, her big blue eyes drawing me in like they were made to do that, making me wonder if I could drag myself from them even if I wanted to. Finally, she blinks, quietly says, "I think I've done enough architectural research for one day," then moves toward the stall.

When she emerges in the black dress, the transformation is striking. Not just in the way the dress fits her, though that certainly commands attention, but in how she carries herself, like she's reclaimed her armor.

"Much better," she says softly, more to herself than me as she eyes herself in the mirror.

I maintain my position against the counter, watching as she gathers her composure along with her things. "The black dress was always the right choice." Because it was *her* choice.

Her eyes meet mine, gratitude softening them, and fuck if I wouldn't trade anything for another look like that.

She smooths her hands down her dress. "Thank you. For everything." A smile threatens. "Though you really didn't need to buy me multiple brands of tampons and pads." Now, she allows the smile to settle in place. "It tells me you'll be great when Luna's older and needs her father's help surviving period hell."

"I seriously doubt that shopping for supplies for you is enough training for a teenage daughter's period hell."

She rolls her eyes but there's amusement there too. "Only you would use the word 'training' when it comes to raising children."

We're interrupted when the bathroom door is pushed in and two wedding guests enter, sisters who are friends of my parents, both in their sixties.

The older sister comes to a halt as she assesses Amelia and me. Then, with an arrowed brow, she greets me, judgement threading its way through every letter of my name.

She thinks I've fucked Amelia in here.

It's a fair assessment based on some of the shit I got up to in my early twenties that became gossip fodder in Manhattan. A Black son not following in his father's or older brothers' respectable footsteps was a hot talking point that my parents were never happy about, but not one I ever cared to change. Watching buttoned-up socialites cast disapproving looks my way always amused me. Particularly since I knew what some of the husbands in New York were getting up to behind their wives' backs.

However, the way Amelia straightens lets me know she's not finding this as amusing as I am, so I take charge of the situation to put things right.

"Deborah." I push off the counter and move toward her. "This isn't what it looks like. Amelia had a dress malfunction and required my help."

Her expression tells me she's not buying a word of what I said. "I can imagine."

"I can see you don't believe me, but—"

"I got my period," Amelia blurts. "And it . . . well, my dress was ruined." She holds the garment bag up. "Gage came to my rescue and brought me a new dress."

Compassion immediately fills Deborah's face. "Oh, dear, we've all been there." She shakes her head. "Periods were the bane of my existence, and as I got older, they only got worse. Actually, they were horrendous, often flooding my underwear and staining my outfits."

"Right," I say, glancing at Amelia. "I'll leave you to it."

Her eyes crinkle with enjoyment. "What? You don't want to stay and further your period training?"

It's on the tip of my tongue to tell her I'd happily further my period training if it was just the two of us here, but I don't want to utter those words in front of one of the biggest gossips in this city. "I've got years before I'll need that training."

The last thing I see before I leave the bathroom is a smile gracing Amelia's face. It's warm and genuine, and it leaves me wondering just how many layers she's hiding behind that carefully constructed facade.

CHAPTER 3
GAGE

I RETURN to the family table after leaving Amelia and making sure Luna and Sarah are still safe on the dance floor. Ethan, my youngest brother who just got married, sits next to his wife who's five months pregnant, his hand resting possessively on her thigh while she talks excitedly with our mother about their upcoming honeymoon.

I take the seat next to him and lean in to say quietly, "Mom hates that you guys are going away for a month. I think she had plans to help Madeline decorate the nursery."

Ethan turns to me, grinning. "I've no doubt she'll let herself into our condo and decorate without Maddie."

"You gave her a key?"

He shakes his head. "Fuck no. My *wife* gave her a key."

Our brother, Hayden, overhears. "From what I've heard, they're besties now."

"That's pretty accurate," Ethan agrees.

I arch a brow at Hayden. "Besties? Since when do you speak in slang?"

He reaches for his scotch, and before taking a sip, says, "Since I've had to listen to Liv go on and on about it at work."

Olivia is one of our other sisters-in-law. Callan's wife. She was our neighbor growing up, our lives all intertwined long before she married our brother last year. Liv's a lawyer and works for Hayden at his law firm.

"Olivia and Madeline are close?" I ask. This is information I would usually know. However, my custody problems with my ex-wife have been taking up a lot of my attention the last few months and I've lost track of some family dynamics.

Olivia hears her name and joins our conversation, "What?"

Ethan looks at her. "Gage was asking if you and Maddie are close."

She smiles. "Oh, us girls are all close. Though your mother might be winning the race for Maddie's favorite family member."

"That's because Mom's already taking over the nursery planning and Madeline loves all her ideas," Callan comments from across the table, drawing everyone at the table into the conversation now.

"I'm not planning anything," Mom protests, but her eyes light up at the mere mention of it. "I simply showed Madeline a few Pinterest boards. And some paint samples. And possibly called my interior designer—"

"Mom." Ethan's voice carries that mix of affection and exasperation I've heard him use with her since Madeline joined our family and won our mother's heart. "We talked about this."

"What your son means," Madeline cuts in, her hand

resting on her bump, her smile directed at her husband before she glances at Mom, "is that we'd love your input when we get home."

"A month," Mom sighs dramatically. "What could possibly take a month?" This is the frustration of a woman who only had sons. She now has three daughters-in-law and is more than making up for not having had girls to dote on until now.

"Well," Callan drawls, "when two people love each other very much—"

"Don't you dare finish that sentence," Olivia warns, but there's a smile in her eyes.

"I was going to say that they need time to see Europe," Callan protests as he places his arm across the back of her chair and grins at her.

Olivia rolls her eyes but angles herself closer to him so she can brush her lips across his.

"Speaking of vacations," Bradford, my eldest brother, cuts in smoothly, "where are you two starting your honeymoon?"

"Paris," Madeline answers, but Ethan shakes his head.

"No," he says, smiling at his wife's confusion. "I've got a surprise planned in London first."

"Another camera shop?" Kristen, Bradford's wife, teases, referencing the time he dragged us all on a shopping expedition that was meant to be a quick stop before lunch on one of our family weekends away.

"That was one time—"

"Two hours, baby brother," I remind him. "Luna almost finished an entire coloring book while you drooled over vintage lenses."

"It was a rare find." He shrugs but the grin on his face says he regrets nothing.

"Everything's a rare find with you," Callan points out. "Remember when he convinced Maddie that vintage guitar he found was 'investment shopping'?"

"Oh, like you're any better?" Olivia challenges. "Mr. I-need-another-watch-because-this-one-only-tells-time-in-three-zones."

The conversation shifts into my family good-naturedly teasing each other and I find myself watching them rather than fully listening. Bradford and Kristen with their subtle touches and shared looks. Callan and Olivia sharing a connection that is twenty-plus years deep. Ethan and Madeline, still in their wedding-day glow but so in tune with each other.

While I'm taking it all in, a familiar feeling surfaces. The one I do my best to ignore. The one I've been outrunning for a long time.

For years, I've told myself I don't want this. That I don't need it. That Shayla and I gave it our best shot, and I'm better off focusing on Luna, on work, on anything but the wreckage I left behind.

But watching my brothers now, happy and settled, it's harder to ignore the thoughts creeping in. The ones that whisper late at night when Luna's asleep and everything's too quiet. The ones that ask if maybe I do want this. If maybe I always have.

Today, though, the feeling is different. It's the hollowness that comes from the realization I've never really had any of this. Not the way they do. Shayla and I burned too fast. The honeymoon period barely had time to settle before we were preparing for a baby, trading late nights out for sleepless nights in. And somewhere in the middle of all that, she changed. Or I did. Or maybe we both did, and neither of us knew how to fix it.

I shift in my chair and scrub a hand over my jaw, forcing the thought away. It's done. No changing it now.

Still, sitting here, watching my brothers build the kind of lives I thought I didn't need, I can't help but wonder if maybe I've been lying to myself. And worse, if Luna's missing out because of it.

Movement catches my eye and my attention shifts. Amelia glides through the ballroom toward the exit in that black dress, breathtakingly beautiful, and for a moment, my mind goes completely blank. The fabric moves with her like it was created for this purpose, emphasizing curves she usually keeps concealed under casual jeans and T-shirts. Her long dark hair falls in waves past her shoulders and her pale skin is a striking contrast against the dress.

She walks with grace, head high, but there's a slight uncertainty in the way she smooths down her dress.

"Interesting," Hayden murmurs beside me.

I drag my focus back to the table. "What's interesting?"

"You watching Amelia."

Before I can respond, my phone buzzes. The moment I see my ex-wife's name, tension coils in my shoulders.

SHAYLA:

Michael and I have to fly to LA
unexpectedly. We won't be home until
Thursday, so you'll have to have Luna
until then. I also need you to take her on
Friday night because I have a work thing
now. I'll switch and have her next
weekend.

The familiar surge of frustration rises. Another change to our agreement. Another disruption to Luna's schedule. Another fucking game.

"Everything okay?" Hayden asks quietly.

I show him the text.

Like she's been doing for longer than I care to admit, my ex is changing plans at the last minute. And while I'd happily have my daughter full-time, Luna needs her mother, and she needs her consistently. She needs to know she can count on the routine in place, which isn't something she's had since Shayla's fiancé, Michael, has been on the scene.

I've allowed a lot of these plan changes, not wanting to alienate the mother of my child, but I've reached the end of my patience.

Hayden looks up from the text. "You need to hire Blair."

"No."

"She's the best family lawyer in New York."

"She's a fucking shark, Hayden."

"Sometimes you need a shark." He gathers his thoughts in the way he always does before speaking. Hayden isn't one to speak rashly or without consideration. "This has been going on for too long, Gage. The constant schedule changes, the last-minute demands.

Luna needs stability and, I hate to say it, but Brett isn't cutting it."

He's right about all of this. Brett, my attorney, is the best at what he does, but family law isn't his specialty. However, Blair is the last attorney I'd hire. Mostly because she *would* cause a divide between Shayla and me, but also because she and I can't be in a room together without arguing over something.

"What about Justine Brown?" She's one of the best, and she works for Hayden, so I'm not sure why he hasn't suggested her.

Hayden shakes his head. "She's just started maternity leave." His eyes bore into mine. "Hire Blair. Let her fix this for you."

I stand abruptly, needing space from both the conversation and the knowing look in my brother's eyes. "I need some air."

The tension in my shoulders eases slightly as I step out of the ballroom, but my mind keeps circling back to my problems with Shayla.

I'm in the middle of sorting through this mess in my mind when I spy Amelia standing a short distance from me, reading something on her phone. Even from where I am, I can see she's agitated, and as I move closer, I hear her agitation.

"Unbelievable," she mutters. "Un-fucking-believable."

Interesting. I've never observed Amelia like this or heard her swear. I find myself moving even closer to her as she starts stabbing at her phone, typing something in an angry rush.

"Everything okay?" I ask.

She startles, nearly dropping her phone. "Oh! I—"

For a moment, I see her trying to slip her mask back on, but then something in her snaps. "Actually, no. Everything is *not* okay. My mother—*my absolutely infuriating mother*—is texting me about how excited she is that James and I will be attending her anniversary party together next weekend. *Together*! Which is fascinating news to me since I'm definitely not attending anything with my ex-husband. But apparently, he's been having lunch with my parents and helping my father with his golf swing—his golf swing!—and now my mother is sending me links to dresses she thinks would be perfect for me to wear to the party with him. As if there's still an 'us.' As if he hasn't—" She cuts herself off, eyes wide, lips smashed together.

I watch as she catches herself, her cheeks flushing. It's the most unguarded I've ever seen her.

"I'm sorry," she says quietly. "That was . . . a lot."

"Don't apologize. Seems like you needed to get that out."

Her phone buzzes again and she closes her eyes briefly, exhaling slowly. "That'll be another text about china patterns or seating arrangements or how James always remembers which wine my father prefers."

"Want me to reply? I guarantee your mother won't harass you again."

A laugh bubbles out of her unexpectedly. It's real, not the polite chuckle I've heard from her before. "Don't tempt me." Her eyes hold mine, all her walls down. "Thank you. For earlier, and now."

"For what? Offering to destroy your relationship with your mother?"

"For not . . ." She waves her hand around like she's

trying to pluck the right words from thin air. "Most people either tell me I need to try harder with James for Sarah's sake, or they launch into a speech about how I should take him back because he's such a 'good man.'" The air quotes are audible in her tone.

"People who think they know what's best for others usually don't know shit," I say, and watch surprise flicker across her face at my bluntness.

Luna's voice carries from behind us. "Daddy! Come see what Sarah taught me!"

"Go," Amelia says softly. "I should deal with this." She holds her phone up.

I nod but find myself hesitating. "Sometimes the right choice is just saying no."

She doesn't respond, but the look in her eyes says she's contemplating what I said.

Inside, Luna's waiting to show me some complicated dance move that apparently requires trying to spin in three different directions at once. But my mind keeps drifting back to Amelia, to the vulnerable moments with her today.

Since my divorce, I've kept things simple with women. A date to a gala. Dinner. Sex. Nothing more. Clean edges, no complications. The whole marriage and divorce clusterfuck taught me that lesson well.

I don't let women matter beyond the moment. It's been a rule I've chosen to live by.

Somehow, though, Amelia Sinclair has slipped past those defenses. She's on my mind like no one has been since Shayla and I'm not sure I want to do anything about that.

CHAPTER 4
AMELIA

THE WEEK after the wedding comes in hot.

Sarah and I got back to New York late Sunday afternoon, and I went straight into planning mode, my usual Sunday routine. Between work, Sarah's school and extracurriculars, the never-ending housework and mom duties, and the rare moments I steal for myself, planning isn't optional. It's survival.

Monday was beyond hectic, ending with a late bedtime of one a.m., and I wake on Tuesday with a headache. It lasts all day, and my ex-husband does his best to intensify it when he texts while I'm walking to collect Sarah from school in the afternoon.

JAMES:

I spoke with your mother this morning.
The party plans sound wonderful. I know
how much these events mean to your
parents.

ME:

I've already told you I'm not comfortable attending together.

JAMES:

Let's be adults about this, Amelia. Your mother is counting on us.

ME:

You're manipulating the situation.

JAMES:

I'm simply trying to present a united front for our daughter and maintain our family connections. You know how this works. Appearances matter. Think about how it will look if we can't even attend one party together.

ME:

You mean think about how it will affect your image with my father's contacts?

JAMES:

You're being dramatic. This hostile attitude isn't like you.

I stare at his last text, my teeth clenched. Even through messages he manages to make me question myself. Makes me feel like I'm the unreasonable one for having boundaries. For saying no.

But I *am* saying no. Finally.

I toss my phone into my purse and inhale a long breath while increasing my walking pace. I'm already running late for school pickup, and my mind is scattered in too many directions. The party drama with James. The contract negotiations for scoring *Velocity Reign*, potentially the biggest action film of next year, starring Hollywood's most bankable leads. The fact that my usually meticulous schedule is edging toward unmanageable lately.

The movie is an incredible opportunity. Game-changing, career-defining. All those cliché phrases that happen to be true in this case. But the workload . . . I'm already calculating the hours, trying to figure out how to balance it with Sarah's schedule and basic life maintenance.

My phone buzzes again. Probably James with another carefully worded guilt trip, or my mother with more party suggestions, or my agent with contract updates. I ignore it.

I make it to Sarah's school a few minutes late, power walking through the sunny courtyard like my life depends on it, in heels that weren't made for this. And because the universe has a sense of humor, I nearly collide with Gage Black.

He's radiating that effortless control that makes me both envious and wary. His dark suit is impeccable as always, not a single crease in sight, and tailored to his frame. A blue Kiton pinstripe if I'm not mistaken, which I'm not. Having been married to a man who demanded only the best in everything, I dedicated enough hours to suit research to know what I'm looking at. And those black John Lobb Oxford shoes he's wearing? They're polished to a shine that would put a concert piano to shame.

"Amelia." The low rumble of his voice wraps around my name, affecting my pulse in ways I refuse to acknowledge. He's devastating with his thick, dark hair, and a beard that only makes him more dangerously masculine. A strong jaw, eyes that promise things no good girl should want, and a mouth that looks made to ruin women all combine to make him unsettlingly magnetic.

On top of all that? He's built like he could pin you against a wall without breaking a sweat, all broad shoulders and raw power. Anyone with functioning eyes can see that he's the kind of handsome that makes intelligent women forget their own names. And the worst part? He knows it. Every inch of him knows it.

"Those heels must be killing your feet," he says, his gaze zeroing in on my shoes.

"I, uh, I got caught late at a meeting with my agent and didn't have time to change shoes." I have no idea why I'm explaining myself to him, but here I am.

His gaze meets mine again. "I don't think I've ever seen you wear heels to school pickup."

I blink. Hopefully, only on the inside. Then, with a slight arch of my brows, I say, "You're keeping a record of my outfits?"

Before I can fully process this or wonder why he's keeping track of what I wear, Sarah's teacher, Mrs. Liu, approaches with a bright smile that immediately sets off warning bells.

"Mr. Black, Ms. Sinclair! I'm so glad to catch you both." Her smile practically turns into a full beam as she directs most of her attention to Gage. "As you know, Stephanie Monroe has been planning the class's science fair on her own. Unfortunately, due to a personal crisis, she can no longer manage it, which means we need someone to take over." She glances between us, that beam still beaming. "Since I know you both to have a flair for organization and an interest in science, I thought you'd be perfect for this!" The only thing she doesn't do is clap her hands together at the idea. I'm willing to bet she's *this* close to doing that though.

"Ah, no, I don't think—" I start, but Gage cuts me off.

"We'd love to."

I gape at him.

Is the man serious? Neither of us have the time for this. The fair is only a few weeks away. Plus, co-planning anything with Gage Black is not on my bingo card for this year, or any year for that matter.

"I'm not sure either of us have the time—"

Mrs. Liu isn't interested in a word I have to say. She's in the Gage Black Fan Club and has been for as long as I can remember. That beam she was beaming? I'm not sure how she's not blinding him right now. "Excellent," she says to him. "I know that you will plan an amazing fair."

I'm sure she meant to say she knows *I'll* plan an amazing fair. I mean, come on. Gage might be a good dad in many ways, but I can't see him giving up his precious time for this. James sure as hell wouldn't.

And from what Shayla's told me, she has to do most of the heavy lifting when it comes to their daughter. Apparently, he'll show up and claim the credit for being an amazing father, but behind the scenes Shayla's the one making it look effortless. Much like what I do.

Gage and Mrs. Liu discuss some logistics while I try to keep up. Mostly, though, I'm trying to wrap my mind around Gage just agreeing to this. Agreeing on my behalf without even so much as a "Do you have time for this?" Like it was nothing. Like we both don't have demanding careers and complicated schedules and a weird tension between us that I'm trying to ignore.

"I'll call you tonight to set up our first planning

session," he says as we walk away from the girls' teacher, toward the playground where Sarah and Luna are waiting.

"Right." I nod like I believe him.

"I'm detecting a tone." He slows his strides and when I glance up at him, I find him watching me with narrowed eyes.

"You are." I come to a stop so we can have this conversation away from the girls. "I highly doubt you're serious about helping."

He looks down at me, his dark eyes as intense as always. "Why wouldn't I be serious?"

"Because it's a massive undertaking? Because we both have full schedules?" *Because my ex-husband always left me to manage everything, and I'm drowning just thinking about adding one more thing to my plate.*

"We'll handle it." His voice carries absolute certainty. "I'll make sure of it."

I want to believe him. But Shayla's words echo in my head. *He never follows through, Amelia. I'm always left to do everything myself.* "Just . . ." I take a breath. "If we're doing this, I need to know you'll follow through. I can't take on the whole thing myself. Not with everything else I've got going on."

He doesn't even hesitate. "I always follow through, Amelia."

His promise stays in my mind all afternoon and my overthinking is next level. Because as much as he said he'd contribute, I still have my reservations.

Later, I'm in my kitchen attempting to salvage a stir-fry that's quickly turning into a culinary disaster when my phone rings. Gage's name on the screen is a surprise.

I hesitate for a second before answering.

"Tomorrow morning," he says without preamble. "Eleven a.m. You name where you want us to meet. Or if that time doesn't suit, let me know what works for you."

Just like that. No small talk, no pleasantries. Straight to the point. Which is good. Efficient. And he's doing what he said he would. But for some reason, he's scrambled my brain with this call.

I often feel like I'm on the back foot with Gage. He has this unnerving ability to throw me off balance without even trying. It's not that he plays games. Far from it. He's too direct for that. It's just . . . him. Everything about him.

I swipe the burner too high, and the stir-fry starts to sizzle aggressively. I quickly turn it down, gripping the spatula a little tighter than necessary.

"Uh." I clear my throat. "The coffee shop on Lexington and 82nd works."

"Done."

I expect him to hang up, but instead, there's a beat of silence.

Not awkward, not tense. Just there, lingering. Like he's waiting for something.

Like he wants me to say something.

But my brain refuses to cooperate, so I say nothing.

Another second passes before he murmurs, "See you in the morning, Amelia."

The line goes dead, and for some ridiculous reason, I just stand there, staring at my phone.

I don't know what rattles me more—that he called, or that I'm still thinking about the way he just said my name with a thread of anticipation in his voice.

CHAPTER 5
GAGE

BLAIR WHITNEY'S office is exactly what you'd expect from Manhattan's most ruthless family lawyer. Sharp edges, sleek lines, and not a hint of softness in sight.

Just like the woman herself.

I find her behind her desk at seven a.m. on Wednesday morning. The air around her hums with a don't-waste-my-time warning that most would take heed of.

She doesn't look up from whatever document has her attention. "Unless someone's dead or dying, I don't take unscheduled meetings."

"I'm neither, but you'll take this meeting." I settle into one of her visitor chairs without waiting for an invitation.

Now she does look up, one perfectly shaped eyebrow arching. "Gage Black. To what do I owe this unwelcome interruption?"

"I need a lawyer."

"You have a lawyer. We've discussed him many times."

"I need a family lawyer."

I've got her full attention now and a smug expression settles across her face as she leans back against her leather chair. "I see you're finally ready to listen to me."

I don't know what it is about Blair, but she never fails to rub me the wrong way. We're not even five minutes into this conversation and I'm ready to leave. However, I push past that and remind myself why I'm here. Luna.

"You told me months ago that when I was ready, you'd help me."

"Did I?" She taps a nail against her desk. "That doesn't sound like me."

"Quit the bullshit, Blair."

Keeping her eyes firmly on mine, she sets her pen down with deliberate precision. "No."

Her response is unexpected. "Excuse me?"

"No," she repeats, like I might have trouble with the word. "I won't take your case."

"Why not?"

She studies me for a long moment, then says something that catches me completely off guard. "Because I refuse to help you turn Luna's mother into a ghost."

"That's not what I want, and you know it. I've told you enough times that I don't want to alienate Shayla."

"Right, but here we are after a long time of you putting up with her shit. You've reached the end of your patience." She leans forward. "You're finally ready to play hardball and we all know what that means in Gage Black's world."

"You have no idea of what I want."

"No?" Her gaze pins me in place. "Let me guess. You want full custody. You want to control all the decisions. You want—"

"I want stability for my daughter."

"And you think the best way to achieve that is by hiring the lawyer known for scorched earth custody battles?"

I lean back, studying her, trying to figure out what's going on here. "For a woman who's been telling me for a long fucking time to find a new lawyer, you've changed your tune a hell of a lot. What's changed?"

She's quiet for so long I think she won't answer. Then she says, "My father controlled my mother."

Her admission strikes me silent.

"He controlled everything. Everyone. A master manipulator. When my mother finally left him, he used every legal means possible to cut her out of my life." Her smile is bitter. "He succeeded."

"Blair—"

"I was twelve when I last saw my mother." She pauses, her gaze piercing me in a way that says she wants me to pay close attention to what she's saying. "Do you know what that does to a child? To watch one parent systematically destroy the other?"

"That's not what this is."

"No?" Her tone is hard. "You came to me because I'm ruthless. Because I fight dirty. Because I win." She shakes her head dismissively. "Find another lawyer. I'm good at what I do, but what I *don't* do is cut children off from a parent."

My jaw clenches. "Are you finished? Do I get to speak now?"

"I'm finished, but there's no point in you responding." She leans toward me. "I know who you are, Gage. You're a ruthless guy who always gets what he wants. I'm not going to be your lapdog making that happen."

"Fuck, Blair." I stab my fingers through my hair, pissed off and frustrated that she's refusing to listen to me. Desperate in a way I never am to make someone hear me out. "You might think you know me, but I assure you that you don't. I have never wanted to destroy Shayla. I grew up in a home with a mother who was emotionally absent. I saw what that did to my family and I never want my child to experience being cut off from her mother in any way." I pause, trying to rein in my tendency to use cold, direct language when negotiating. "And now, knowing your history, I want you more than I did when I walked in here."

Her eyes spark with curiosity. "Why?"

"You'll keep me in check if I do push too far. And I now know that you won't completely alienate Shayla, which was always my concern with hiring you."

I watch her brain work and admit that while I've usually dismissed this woman because of the agitation between us, I'm now intrigued.

Finally, she says, "I'll think about it and let you know today."

"Within the hour."

I receive another arched brow. "I don't play well with that style of command, so you may want to rethink your desire to hire me."

I stand, buttoning my suit jacket. "I want to hire you. At any cost. We'll figure out how we work best along the way."

At that, she rolls her eyes. "Seriously, I have no idea

why Liv finds you endearing." Her best friend, my sister-in-law, and the reason I've had to endure Blair in my life.

I ignore that. "I'll loop Hayden in. He'll keep both of us in check."

"First of all, I haven't said yes yet. And second, I know for a fact that Hayden won't touch family law."

Interesting. She seems quite confident about what my brother will and won't do.

"He will for me," I counter.

She turns silent, and I see her brain working again. A few moments later, she nods, decisive. "Okay, yes. Have your lawyer send me everything I need to get started and make an appointment. Make sure Hayden is with you at that appointment." Then, gesturing at her office door, she says, "Now get out of my office. I have work to go over that you interrupted."

I'm almost to the door when she calls after me. "Gage?"

I turn.

"Don't make me regret this."

THE COFFEE SHOP Amelia chose is exactly what I'd expect from her. Understated but elegant and tucked away from the noise of the city. She's already there when I arrive, laptop open, wearing jeans and an oversized white blouse. Her hair is pulled back in a neat twist that emphasizes the graceful line of her neck.

I head to her table and when she looks up and spots me, I nod toward the counter. "Coffee?"

With a shake of her head, she says, "I've already ordered. Thanks."

I get the distinct impression that even if she hadn't, she wouldn't have accepted a coffee from me.

After I place my order, I take the seat across from her, pulling out my phone to find the email Mrs. Liu sent us last night. I'm interrupted by a text from my assistant.

> **LUCY:**
> Just a heads up. Max is PISSED that you canceled on him this morning. Prepare for an incoming call from him.

> **ME:**
> I won't be taking calls for the next hour or so.

> **LUCY:**
> Why must you make my job harder than it already is? Seriously, Gage, this meeting has been planned for A MONTH. I hope that whatever you canceled it for is worth it.

I glance over at Amelia, trying to convince myself that I pushed my meeting with Max for Luna rather than for the opportunity to spend time with this woman who doesn't want my attention but who has it anyway.

Switching from my texts to my inbox, I locate the email about the science fair as Amelia says, "Okay, so we've been given a mess to clean up."

Right. Straight into it, which isn't my preference.

"First, how are you?" I place my phone down.

She frowns. "I'm good. Why?"

"One of our last conversations was about your mother and ex upsetting you. Did you manage that situation?"

Still frowning. "You say 'manage' like figuring out personal relationships is a simple matter of negotiation."

"Well, isn't it?"

She stares at me like she can't believe what I've just said. "Maybe it is for you, but for me, it's never that simple. It's not checklists and outcomes. It's a mess of emotions, unspoken thoughts, and trying to keep the peace without losing myself. That's not something you just *manage*."

I file that away. Amelia doesn't do simple. She does layered. Complicated. Raw. And I'm beginning to think she's never had someone who wanted to navigate all that with her.

"I didn't mean it's simple, Amelia." My voice lowers, the weight of my own past pushing through. "I know all about messy. The emotions, the history, all of it. And I've learned the only choice is to face it head on and manage what you can."

She's quiet for a long beat, her gaze shifting away from mine before coming back to me. "No. I haven't managed that situation yet." Her voice is softer now and it seems like she's going to elaborate, but she clears her throat and says, "Let's get back to the science fair. We've got a lot to go over."

I'd have preferred some more personal conversation before moving onto the fair, but I follow her lead because I'm a man who's learned when not to push, and Amelia's making it very clear not to right now.

"It's a hell of a mess," I agree. "I think we should just toss it all and start fresh."

Amelia's eyes go wide. "What? No."

"Why not?" I point to the teacher's email on my

phone that includes an array of unfinished spreadsheets, vague notes, and unhelpful Pinterest screenshots that the previous parent was trying to pass off as a plan. "That's a Pinterest graveyard, a half-baked science experiment of its own. There's nothing useful for us to work with."

Eyes still wide, like I've just suggested the worst idea she's ever heard, she says, "Stephanie put a lot of time into these plans, and I think we should honor that. How would you feel if everything you'd worked hard on was scrapped by the people who took over your project?"

"I'd feel grateful that they took my mess and fixed it."

Her brows furrow, her shoulders square like she's ready for battle. "Gage. No. She did the best she could."

Stephanie Monroe is a well-meaning but control-freak mother who insisted on managing the science fair alone. Other parents offered to co-plan it with her, but she refused. Then, her marriage broke down, and here we are. In a fucking mess because Stephanie might like control, but she appears to lack any kind of organizational skill.

She may have done the best she could, but frankly, her best doesn't cut it.

I don't say that to Amelia, though, because I'm a smart man and I know when I'm fighting a losing battle. Instead, I say, "Okay, let's go through it all and come to a compromise on what to keep and what to improve on."

She's not having any of my bullshit "what to improve on." She gives me a look. A pretty pointed one. "You do realize Stephanie's enduring a lot of gossip over all this, right? The last thing I want to do is hurt her more."

Amelia's not the first woman to accuse me of being ruthless, but she's the first to do it without bite, and without directly naming it. She simply lays out the facts for me to reconsider. I find it fucking refreshing.

"Okay." I lean back against my seat, ready to listen. "What do you suggest?"

Surprise flickers in her eyes. Then, I'm given a smile, and fuck, her beauty only intensifies when she smiles like that. I may even agree with whatever she says if she keeps smiling at me like that, damn the consequences.

She retrieves a planner from her purse and opens it to a color-coded list that looks fairly extensive. "I've taken Stephanie's ideas and expanded them."

She launches into her suggestions for budget adjustments, volunteer recruitment and organization, logistics planning, communication with parents, the event schedule, and the set-up on the day. I'm impressed with not only the amount of work she's already done on this, but also with every idea she shares.

We spend an hour going over it all, coming up with a plan for how to move forward. We've just finished agreeing that I'll draft an email to send to Mrs. Liu by end of day tomorrow detailing everything when Amelia's phone rings. She checks caller ID, and her instant scowl tells me she doesn't want to answer the call.

"Sorry." Her face twists with apology. "If I don't take this, he'll just keep calling."

When she answers with a curt, "James", I understand her grimace. It's her ex who I've gathered isn't her favorite person these days.

I take the opportunity to check my emails for anything urgent. I try not to eavesdrop on Amelia, but her voice, and the tension in it, pulls my attention.

Apparently, she was supposed to be at home this

morning so James could drop something of Sarah's off. She apologises for forgetting but the strain is clear in her voice. He must ask her where she is because she tells him she's working on the science fair with one of the class parents and won't be home for a little while.

It's at this point that my phone rings. I answer immediately when I see Hayden's name on the screen. I left a message for him this morning after I saw Blair.

"You got my message?"

"Yeah, and I don't really have the time to get involved."

"Blair will do all the work. I just need you to keep an eye on her."

I overhear Amelia's voice turning sharper. "No, James, I'm not on a date, though if I were, it wouldn't be any of your business."

Interesting that he's grilling her about her dating life.

"So," Hayden says, "You don't trust the attorney you've hired."

I'm distracted by Amelia abruptly standing and striding out of the coffee shop, still on the phone, her displeasure with the conversation blazing from her.

"Gage," Hayden nudges. "There's no point hiring Blair if you're not going to let her do her job. And she's not going to want me watching over her."

"She explicitly told me to make sure you're with me when we meet next."

He turns silent for a moment. Then says, "Right. Okay."

I frown at the note of uncertainty in his voice. "Is that 'okay' as in yes?"

"Yes. Let me know the details and I'll make time for it."

It's unusual for Hayden to bend to my requests so easily once he's already said no. If I wasn't so distracted by Amelia, I'd dig into that with him. Instead, we end the call, and I give my full attention back to the woman who is now standing on the sidewalk gesturing wildly with her hands while saying something to her ex that looks a lot like *fuck off*.

Her entire body is rigid when she walks back inside.

"Sorry about that," she says as she sits, her face tight.

I nod but don't speak. Not yet. I want to know if she'll open up further.

She takes a sip of her coffee, staring at her planner like it holds all the answers she needs in life.

"Is it always like that?" I ask quietly.

Her eyes cut to mine. "What?"

"With him."

I see her shutting down before she even contemplates answering me. "Let's just get back to finalizing these plans. I have another appointment soon."

Not wanting to push her further away, I give her what she wants.

We finish planning, but my focus is shot.

I came here for science fair logistics. Now all I can think about is Amelia, and the fact I want to demand a meeting every day just so I can spend more time with her.

CHAPTER 6
AMELIA

THERE ARE days I wonder if the universe is actively trying to see how much stress I can handle before I crumble. Today feels like one of those days and it's not even nine a.m. yet. Mind you, I've always hated Thursdays. The day of the week the universe likes to whisper, "You're almost there," only to kick you in the shins and remind you there's still one more day to go.

I've had my mother on the phone to me this morning about the anniversary party this weekend. Asking why I refuse to take James. After that torturous conversation, my agent called about the *Velocity Reign* contract and some clauses the production company want added that he knew I wouldn't be okay with. I stood my ground and refused them, but the decision has my stomach in knots. Then, as if those two phone calls weren't enough, Sarah forgot her homework, which meant an emergency detour back home, making us late for school. If there's a prize for the world's most efficiently frazzled parent, I'm in the running for it.

I dash through the school courtyard, mentally calculating the minutes I have before my first work meeting. Sarah skips beside me, chattering about a science project idea involving "music that makes plants grow faster, but not Taylor Swift because Luna's already tried that, and it didn't work."

When we reach the drop-off point, my gaze immediately finds Gage, a habit I'm trying not to analyze too closely. He's standing near the entrance in a charcoal suit, looking like Wall Street meets runway. He appears calm and composed, making me wonder yet again how he always looks so unruffled by life.

Luna spots us and waves excitedly, tugging on her father's sleeve to get his attention. I notice the way his expression softens when he looks at his daughter. It always does.

"Good morning," he greets when they reach us.

I ignore the hint of gravel in his voice that I like a little too much. "Morning."

After some awkward small talk about the unpredictable March weather, the kind where every word feels too loud and every silence too long, we say goodbye to the girls. I then push past the weird energy between us and direct our attention to the science fair. "I wanted to check about that email draft you were going to send me. I haven't received it yet, and I was hoping to review it before we send it to Mrs. Liu."

His voice carries the trace of an amused smile when he says, "I'll have it to you by noon like we agreed."

"Right." I try to leave it at that, I really do, but the obsessive part of me mourns the loss of an extra eight hours to overthink every possible disaster, so I find myself pulling my planner from my bag and flipping to the page covered in color-coded notes. "I want to make sure we're aligned on some things." I glance up and find him watching and listening intently. "I've drafted preliminary exhibit layout zones based on project categories, available table space, and fire safety compliance. Plus, I've made a list of suggested display guidelines to prevent a sensory nightmare. We don't want glitter bombs and baking soda volcanoes competing for attention."

The corners of his mouth twitch, and I realize I'm doing that thing I do where I get overly specific and detailed about things most people wouldn't even think to question.

"Layout zones and fire compliance?" he says, and there's definitely amusement in his tone now.

"Yes," I say firmly. "I don't want an actual chemical reaction happening in the corner because two projects got too close together."

"You're serious."

"Of course I'm serious."

"Amelia," Gage says, taking a step closer. "I've got it handled."

"I know, but—"

"I promised you I'd follow through, and I will." His dark eyes hold mine with unwavering certainty. "The email will be in your inbox by noon, complete with layout zones, fire safety compliance, and display guidelines, which you can, of course, add to if I miss anything."

I want to believe him. I desperately want someone else to share this load. But experience has taught me that when someone says, "I've got it handled," what they really mean is "I'll do the bare minimum, and you'll end up handling the fallout."

"Okay," I say, trying not to sound too skeptical. "But please don't be late. I have a meeting later this afternoon, and I'd like time to go over everything before sending our ideas to Mrs. Liu by end of day."

He nods, his eyes still firmly on mine. "I'll ensure you have plenty of time to go over it."

I'm still thinking about this when I step inside my studio thirty minutes later, still feeling the echo of anxiety over not knowing if I can count on him. However, my studio is my sanctuary, and the tension in my shoulders begins to ease. This is the one place where I don't have to be perfect, where chaos doesn't feel like failure but like possibility.

After I divorced James, I bought and combined two condos, transforming one into a professional recording studio with state-of-the-art equipment and perfect acoustics. It's totally separate to our living space, but close enough that I can be there for Sarah if she needs me.

I settle at my workstation, pulling up the cues for the big action sequence in *Velocity Reign*. I haven't signed the contract yet, but that doesn't mean I haven't started working on it. The director wants something that "reinvents tension" for the climactic chase through the streets of Bangkok. I've been experimenting with layering traditional Thai percussion and wind instruments over distorted synths, letting the rhythm build and fracture in unexpected ways.

My studio hums with creative mess. Sheet music from yesterday's session still litters the floor, a scattered map of half-finished thoughts, and my three keyboards form an arc around me. The vintage Moog I splurged on after landing my first big film score, the weighted Yamaha for classic depth, and the cutting-edge Roland for everything digital.

Against the far wall, a battered upright piano waits beside an acoustic guitar and a cello I haven't touched in weeks. A set of hand drums from a trip to Chiang Mai sits under the window, half-buried beneath film scoring manuals and notebooks filled with jumbled thoughts.

It's cluttered, but it's mine. The only place I ever feel fully myself. The version no one else gets to see.

I disappear into the music. Times becomes irrelevant. There's only the flow of creativity, the satisfying click when a chord progression finally falls into place, the frisson of excitement when a melody line takes a turn that works beautifully.

This is who I am when no one's watching. Passionate, messy, completely absorbed.

My hair gradually escapes its neat twist as I run my fingers through it in concentration. I kick my shoes off, pace the room, occasionally singing fragments of melody or tapping complex rhythms on any available surface.

In here, I'm not James's ex-wife, or Sarah's always-put-together mother, or the quiet woman at school functions. I'm just Amelia, a composer who hears the world in counterpoint and harmony.

My phone chimes at 10:45 a.m., pulling me out of my musical trance. I assume it's my agent with more contract details, but when I check, it's an email from Gage.

Holy shit. He actually sent it on time. Earlier, in fact.

When I open the attachment, my jaw nearly drops. This

isn't just a draft for me to add to or improve. It's comprehensive, thoughtful, and detailed. He's included everything we discussed, including the things I mentioned this morning, plus aspects I hadn't even considered like contingency plans for common issues like absences on presentation day.

Without thinking, I text him.

ME:

> Did you really write this, or did you have an assistant do it?

His response comes quickly.

GAGE:

> Hello to you too, Amelia.

I can almost hear his dry tone.

ME:

> Seriously, this is extremely thorough.

GAGE:

> You sound surprised.

ME:

> I am. Most people's idea of "thorough" is not this.

GAGE:

> I'm not most people.

No, he certainly isn't.

ME:

> The display guidelines are particularly impressive.

GAGE:

We can't have the fair turning into a
circus of glitter and vinegar.

I can't stop the smile on my face and find myself madly texting a reply to that.

ME:

Your sarcasm is noted.

ME:

Thank you. This is excellent. I'll send it to Mrs. Liu today.

GAGE:

Great.

I think our conversation is over, but another text comes through.

GAGE:

For the record, I always follow through.

ME:

I'm beginning to see that.

I'M early for school pick-up today and position myself near the playground where I'll easily spot Sarah. My mind is half-stuck on a particularly tricky transition in the cue for the Bangkok chase sequence, my fingers absently tapping out the rhythm against my thigh.

That's when I notice Shayla across the courtyard, her designer handbag dangling from her wrist as she gestures emphatically to another mother. She hasn't seen me yet, which gives me a moment to observe her unnoticed.

Shayla and I became friends gradually over the past year. She's glamorous in a way I've never aspired to be, and beautiful in the kind of way that makes the world pause. Long, sleek dark hair. Flawless, sun-kissed skin. Eyes so vividly green I sometimes forget what I was saying mid-sentence when talking with her. And her face? Don't get me started. Perfect symmetry, full lips that look designed rather than inherited, not an ounce of lip filler or botox in sight. It's as if on the day she was born, God decided to outdo herself.

Shayla is an influencer with millions of followers. She posts about beauty, fashion, and a curated version of motherhood, all filtered through a lens of effortless perfection. Her content walks the line between aspirational and unattainable. The kind of posts that show her in a silk robe with a green smoothie, writing captions about balance while her makeup is professionally done and not a single toy is out of place in the background. She's got a verified checkmark, brand deals with luxury labels, and enough celebrity followers that the gossip accounts regularly speculate about who she's dating, even though she's not technically single. Last I heard, she was engaged to Michael Trent, the movie producer who's as famous for his taste in women as he is for his blockbuster hits.

We have nothing in common. But motherhood has a way of bringing women together, especially when your ex is the kind of man who leaves emotional landmines in his wake.

She's painted a picture of Gage as controlling and emotionally distant. A workaholic who left her to shoulder the parenting alone while he built his empire. I've sometimes struggled to reconcile that with the Gage I've seen, but having firsthand experience with an ex who shows one face to the world and another to me, I haven't questioned her version of events.

Today, however, she gives me reason to.

When she sees me, she smiles and waves me over.

"Amelia! How are you, darling?"

She always calls me "darling." I always ignore the falseness of it.

"I'm good. You?"

The mother she's been talking with, a woman I've only met once, laughs. "Oh, god, don't ask her that unless you want to hear all the ways her ex is ruining her life."

I frown, glancing between them. "Oh?"

Shayla waves a hand, dismissive. "It's nothing new. You know all about Gage and his bullshit."

Her friend, Clare, is far less inclined to move on. "This was a particularly asshole move, though, Shayla."

"Yes," Shayla agrees but offers nothing further.

Clare, clearly invested, fills the silence. "That man." She shakes her head like the verdict is already settled. "Last month, he bailed on Shayla when she needed him to take Luna for the weekend so she could be with Michael in LA for his movie premier. And now? He's refusing again. Shayla's got an important work event and Gage won't budge. He's jealous and using Luna to manipulate Shayla."

This time, I manage to stop my frown.

None of that matches what Shayla told me last

month about that same weekend. Then, she'd told me how amazing her fiancé is and that he was desperate to spend more time with Luna. She talked up how special Michael is. She said they wanted to take Luna to LA for that weekend so they could have a fun family time after the premiere, but that Gage wouldn't give up his scheduled time with his daughter. She said Gage is doing everything he can to stop Michael being a part of Luna's life.

I glance at Shayla, catching the moment she schools her features into disinterest, smoothing her expression into a glossy blankness.

I feel the need to defend Gage. "He's helping me plan the class Science Fair at the moment."

Clare blinks. Shayla's mouth parts slightly, but no sound comes out.

"What?" Clare huffs her disbelief. "He's putting his name to it while you do all the work?"

I shake my head. "No. He's showing up and suggesting some great ideas." I meet Shayla's gaze. "Maybe he's paying attention to your requests for help."

Her eyes narrow ever so slightly, and her nostrils flare, a subtle, but telling, flash of irritation. "I doubt it. Gage only pays attention to what he wants."

Clare immediately nods in agreement, but I'm watching Shayla now. Watching the cracks show.

Because nothing she's said lines up with the man who sent me that email this morning. Who took the initiative and arranged our meeting yesterday. Who did everything in his power to ensure Luna and Sarah had a magical weekend in Nashville.

A cold unease curls in my stomach.

Has Shayla been exaggerating, or outright lying, about Gage?

And if so, why?

Before I can fully process this, Sarah comes running over, her backpack bouncing with every step. Luna follows, just as breathless.

"Mommy! Can we get donuts on our way home?"

I push the question aside for now. "Sure, sweetheart."

But the feeling lingers. Gage Black may not be the man I thought he was at all.

CHAPTER 7
GAGE

MID-MORNING FRIDAY, I receive an email from Mrs. Liu that she's also sent to Amelia. She's happy with the plans we've made so far. She's also forwarded a list of volunteer parents that Stephanie just sent her. It's disorganized as hell, and I can't make sense of who actually volunteered, who was added without agreeing, and who has now bailed.

I'm in the middle of perusing the list when I receive a text from Amelia.

> **AMELIA:**
> Have you seen Mrs. Liu's email?

> **ME:**
> Reading it now. Trying to make sense of the volunteer list.

> **AMELIA:**
> I think we should contact everyone to see if they still want to volunteer.

> ME:
>
> It'd be more efficient to just ask everyone to sign up again.

She takes a minute to come back to me.

> AMELIA:
>
> Okay, but we need to do that ASAP.

> AMELIA:
>
> We also need to do more work on the budget ASAP.

She's right about that. It's a complete fuckup. Unrealistic.

> ME:
>
> Let's find time to go over it tonight when I collect Luna.

> AMELIA:
>
> I thought Shayla was collecting her.

> ME:
>
> Change of plans. She's busy. I'll try to get there by five.

> AMELIA:
>
> Okay. See you then.

> ME:
>
> We'll make it happen, Amelia.

She doesn't text a reply, and I find myself still watching my phone ten minutes later. Waiting.

It's been years since a woman's silence has held my attention like this. In fact, only one woman ever has, and it wasn't depth that pulled me under. It was the sex and the intoxicating rush of being made to feel like I was her entire world.

I was young back then and had no fucking idea.

I didn't know physical attraction and good sex weren't enough to hold a relationship together.

Now?

This interest?

The way my thoughts have started returning to Amelia throughout the day, and the way I'm so fucking eager for a text from her?

It's not about her looks, though she's fucking stunning.

No, what holds me is a woman who reads about war, writes music like a poet, mothers like a lioness, cares deeply for others, puts herself last, and shows up every day with the kind of vulnerability I rarely see.

It's the way she walks into a room like she has no idea she's the most captivating thing in it. The way she prioritizes what matters while the rest of the world drowns in superficial bullshit. The way she bends under the weight she carries but refuses to break.

I'm fascinated by her mind and the way it never stops. Overthinking, organizing, and obsessing over the smallest details like they're life or death.

I want to know every corner of it.

And fuck, I shouldn't want that.

Not when her daughter's friendship is the only one that's ever mattered to Luna.

The only thing I should want is to keep things from going to hell between us because we wouldn't be the only ones who got burned if that happened. It'd be the girls too.

I lean back and scrub a hand down my face.

The first woman I've wanted for more than dinner and sex in a long time, the only one who could crawl under my skin and make me like it, and she has to be my daughter's best friend's mother.

I'm in the middle of that thought when my office door crashes open and Shayla storms in like a goddamn hurricane.

"I have an assistant for many reasons, Shayla," I drawl, lifting my gaze to her. "And one of those reasons is to only let people in here who have an appointment."

"Don't," she snaps, striding to my desk. "What the hell is this?" She waves a crumpled letter like it's offensive to her.

I stand, slowly taking her in. She's dressed immaculately, of course. Designer dress. Blown-out hair. The usual. But there's a crack in the veneer today. Her eyes are wild, and there's a flush on her cheeks that has nothing to do with makeup.

"I see Blair's letter reached you." My cold tone should let her know I'm not in the mood for her today.

"This isn't you," she hisses. "You don't handle things this way."

"I do now."

Blair's letter was exactly what it needed to be. Firm, direct, and leaving no room for Shayla to keep letting Luna down. It outlined our custody agreement in black and white, noted every time she'd violated it over the past year, and made it clear that any further breaches would put us in court. No more changing plans and dumping Luna with me when she wants to party or when it simply doesn't work for her. No more unilateral decisions. Blair warned her that if she kept this up, I'd file to modify the custody order, and I wouldn't hold back.

Her perfectly glossed lips purse, and from experience, I know this will go one of two ways. She'll either start yelling or begin crying. Always the victim when things don't go her way. Today, though, she'll find I don't have my usual patience for any of it.

"You chose Blair Whitney?" she says, voice dipping, softer now. The same quiet she always uses when she wants to pull me back in. "You know how she is, Gage."

"She's the best." I'm not buying into the nostalgia she's peddling. It's not us against the world anymore, no matter how often she tries to use that tactic on me. "She's exactly what Luna needs."

"She's a pit bull," she spits, dropping the soft act like it was never there. "You've never once involved anyone like her before. Why now?"

Truth is, I've let Shayla run rings around me when it comes to Luna. Not because I don't care, but because every time I've pushed back, Luna's paid the price. Less attention. Less affection. More whispered bullshit like, *"Daddy doesn't care about us,"* slipped in right when Luna's defenses were down.

The worst has been watching my little girl shrink in on herself recently, trying to be the perfect daughter so her mother might love her a little louder. It's gutted me.

I could fight Shayla, but Luna? She was the one who'd bleed for it.

I hate playing hardball with my ex, but I will go to the ends of the earth for my daughter.

I walk around the desk, moving in close to her, my entire body vibrating with anger. "I'm doing what I should have done a long fucking time ago, Shayla. I'm protecting our daughter."

Her lip curls. "No. You're punishing me."

"Fuck, can you hear yourself? Where's the woman I married? The woman I thought would be the greatest mother alive? She sure as hell wouldn't whine about me trying to punish her."

"God, you're an asshole." Her eyes glitter with hatred. "You're going to rip this family apart."

I stare at my ex and wonder for the millionth fucking time how I ever loved her. "You've already ripped this family apart. I'm trying to make things right for Luna." I snatch Blair's letter from her and angrily shake it between us. "*From now on*, Blair's handling everything for me. You want a switch of nights with Luna? You go through Blair. You want to pick her up an hour later than our agreement? You go through Blair. You want anything at all from me? You go through Blair."

She draws back slightly, stiffening at my tone. "You think you're a saint. Like you're the best father out there and I'm the worst mother. Do you have any idea how hard it is being a mother in this world that's not made for women? I'm doing my best while trying to juggle mother-hood and work."

"Are you fucking kidding me?" I clench my jaw. "You have two nannies, a housekeeper, a driver, a personal shopper, and a goddamn spiritual guide, whatever the hell that is. All paid for by me. The only thing you're juggling is the attention you gain from Insta-*fucking*-gram." *Fuck.*

"You never understood me! And you still don't!"

She's right about that. But I'm not getting into this shit with her today.

"We're done here." My tone is colder than it's ever been with her. "And I'm done with pretending this is working. It's time you start showing up for Luna."

Her eyes go wide, flickering with shock for a split second before she gathers herself and we're back to the practiced Shayla. The woman who stopped knowing how to be real a long time ago.

She squares her shoulders. "You keep acting like I don't care. Like I don't love her. But I do."

"Then show her that. Show her she matters more to you than your followers or your image or your next event. Be her mom, Shayla."

She slaps me. Exactly as I knew she would.

Then, she pivots and stalks out, heels echoing like rapid gunfire.

I exhale, the weight of this shit settling deep.

I didn't want this.

None of it.

I just wanted Luna to have two parents who loved her enough to put her first.

But I realize I may have been wrong.

Maybe Shayla doesn't have it in her to love Luna more than herself.

AFTER A LONG DAY, the argument with Shayla looping in my mind like a bad movie, I arrive at Amelia's just before five and find her unraveling.

The elevator doors open and I step into her condo,

the scent of something buttery and rich filling the space. Comfort food. Underscored by the sharper edge of garlic, it's the kind of smell that lets you know you've walked into a home, not just a house.

Classical music blares from the baby grand in the living room. Not playing, but *blaring*, as Luna hammers out a dramatic melody with all the enthusiasm of a six-year-old trying to summon a thunderstorm.

Sarah's voice cuts through from the kitchen, loud and argumentative, locked in a tug-of-war with Amelia about some injustice I can't fully catch. Probably homework. Or dessert. Or socks. Kids will go to war over any of them.

And then there's Amelia.

She's at the stove, one hand clutching a wooden spoon, the other gripping the counter like it's the only thing keeping her upright. Her hair is half up, half falling out of its twist, strands sticking to her cheek. Her blouse is untucked on one side of her jeans, her phone wedged between her shoulder and ear, though I can't tell if anyone's actually on the other end. Her eyes flick to me, wide and glassy, and in that second, I see her entire brain short-circuiting behind them.

I've been here before, but only as far as the living room. That space, like her, has always felt polished to the point of untouchable. Neoclassical perfection with its pale walls, high-end textures, and expensive restraint. But now? The kitchen's a battlefield. Open cookbooks with sticky tabs jutting out. A pasta box half-torn on the counter. A trail of grated cheese marking territory across the island. Whatever polish I thought lived here all the time is nowhere to be found. And I don't think she has it in her right now to handle this alone.

She doesn't even register me fully before I move.

Jacket off. Sleeves up. I'm in her space, my hand closing around the spoon before she can process it.

"I've got this," I murmur.

She looks at me, lips parting, breath catching. "You don't have to—"

My look is determined. Steady. Final.

She clamps her mouth shut. A full beat passes. Then she exhales, nods once, and steps back, letting me take charge.

I turn down the heat, stir whatever's in the pot—some kind of creamy pasta—and open the oven to check on the garlic bread browning inside.

Sarah's still arguing. Luna's banging away at the keys like she's performing for Carnegie Hall. Amelia's put her phone down and is pacing now, trying to calm Sarah while pressing her fingers to her temples like she can physically push the stress back into her skull.

I glance over at my daughter. "Piano recital or end-of-world score?"

Luna stops playing just long enough to grin at me. "I'm composing a villain theme."

Of course she is.

Amelia shoots me a look. "Sorry. I told her to turn it down."

I shake my head. "It suits the mood."

She stares at me for a second like she can't figure out whether I'm mocking her or offering grace. "Are you enjoying this?" she asks with a tilt of her head and furrowed brows.

I let my grin curve slowly. "Immensely."

Her eyes narrow. "That's cruel."

"I could have simply grabbed Luna and run. That would have been cruel. I'd say I'm showing mercy."

She rolls her eyes and goddamn if I don't like that. "Seriously." Then a shake of her head. "Men."

My grin only grows. Earning an eye roll from Amelia feels like an achievement. Not to mention that muttering about men that she's doing.

And despite the stress still etched in her face, she's stunning like this. Frustrated, stubborn, and trying to hold her world together with nothing but sheer force of will. I should not want to be the man she leans on.

I grab the garlic bread from the oven and meet her gaze again. "I'd like to point out that this would have burned under your watch."

That doesn't earn me another eye roll but close to it. "It's a good thing it was also on the receiving end of your mercy then. Whatever would we have done without your assistance?"

A laugh barks out of me, and I can't remember the last time a woman caused that. "You'd probably have set the place on fire by now. You're lucky I showed up when I did."

Her reaction isn't immediate. First, it's the twitch of her lips, like she's fighting to hold it in. Then comes the spark in her eyes, like she's seconds from losing the battle. And finally, her laugh breaks free, soft and real, hitting me like a clean shot to the place I swore I'd locked up for good.

"Mommy!" Sarah's voice breaks the moment, dragging Amelia's eyes from me. "I want my book!" She plants her feet, folds her arms tight, and lifts her chin defiantly, every ounce of her radiating six-year-old fury and royal injustice.

"And you know why you can't have your book, Sarah," Amelia says, not giving an inch. "Now, please go to your room and take ten minutes to calm down."

Her tone is firm enough that Sarah scowls, lips pushed out in a dramatic pout, then backs down and stomps off in the direction her mother pointed.

Amelia tilts her head back and inhales a long breath. As she releases it, she looks at me. "You and Luna should stay for dinner."

"To protect Sarah from harm?"

Her laughter is immediate this time. "Yes. Who knows what I'll do to her if you're not around to stop me."

We take a moment, just watching each other, and then I smile. "We'd love to." I turn to Luna who's still composing her villain theme, surely contributing to the headache I suspect Amelia has. "Sweetheart, that's enough now. Go wash your hands for dinner please."

"And please tell Sarah to wash hers, too," Amelia calls after her.

Once we're alone, I assess Amelia. "How bad's the headache?"

Her fingers absently find her temple again. "I'm okay."

"Says the woman who looks like she just survived a war."

She nods slowly and I swear I see a wall coming down as she practically begs, "Tell me you survive wars too. I need to know I'm not doing everything wrong."

"Fuck, sometimes I survive more than one a day." I pause before adding, "You're not doing anything wrong, Amelia. You're the best mother I know."

She blinks. Then stares at me for a long moment that stretches between us, fragile but charged. Neither of us move. Neither willing to be the one to look away or speak first, and fuck if I don't want to reach out and tuck that stray strand of hair behind her ear just to see if she'd let me.

But I don't.

Instead, I hold her gaze and let her have the space to decide what to do with whatever just passed between us.

"Thank you," she finally says, her voice soft and raw with emotion, like tears are threatening. "I needed to hear that."

I want to kick her ex's ass for not being the one to make sure she knows that. For not telling her every goddamn day that she's a phenomenal mother.

I shift gears because she's looking at me like I just pulled the pin on a grenade of emotions inside her. And fuck, I get it. Sometimes we just need a moment to pull ourselves back together. "Go round up the girls." I keep my voice steady. "I've got the rest of dinner handled."

She hesitates for only a second before nodding and slipping out of the kitchen, leaving me with a million thoughts I never saw coming and am not sure I'm ready for.

We all survive dinner, though I can see that Amelia's had a rough day and that her daughter is pushing all her buttons. So, I take charge, directing the conversation with the girls, getting them talking about the project they're collaborating on for the science fair.

Amelia's the reason this weather project isn't a total mess. She's the one who helped steer them into choosing a weather forecasting project rather than one of the usual experiments kids this age love. And the one who has helped them come up with some great ideas. They're tracking weather patterns like tiny meteorologists in training, and will present their own forecast at the fair, complete with charts and a "live report." It's smart, fun, and just enough chaos to keep kids engaged.

As we're clearing the table after dinner, Luna announces, very dramatically, hands flying like she's the star of a show, "I'm gonna pretend there's a giant storm coming that will blow all the playground equipment away."

Sarah frowns. "But that's not what we're predicting. There's no storm coming."

"It's for the video," Luna says, clearly exasperated that this needs explaining. "I'll do the serious weather voice too. Like this"—she clears her throat—"A storm is coming . . . and only the brave will survive!"

Sarah looks at her like she's deeply concerned. "I think I should say the science stuff first. Then you can do your thing."

Amelia snorts quietly and our eyes meet. A silent *this is going to be fun* passes between us.

I glance at the girls. "How about you two go and work on this some more while we clean up?"

They don't hesitate, and a second later, Luna is pulling Sarah by the hand while exclaiming, "We need to write scripts!" The last thing we hear is Sarah saying, "No, we need to learn more about forecasting before that."

Amelia laughs once they've disappeared, and as I

carry the plates into the kitchen, she says, "Luna is so you."

"How so?"

"She's take charge. Confident in herself, in her place in the world. And so damn smart." She reaches for the plates to begin filling the dishwasher, her eyes sparkling with mischief as she adds, "That flair for the dramatics though? That has to be Shayla. I can't imagine you ever being dramatic."

I arch a brow. "What, you don't think I've got a dramatic bone in my body?"

She tilts her head, playing innocent. "Do you?"

"I've got a six-year-old composing villain music like she's Hans Zimmer on a vengeance arc. Where do you think she gets that from?"

Amusement flickers across her face, then shifts, like her brain just flagged something worth a second look. "I'm impressed you know who Hans Zimmer is," she says, quieter now, the playfulness stripped from her voice.

I pass her a bowl for the dishwasher, keeping my tone casual even though I caught the way her focus shifted to seeing me a little differently. "There's a lot you don't know about me."

"Yes," she confesses. "I've realized that."

Her admission lands low in my gut but I don't have time to sit with it because Luna barrels back into the kitchen like a one-kid parade. "Dad! We just had the *best* idea!" She's pure electricity. Wide-eyed, breathless, buzzing with excitement.

"Tell me," I say as Sarah joins us, looking just as excited.

"Well, you know how we're recording our weather forecast?"

I nod.

"We need badges! And our own news channel name! And you *have to* do the video editing like you did for the video we made Uncle Ethan and Aunt Maddie!"

Luna will always be the best thing I've ever done. Nothing compares to watching her grow into herself. Confident. Fierce. Unapologetically Luna.

I ruffle her hair. "You've got it. We'll get badges and figure out your news channel name."

Sarah steps forward, anticipation shining in her eyes. "And you'll do the video editing, right?"

I meet her gaze with a smile. "Absolutely. And your mom can compose your channel's opening music."

"Yes!" Luna says, bouncing now. "This is going to be so good!"

Within seconds, Luna's dragging Sarah back to the bedroom, already plotting their next move.

"Do you always just volunteer people for things?" Amelia asks once we're alone. There's no annoyance in her tone, but still, I can see she wishes I wouldn't do that.

"Fuck, sorry. I got caught up in the girls' enthusiasm." I want to kick my own ass now for adding another thing to her plate. "I'll find someone else to help—"

"No," she says, placing her hand on my arm, stopping me. "It's okay. I'll do it. Just, please"—her voice trails off, but everything she's trying to say is right there in her eyes —"I'm busy."

"I hear you. I'll ask you before just assuming you have time for something, or that you'd even want to do it."

"Thank you."

The thread of quiet surprise I hear in her voice, along with the way she stumbled over voicing her request make me wonder how often she feels like people consider her.

While I'm contemplating that, she reaches for the dishcloth and eyes me, her playfulness sparking again. "It's no wonder your company is so successful. You probably boss everyone into brilliance by noon."

My gaze locks onto hers with an intensity I can't dial back. Not when she's meeting me with this much fire. "You haven't seen my bossiness, Amelia."

Her eyes widen a little and a subtle flush colors her cheeks. "No?" There's a slight catch in her voice.

"No. You've seen me being polite."

The air shifts. She hesitates, just a beat. "What does bossiness look like on you then?"

"You'll know when you've met it."

Her breathing slows. Just a fraction. But I catch it.

So does she.

It hangs between us, the moment stretched tight, heat curling at the edges. We both know what I was referring to.

And hell, I'm fighting myself every second I watch her.

I want to know what she's thinking.

What she's *overthinking*.

Where her mind's letting this go.

And just when I see her chest rise, as if she's about to say something, the elevator dings. Footsteps echo, fast and purposeful. A moment later, her ex strides into the kitchen like he owns it, and Amelia's entire body tenses.

His shock at seeing me here is more than clear. As is his displeasure.

He halts mid-step. "Gage." One word. Flat. Frosted. Then he turns to Amelia. "I wasn't aware you'd have company."

"And I wasn't aware you'd be dropping by," she retorts coolly.

"Am I not allowed to surprise my daughter with a visit?"

"Actually, no, you're not. We have a custody agreement, James, and it'd be nice if you started following it."

"You know," he says, his tone superior, "most women would be over the moon to have a partner who is attentive, Amelia."

"You've forgotten we're no longer partners, James."

"Oh, we'll always be partners, sweetheart. I'm the father of your child, after all."

Fuck, he's a manipulative bastard.

Every word's calculated. Every smile, a trap.

No wonder she's so guarded.

"What do you want?" she demands, looking like she's *this close* to unleashing all her thoughts and feelings on him. "In case you can't see, I'm busy."

His eyes come to mine again, and I see his deep hatred of the fact I'm standing in this kitchen. "I can see that." Narrowing his gaze at me, he says, "You're who she's planning the science fair with?"

Before I can answer, Amelia grits out, "Oh my god, James. *No*. Stop."

His head swings immediately in her direction. "No? This isn't science fair planning?"

I've had enough of this asshole.

"No, not science fair planning," I cut in. "Not that it's any of your business."

That earns me a glare. "It is my business if you're a man she's bringing into my daughter's home."

I arch a brow. "*She's*? I think you meant to say "Amelia.'"

That old saying, "if looks could kill", rings true right now. James wants me gone.

"I'd like a minute with my wife," he snarls.

I try like hell to allow Amelia the opportunity to correct him. But I can't hold back. "You mean, your *ex*-wife."

His jaw clenches. "This doesn't concern you."

"Enough!" Amelia snaps, completely done with his bullshit. "Gage isn't going anywhere, so how about you just say what you came here to say, and then leave."

There's that steel I keep catching glimpses of.

Casting one last filthy glare my way, James turns to her. "I came to discuss your parents' party. I'll pick you up at six tomorrow night."

"*I've told you* I'm not going with you," she says, firm enough that even I'd think twice.

He blows right past that clear boundary. "There's no need for hostility. I'm just trying to honor your parents' wishes for a united front."

This guy isn't here for his daughter. He's here to rattle Amelia's cage.

"The reason she can't go with you," I say, "is because I'm taking her to the party."

Within a second of uttering that lie, I've got both of them staring at me. James is furious. Amelia, stunned.

She quickly recovers, though, and instead of pandering to his inflated sense of entitlement, she simply says, "I told you we couldn't go together."

James stiffens. His jaw ticks. For a second, I think he might argue.

Instead, he smooths his expression and levels her with a disappointed look, the kind meant to shame. "That's unfortunate. I really thought you'd want to honor your parents on a night that matters to them."

He gives her one last look that's cruel enough to bruise without laying a hand on her, and then he's gone.

After he leaves, the air is thick with the kind of silence men like him leave behind. Men who gaslight like it's a damn art form.

I study Amelia. "You okay?"

Shoulders back, spine straight, she nods. I see her though. She's not okay, but she's holding. "Welcome to the disaster of my life. That's pretty standard for James."

Fuck.

It's clear she doesn't want to talk about it because she deflects quickly.

Giving me a look that's the equivalent to a raised brow, she says, "Nice work there, by the way. What happened to never volunteering me again?"

I can't help the smile tugging at the edge of my mouth. She's quick. Sharp. And calling me out like it's a sport. A sport I like more than I should. "I'd say I volunteered *myself*."

She crosses her arms, and that glint in her eyes? It holds a challenge I want to lose. "Right. You were just showing me mercy again."

"I knew you'd catch on."

"You do realize that you now have to take me to a party, don't you?" There's an eye roll in there somewhere. I'm certain of it.

"I do."

She shakes her head as a slow smile spreads across that beautiful face of hers. "No, it's okay. I'll just tell him something came up and you couldn't make it."

"I'll take you."

She blinks. Likely at my decisive tone. And instead of responding, she silently watches me while *I* watch her brain do a whole lot of thinking.

"Okay," she finally decides, dropping her arms to her sides. "Pick me up at six but be here ten minutes before that. It's black tie. And if you truly value your life, you will not, under any circumstance, agree to anything, *not one tiny thing*, on my behalf if my family asks for something." Her eyes bore into mine like she's extracting a signed agreement from me. "Are we clear?"

Christ, I had no idea how much I'd like being ordered around.

"You want me to pick you up at six but be here ten minutes before that?"

"Yes."

"Why? Are you planning to spend ten minutes issuing more orders?"

That gets me my eye roll. But there's a smile there too.

"I'll be here ten minutes early," I agree. "And I won't offer you up for anything."

"See, I knew you were a smart man."

We finish cleaning the kitchen after that. The girls pop in and out, and we talk science fair plans like it's business as usual between us.

But it's not.

Far from it.

I just made plans to take her to a party. Lied to her ex. Promised to behave.

For a guy who wasn't supposed to get involved, I'm doing a hell of a job.

CHAPTER 8

AMELIA

Gage arrives fifteen minutes early to collect me for my parents' party. The second I spot him stepping out of the elevator, I suspect mistakes were made. The moment he closes the distance between us, I *know* they were.

It turns out that Gage Black in a tuxedo is a whole situation.

Broad shoulders, precision tailoring, and the kind of presence that makes it hard to remember what day it is.

He smells expensive.

He looks like sex and danger dressed in formalwear.

He moves like the room already belongs to him.

His eyes sweep over me.

Slowly.

Thoroughly.

Deliberately.

And I feel it like a touch that lingers longer than it should.

Every cell in my body apparently got the memo that he's hot. None consulted me.

"You look beautiful," he murmurs.

I don't have the bandwidth to fully appreciate that. I'm too busy holding myself together because *this* is a lot. And I made an error in not anticipating any of it.

Holy god.

This was supposed to be strategic. A neat solution to a James problem.

But then he showed up like this.

And now we have a situation.

"Thank you." I try to gather myself. I really do. But it's as if my entire body is staging an ambush, and I find myself throwing out, "You clean up disturbingly well yourself."

Heat flashes in his eyes. Then comes the quiet quirk of his mouth. That smug little move that says he's not going to let what I just said go. And that he's going to enjoy every second of it. "That sounded suspiciously like a compliment."

Abort. Abort. How did we get here and where is the reset button?

I wave him off, trying hard to look more in control than I am. "That was an outlier. It won't happen again."

That damn mouth of his just won't let this go. It's a full smirk now.

"That's a shame," he says, smooth, unhurried, and way too pleased with himself.

And, oh boy, we're in new territory now.

The kind that's far too sexy to be in with the father of my daughter's best friend.

"Right," I say, stumbling over my words as I attempt to steer us out of danger. "We should, ah, we should, go."

His full smirk eases into a half-smirk, which I didn't

even know was a thing. This man doesn't follow rules. He sets them. "What happened to the ten minutes of you bossing me around that I was looking forward to?"

Seriously.

He's a whole-ass situation.

I stab at the call button for the elevator and give him a pointed look. "I'm going to ignore that." Then I move right along, shifting us into safer territory. "How did you go getting Luna to sleep last night? Was she as hyped up as Sarah?"

His smirk is replaced with a knowing smile. He lets me have the out, though. "Yeah, it was pretty late when she finally fell sleep."

In the elevator, the conversation flows. It's light, comfortable, safe. Gage tells me Luna's bowling. I mention Sarah's at a sleepover. He's relaxed and doesn't miss a beat. Meanwhile, I'm over here trying to string words together and act normal while his scent rewires my nervous system.

I'm relieved when we exit the elevator and walk out to the sidewalk. I inhale as much fresh air as I can while Gage hands over the valet ticket. I also try to unscramble my scrambled thoughts.

And then I see his car.

Sleek. Dark. Sinfully low to the ground and completely unnecessary in this city.

Of course it's a McLaren GT. And I only know that because my brother once called this car a "precision-built orgasm on wheels."

Gage opens my door for me, and we exchange a glance as I get in. A glance that only bewilders me more.

Gone is the smugness. The teasing. The laid-back smile.

Now, there's *interest*.

He's taking his time enjoying me.

And good god.

I was not prepared for this.

Or for how much I like his attention.

I settle into the seat while he rounds the car, and it takes exactly three seconds for my brain to glitch out.

The leather is warm against my body. Soft, expensive, and entirely too intimate.

It's his scent too. That lethal mix of something spicy and male and wholly unfair. It's all through the car.

I remind myself that my olfactory response is primal. That pheromones are real. That this is just biology misfiring, not actual attraction.

And yet.

The thrum in my veins says otherwise.

So does the fact I just pressed my knees together.

This is fine.

Everything's fine.

A moment later, Gage is in the car with me and we're on our way.

We fill the time talking about my family. How long my parents have been married, my siblings, the fact that my parents requested no children at the party tonight. Gage appears surprised that not even Sarah is allowed, a sentiment I share.

And even though I'm still recovering from the full sensory experience he is tonight, I like talking with him. It's easy. Gage's calm energy grounds me.

And the way he handles traffic, completely unbothered? I like it a lot. He doesn't fidget. Doesn't check the time. Doesn't sigh or tap the wheel like he's too important to be stuck here. He just sits with one hand on the wheel, like he's got all the time in the world to be with me.

When we arrive at my parents' building, Gage pulls into the private drive. We leave the car with the valet and take the elevator up to their residence. The doors open into the foyer, and a few moments later, we step into the great room. Tonight, it's been transformed into something closer to a ballroom. Towering florals, polished floors, a string quartet in the corner, and enough couture to rival fashion week.

I'm suddenly reminded of what I hate about these things.

The people.

Gage must sense my hesitation. His hand comes to the small of my back and he bends his mouth to my ear. "Everything okay?"

Yes.

No.

I stop and turn into him, and because he didn't see that coming, he collides with me. His hands come to my hips to steady me, and honestly, this man should be banned from being in my presence.

It's complete hormonal chaos inside me.

"Fuck," he curses softly, caught off guard. "Sorry."

"No, that's on me," I say as my brain malfunctions at the question of where to put my hands. They went straight to his abs when we crashed into each other.

I try to step back but there must be someone behind me because Gage's hands tighten on my hips, keeping me right where I am, which is approximately way too close to him.

He nods to the person, waits until they pass, then lets me go. His gaze returns to mine, curious. *Why did I suddenly turn around?*

"I don't do well at parties," I confess. "It's too many people, and too many"—I gesture with one hand while trying to find the right word—"expectations."

I don't think he's surprised by my admission. "Okay, so we're not staying too long."

He says that like it's simply a fact he's updating in his mind. He's not taking it as a decision to be argued over or a choice of mine that needs to be changed.

I'm not used to that. To someone hearing me and not trying to talk me out of what I need.

"That's my preference."

His response is immediate. "Well then, lead me to the food straight away because I only agreed to be your date for that."

My head pulls back a little. "You *agreed* to be my date? I recall you forcing yourself upon me."

"You can't help it if your memory is hazy. It's a good thing you've got me to remind you."

I shake my head while trying not to laugh. "At the rate you're going, I won't be keeping you around."

"Have you forgotten you're stuck with me for a few weeks?"

It's a simple question but the look in his eyes isn't. There's heat there for the second time tonight. I swear I'm not imagining it into existence.

My mother's voice cuts through the moment.

"Darling, you're here." She leans in for air kisses. "You

look lovely. Though, black again, Amelia? You know, color won't kill you."

I don't respond. I never do when she says things like that. It's easier to let it skim right over me than to explain my reasons.

My dress is black. Quietly elegant. It smooths itself over my body like it was custom-built to highlight every curve I usually hide. One bare shoulder. A sharp drape across my chest. A thigh slit that shows more leg than I'm usually comfortable with.

I chose it for her.

Not the color. I couldn't go that far. But for the silhouette, the cut, the boldness. I thought maybe this time she'd approve. She's always wanted me to be bolder. Brighter. To dazzle and own the room instead of trying to disappear into it.

Of course, this dress still isn't enough. It never is.

Gage shifts beside me.

I don't look, but I feel him. Tall, solid, and very, very quiet.

Mom looks at him. "Gage." She smiles but it doesn't quite reach her eyes. "It's lovely to meet you."

She wasn't thrilled when I told her last night that Gage would be my date instead of James, and she's not trying hard to hide that from him.

He doesn't appear fazed. He reaches for her offered hand and gives the kind of handshake that's firm without trying to dominate. "Thank you for welcoming me into your home."

Mom's assessing gaze remains on him for only another moment before she glances at me. "Larry was asking about your next movie. Have you signed the contract yet?"

My mother has never supported my career. She always imagined something more spotlight-worthy. However, since the last film I scored didn't just become a blockbuster but made me a name in the industry, she's found it useful to know just enough to impress her friends.

"No, I'm—"

Something catches her eye, and she places her hand on my arm to stop me. "Sorry, darling, I need to speak with Cathy."

With that, she glides away.

My gaze follows her across the room, and I let out a slow breath while shaking off the moment. Shaking off the sting of it all.

I turn to Gage and reach for a distraction. "Okay, food?"

He doesn't move. And the look in his eyes tells me he's not about to. "Is that how things usually go with your mom?"

"She's in entertaining mode." I try to shrug it off like it's nothing. But I know exactly what he's asking, and I'm not sure I'm ready to get into that conversation.

I love my mother, and I know she loves me. But her way of showing love isn't bandaging wounds, making comfort food, or pulling me in close when I fall. It's about anticipating the wound before it happens, and doing everything in her power to make sure no one sees it.

That's how she protects me and my brothers. By preventing mess. By controlling outcomes. And I've spent my entire life trying not to be a disappointment she has to clean up after.

Gage's eyes burn with something fierce and unflinching. "She just disregarded you, Amelia. Twice. In the span of a couple minutes. And entertaining or not, that was her daughter she brushed off. Not a guest. Not a stranger. *You*."

I go still.

Not because I disagree, but because I'm used to polite company. The kind that doesn't name things like this.

I swallow down my rising emotions. I don't hate that he named it; I'm just not used to talking about it with anyone but my brothers. "She wishes she had a daughter more like her."

"In what way?"

"In all the ways." When he simply continues watching me with that fierce look like he's waiting for more, I elaborate. "Mom thinks I should try to stand out more. She thinks I'm too quiet, too modest, too . . . average, when she'd prefer I dress up and sparkle more."

"She wants you to use your beauty more than your brains."

Now, I really still.

He's nailed it.

"Yes. And in answer to your original question, yes, she's always like that."

His eyes search mine for a long moment. Then, he curses quietly, but no less intensely than the way he's watching me. "*Fuck*."

I nod slowly. "That about covers it."

He works his jaw, and it looks like he's trying hard to keep all his thoughts to himself now.

I offer him a smile. "Let's forget that happened and move on to food. It is what you came here for, after all."

I turn to walk further into the room but his hand wraps around my wrist and pulls me back. When he's got his eyes on me again, he says, "I won't forget that happened. And just so we're on the same page here, food is the least of my priorities tonight."

His words are like heat on bare skin.

Impossible to ignore and felt long after they're spoken.

Before I can form a response, his grip shifts, sliding from my wrist to my hand. Deliberate but gentle. And then he threads our fingers together and guides me into the party.

Just like that, he's in control.

Of the moment. Of me.

And I'm nothing short of bewildered by it all.

That he called my mother out when no one else ever has.

That he just made it clear he's not here for the food.

That my hand is in his.

That I am here, at my parents' anniversary party, with Gage Black, who up until just earlier this week was a man I wanted nothing to do with, but who I'm now finding difficult to take my eyes off.

That he just made it clear *he's not here for the food*.

Somehow, I manage to keep my bewilderment to myself and smile at my parents' friends like I'm not a hot mess on the inside as I follow Gage. He walks with purpose, his presence impossible to ignore. And the strangest sensation washes over me. For the first time at a party, I feel safe. Like I don't have to be so on guard. I think Gage would step in if I needed him to.

I'm having a moment over these thoughts when my brother appears in front of us.

"Well, hello there, Sir," he says as he runs his gaze down Gage's body, blatantly appreciative. Tim never learned how to keep a thought to himself. His eyes sparkle as he looks at me. "You've been keeping secrets, sis. You never told us that Mr. Periodgate himself was now a permanent fixture in your life."

If the floor swallowed me whole right now, I wouldn't be mad about it.

My cheeks heat as Gage's lips twitch and his gaze comes to me.

"Periodgate, huh?" he asks, and I want to tear that smirk from his face. I also want to shoot my brother.

After silencing Gage with a *look*, I glance at Tim. "He's not a permanent fixture in my life."

"I'd say I am," Gage disagrees, and I just know he's finding this immensely enjoyable. "Quite possibly for the rest of our lives," he continues, and when I blink at him, he shrugs. "I don't see Luna letting Sarah go any time soon."

How my brain hadn't put that together yet is a mystery to me.

"So," Tim says, "what is this, then?" His eyes widen. "Wait. Is this to piss James off? I would throw my support behind that."

"This is a fake date," I explain.

"Fake is a harsh choice of words," Gage says.

I cock my head. "What word would you use? Oh, wait. Let me guess. It's a mercy date."

"A tux is a hell of a lot of effort for a mercy date."

Tim whistles low. "Hot damn. Is it getting hot in here, or is that just you two faking it?"

Some days, I *really* want to kill my brother.

I'm about to make a hard detour in this conversation, but the way Gage is now looking at me . . . I can't look away.

There's heat, and tension, and no faking in sight.

Tim says something else, but it's just white noise.

I'm so lost in this moment with Gage.

My other brother saves the day.

"Earth to Amelia," Colin says, snapping his fingers in front of my face. "Hello?"

It feels like it takes much longer than the actual seconds it takes to drag my attention from Gage. I look at Colin and try to find my words. "Hello. Yes. You're here."

He grins before glancing between me and Gage.

"This is Periodgate Gage," Tim announces, like Colin has no idea who Gage is, and Colin's grin grows.

Honestly, I don't want brothers in my next life. Just give me dogs. Or cats. Or even jellyfish. Just keep the brothers away.

Gage and Colin are shaking hands, all very official like.

I'm planning mass brother extinction.

And Tim's probably over there plotting how to make this even more mortifying for me.

"We heard you bought her enough pads and tampons to last the next few periods," Colin says to Gage, *and I want to die.*

Gage appears entertained by the entire thing.

Before he can respond, Tim says, "How would you

rate her ninja moves out of that bathroom? Ten out of ten? Or do you have some tips for the next time she has to be stealthy?"

"Oh my god," I mutter. "Seriously, men would not cope if they had to endure periods."

Tim shrugs. "I don't know. How hard can it be?"

Gage holds his hands up in a surrender. "I'm backing out of this conversation now. It was nice knowing you two for a few minutes."

Colin laughs. "Smart move. I'm following suit."

Tim's grinning at me. He knows full well I can never hold a grudge with him for long.

I shake my head at him. "You are dead to me."

Tim's phone alerts him to a text he's just received, and after checking it, he says, "Sorry, I have to make a call."

"Divine intervention," Colin says after our brother walks away.

"Hopefully it's his boss giving him hell," I mutter.

Gage laughs. "What does he do?"

"He's a paramedic."

We get into a conversation with Colin after Gage asks him what he does. The two of them talk like they've known each other forever. It's a skill my brother has. Both of them, actually. The ability to connect with ease and talk about anything. I was not blessed with the same ability. Networking and meeting people is awkward for me.

After Colin excuses himself to talk with one of our cousins, Gage says, "I like your brothers."

"You like that they enjoy teasing me."

"You told them about me."

"I told them about my *period*."

"And yet they know all about how I helped you."

"We were texting at the time." I pause before adding very firmly, "I swear, if you smirk again, I will make you regret it."

He doesn't stop watching me with that amusement, but he doesn't smirk. And who knows what he would have said next if we weren't interrupted by a server.

He offers a tray of appetizers. "Beef Wellington or seared scallops?"

I take the scallop and nod my thanks. Gage takes both.

"I'm surprised you didn't ask for the entire tray," I tease.

"I'm holding out for the tray with sliders," he banters, scanning the room like he's on a mission. "You know, real food."

I laugh, and when his eyes return to mine, there's a smile there. It's easy, open, and free.

Never in a million years, would I have ever expected Gage to be like this. And I certainly wouldn't have imagined just how much I enjoy spending time with him.

Feeling brave, and inspired by him to have some fun, I grab his hand while allowing a grin to spread across my face. "Come on, Mr. Periodgate, let's get you some real food."

His laughter trails behind me as I lead him to the server I saw carrying what my parents consider sliders.

"You think anything here comes with ketchup?" he deadpans after I pile mini brioche buns with truffle aioli and Wagyu beef onto a napkin for him.

"We may need to swing by McDonalds for you on the way home," I deadpan back.

He laughs again and then leans in close. "You keep feeding me like this, and I'll start thinking you like me."

My pulse does something deeply inappropriate.

And while I'm having a moment over that, my ex-husband invades our party for two.

"Amelia," he says, moving in close like he's staking his territory. "Your father asked for us to stand together with him and your mother and brothers while he gives a little speech later."

"No," I say.

His brows draw together. "No?"

His confusion is actually warranted. I've never said a flat-out *no* to him.

"No," I repeat, still not offering a reason.

"Amelia," he starts in that condescending tone he likes to use with me. "You're being unreasonable. I think—"

He doesn't get to finish.

Gage's hand settles at the curve of my back, and when he speaks, it's with the kind of unfuckwithable authority that makes people listen. "She said no. And I'd say it's about time you listened to her."

Holy. God.

When Gage Black decides to take charge, he doesn't raise his voice. He doesn't posture. He simply *owns the moment.*

It's the kind of command that doesn't ask for space. It claims it.

James goes rigid. Fury in his jaw, his shoulders, every line of his body.

He doesn't get the chance to respond. Because Gage is already moving.

He presses his hand more firmly against my back. "Amelia and I were just about to dance."

It's clear in his tone what he's not saying.

Back off. Stay gone. Don't test me.

He dumps the bougie sliders on our way to the dancefloor. Uneaten. Forgotten. He guides us through the room, his hand never leaving my back. I go willingly, and not just because I'm glad to be away from James.

No, I want this.

I want to dance with Gage and I'm not putting that feeling in a box to be analyzed later like I would normally do.

I'm not overthinking this.

When we reach the edge of the dancefloor, he turns into me, slides his hand around my waist, and brings his other hand up. Slowly, palm open, inviting.

I place my hand in his.

And then, we're dancing.

His eyes drop to mine, and there's something new there.

Concern.

Restraint.

Like he's reading me second by second, checking for signs of hesitation.

His thumb brushes lightly over my hand. "Tell me if you don't want this."

I'm held by the weight of his gaze.

My thoughts scatter.

Everything slows, especially my breathing.

He doesn't want to push a boundary. He's asking to honor it. It's a line in the sand he's offering me the power to draw.

I move in closer. "I want this."

His grip on my waist tightens. Possessive almost. Like now that I've said yes, he's done holding back.

We dance in silence. It doesn't demand to be filled, but as one song bleeds into the next, the more aware of him I am.

Of how my body fits against his.

Of his scent that makes thinking hard.

Of his hand on my back.

His closeness.

The longer we dance, the harder it is to breathe evenly.

And the more my thoughts tangle.

Especially when he doesn't say anything.

When he just holds me. Like none of this is dangerous.

By the time he speaks, my pulse is a riot and I'm half-convinced he can feel it.

His head tilts slightly as he murmurs, low and dry, "Your mom's giving off strong royal court energy right now. Pretty sure she's currently judging whether I'm worthy to be here with her daughter."

It's so unexpected, so perfectly timed, that it cracks the tension just enough for me to laugh. Not just because it's funny. But because it's so him. And that thought right there is something I know I'll interrogate later.

I now know Gage well enough to know one of his signature moves. He breaks tension, not to escape it, but to hold space for it.

"Careful," I warn with a smile. "She hears everything. You're one insult away from being exiled from the kingdom."

"It'd be worth it," he says, voice lower now, "just for that laugh you gave me."

What are we doing?

My hand slides a fraction higher at the nape of his neck, fingers threading into his hair. Just a little. Just enough to pretend it's nothing. But the flare in his eyes tells me I'm lying to myself.

"You say that now," I murmur as every other sound in this room fades away, "but you haven't seen her silent treatment. It's like winter in Siberia."

"I can handle the cold."

I let my fingers drift down, slow and idle, like my touch doesn't have a motive. Like it's not driving both of us mad.

"You don't scare easy, do you?"

His voice is all gravel and intent when he says, "Not when I want something."

There's no air left between us. Only heat.

And I am *this close* to unraveling.

Gage is watching me closely. He's made his move and is now letting me decide what to do with it.

And that's the problem.

I *don't know* what to do with it.

I'm not built for decisions made in the space of a single breath. I like time. Distance. A clear list of pros and cons. And preferably not decisions that come with ripple effects. That could touch my daughter if I get it wrong.

"I feel like I should have signed a waiver before agreeing to dance with you."

"You still can." His eyes do not let me go.

My lungs forget how to function.

Everything in me pulls tight. Conflicted.

I break eye contact first.

We can't do this.

Inhaling a deep breath and fighting for rational thought, I meet his gaze again.

I clear my throat. "Thank you for helping me with James."

He takes a long moment, eyes searching mine.

I hold my breath.

There's an ocean of feelings in his eyes and I can't tell what he's going to do with them.

Finally, he nods and loosens his hold on me. "Any time."

The disappointment I feel over his retreat is confusing. I asked for space, and he gave it to me. And yet, here I am, feeling all kinds of unexpected feelings over that.

God.

Did I want him to push? To ignore my line in the sand?

I'm so confused by these thoughts. I've never wanted a man to make a choice for me. Not once. And after being married to someone who always did, I swore off men like that.

I thought Gage was like him. I was wrong.

Gage Black doesn't take without consent. Even when everything in his eyes says he wants to. And maybe that's what undoes me the most.

Thankfully, the music stops, and my father appears with a microphone, ready to give his speech.

James doesn't join me and my family for the speech.

I survive said speech.

And Gage and I ease back into safe conversation with no more dancing.

Later, after he's dropped me home and I'm alone in bed dedicating good time to replaying every second of the night in my mind, I receive a text.

GAGE:

I enjoyed myself tonight.

I stare at the message for approximately forever.
Unsure how to reply.
In the end, I don't.
I need at least twelve more hours of thinking before I do that.

CHAPTER 9

@THETEA_GASP

HOLD UP. Who is @ameliasinclair and why is the moody-piano-girlies chat on *fire* right now? This low-key composer (who's kept it VERY under-the-radar despite working on some of the biggest soundtracks in recent years) is suddenly the name on everyone's lips... and not for a good reason. Word dropped last night that she plagiarized another artist's work. And not just any artist. Bestie, drop everything because this tea is so hot it might just unalive us. The accuser is none other than @sofiarayeofficial, the actual queen of breakup ballads and grammy-bait piano tears. #gasp Word is, Sofia's lawyering up. AND she's been spotted leaning on hockey god @macehawkins, who's clearly in his I'll-burn-the-industry-down-for-her era. We stan a cease-and-desist king. We don't know all the deets yet, but Sofia's team has receipts, and the streets (okay, Reddit) are already dissecting timestamps and background noise like it's a CSI case. It's giving shady snake. It's giving courtroom drama with a side of betrayal. And honestly? We're just getting started because this smells of big scandal. Amelia (yes, we had to google her too) is apparently just about to sign on the dotted line to score Velocity Reign, none other than the hottest action flick of next year. She hasn't responded, and we're not sure if that's a classic silent slay or an admission of guilt. Come on, Amelia. Time to clap back. We are so ready for a new Reputation era.

CHAPTER 10
AMELIA

THE MONDAY after the party is sent to do mortal damage to me. I'm sure of it. And not just because it's the day I wake to the plagiarism allegation, but also because James takes the opportunity to try to weasel his way back in again.

He arrives at my condo right after he drops Sarah at school in the morning, sweeping in like he's the boss of me. He acts like he's extremely concerned about my career. Spoiler alert: he's not and never has been. We argued a lot during our marriage about the fact I worked. He had many reasons for being against it, especially after Sarah was born, but really, all he wanted was me home where he could control me.

After spending time pretending to care, he shares his plan to help me fight the allegation, as if there's no possible way I could manage this myself.

After that, it's all downhill between us. We argue for what feels like an entire day but is closer to an hour. He does his best to manipulate the situation into what he can get out of it, which is more involvement in my life.

Toward the end of that hour, I put my fingers to my temple and close my eyes, wishing the stress away. Wishing *him* away.

"Amelia, you can't just ignore this," he snaps when I close my eyes.

I force them open. "I'm not ignoring it, and the fact you think I am shows me just how little you pay attention to what's important to me and to what I say."

"Don't be ridiculous," he starts, but I cut him off.

"Stop treating me like a fucking idiot!"

His eyes widen. I've never sworn at him. And I've never yelled at him like this. Not even when I fought my way to divorce.

When he opens his mouth to speak, I slam my hand up between us like a stop sign. "It's my turn to speak." My breaths are coming faster now, the heat of my anger burning through my chest, my arms, *everywhere*. "We are *no longer married*, James, a fact I'm sick and tired of having to remind you of. That means you don't get a say in my life anymore. It also means you don't get to come into *my home* and gaslight me. And in case you don't know what that means, it's that thing you do where you manipulate me by making me question the validity of my own thoughts—"

"I'm aware of what gaslighting is, Amelia," he says, his eyes hard. "And I can assure you that you're way off base. But then, you always did need me to help you understand things."

I stare at him, incredulous that a human being can be

such an asshole. Then I stab a finger at him. "That! That's gaslighting."

He looks at me like I'm the dumbest woman in the world. "Is there a point to all of this? Or can we get back to me arranging William for you."

His lawyer. Who, over my dead body, is getting anywhere near me again.

I have so much more to say, but I suddenly understand that it wouldn't matter if I spent the rest of my life telling James how badly he treats me, he won't ever hear me let alone listen to me.

With more calmness than I feel, I say, "No, we can't get back to anything because you're leaving."

He carries on in the same exact way he always has with me. He ignores me. "William's sent through a list of suitable PR firms for us to consider. We'll need to issue a public statement."

I take a deep breath. It beats my other plan, which is to grab the sharpest knife in my kitchen and hack him to death. "If you aren't out of my sight within the next two minutes, I will call Dan and have him come up here and personally escort you out."

That gets his attention.

But he doesn't do what I've asked. Instead, he fixes me with a look so venomous my breath catches. "This is because of *him*, isn't it?"

I know he's referring to Gage, but I don't take the bait. "No, James. This is because of me." My voice stays level even though I'm consumed with fury. "This is what I want. It's what I've wanted for over a year." My eyes bore into his. "I want you gone."

"No, Amelia, you want to spread your legs for Gage Black."

His words are designed to shame me. I've had enough therapy to see them for what they are. They come from a place of deep, unmet need. James was never truly loved as a child, and he never healed himself from that. He took that aching need and twisted it into control. And when he feels me slipping away, he throws shame at me like a lasso to drag me back. He tries to make me the one who finally loves him. The one who doesn't abandon him.

I'm a smart woman. I know that. But James has always had a way of getting into the cracks the world creates. The wounds every woman carries, shaped by a lifetime of being told we're too much, not enough, never quite right.

He doesn't create the doubt. He weaponizes it. And sometimes, I lose track of where the world ends, and he begins.

Staring at him now, I see just how much poison he's filled with, and it causes me a moment of clarity I haven't had yet. Whatever part of me still answers to him; she needs to remember her own power.

I don't give him the satisfaction of defending my "shameful" behavior. That's what he wants. I just turn and walk to the call panel by the elevator, jabbing the button for the doorman. When he answers, I ask him to come up.

"What the fuck are you doing?" James barks, storming toward me.

"We're done here."

He doesn't stop. Still doesn't listen. His hand clamps down on my bicep, hard, and he yanks me around to face him. "We won't ever be done," he bites out.

The shock of it hits me first. Then the anger. No one touches me without permission.

"Take. Your. Hands. Off. Me." My voice doesn't rise. Doesn't tremble. It's quiet, lethal, and final.

James has never touched me like this before and he drops his hand like he just realized he was touching something sharp. Confusion flickers in his eyes, then disbelief. He searches my face like he's trying to find the version of me he could control. But she's not there anymore. And he knows it.

The arrogance slips. Just for a second. Just long enough for something else to break through. Fear. Real sinking fear that he's finally lost his hold over me.

"You don't mean that," he says.

I hold his gaze.

I don't flinch.

I don't speak.

And he *sees* it.

I am so done.

The elevator dings and Dan appears. "Hey, Amelia." He flashes me his usual cheery smile. "What's up?"

"Dan," I say, my voice cool. "Mr. Kensington was just leaving."

His smile falters. His eyes flick from me to James, then back again. He catches the tension immediately. "Understood."

He steps forward, subtly positioning himself between us. "Sir, I'll walk you down."

As James moves, slower than necessary, I add, "And Dan? From now on, Mr. Kensington doesn't come up unless I've personally approved it."

Dan gives a short nod. "Got it."

James doesn't say a word as he steps into the elevator.

I don't look away until the doors close between us.

The second they seal shut, my knees almost give out. I don't let them. I stay exactly where I am, spine straight, jaw locked, hands clenched at my sides.

My skin still buzzes where he grabbed me. Not from pain. From rage. From disbelief.

I close my eyes.

Breathe.

Just once.

And then I walk back into my home like I haven't spent the last hour ripping my insides out just to protect myself.

I wish I had the luxury of time to unpack just what happened, but I never have that kind of time. And today, I absolutely do not have it. Not when I have a plagiarism accusation to deal with.

The story broke yesterday, but I didn't see it. I rarely check social media, and I spent most of yesterday in a daze over everything that's happened with Gage.

I woke up this morning to a handful of missed calls from my agent, three frantic texts, and an email marked URGENT. I read the email a few times as the shock sunk in. He advised me the story is blowing up and that the timing couldn't be worse with the *Velocity Reign* contract not fully signed yet. He also advised that he has PR on standby and has looped my lawyer in.

An hour after that email, he called to let me know the studio behind the film is reviewing their position. Apparently, social media is escalating the story into a full-blown scandal because Sofia Raye is the reigning queen of sad girl music, and I just became the villain in her origin story.

I should have known she'd come back to bite me on the ass.

Four years ago, we spent three brutal months working together on a film score. It started promisingly enough. Mutual respect and cautious collaboration. But it didn't take long for the cracks to show.

We clashed over everything. Style. Tone. Tempo. She wanted control of every note, every measure, and when I pushed back, things got ugly fast.

What made it worse was the pressure. It was a big film. A high-profile director. Sofia was still up-and-coming then, desperate to prove herself. I was just trying to get the job done. But instead of working with me, she treated me like competition.

By the time we delivered the final mix, we weren't speaking. I walked away with relief. She walked away with a grudge.

And now, she's repackaged that grudge into a career-ruining narrative.

She's accused me of lifting a theme we supposedly worked on together. That I passed it off as mine, reshaped it, and used it in the score for my last movie, the one that changed everything for me.

It's a lie.

She didn't even like the piece she's claiming I stole. She shut it down the second I played it. But she has just enough evidence to seed doubt. An old scratch file, a few shared credits, maybe a timestamp that can be twisted.

And that's the thing about doubt. It doesn't have to be true. It just has to be loud enough.

Loud enough to scare a studio.

Loud enough to put my contract at risk.

My phone buzzes with another text.

It's from my lawyer who is liaising with the studio and has advised me to stay silent while she reviews everything.

> **LIANNE:**
>
> The studio is flying someone in tomorrow for a meeting. They want to go over everything in person.

My hands shake as I tap out a reply.

> **ME:**
>
> Okay. Where?

> **LIANNE:**
>
> The Langham at 10:00 a.m. I need you calm, composed, and saying nothing until the meeting.

I stare at the screen for a long moment. Calm, composed, and silent are the exact opposite of how I feel. My hands are still unsteady, my heart's racing, and my brain won't stop cycling through every note I've ever written, searching for some piece of music that might have started with both of us and ended up in my work without me realizing.

But I know I didn't steal anything because I'm meticulous. To a fault. I document everything. Every note. Every take. Every second of sound I create.

I also know that doesn't matter right now.

What matters is that the studio's sending someone across the country to meet with me. What matters is that my name is being dragged through headlines I didn't ask for. And if I'm not careful, I could lose everything I've built.

My phone lights up with another text.

GAGE:

Are you okay?

GAGE:

Olivia is a top crisis management lawyer. I imagine you've got things under control, but if you need her, say the word and I'll put you in touch.

I met Olivia at the wedding in Nashville. I liked her a lot.

But holy god.

How did I get to the point in my life where I need to contemplate hiring a crisis manager?

ME:

Thank you. My agent and lawyer seem to have things under control, but I appreciate the offer.

He comes straight back.

GAGE:

You didn't answer my question.

It's not the only text of his I haven't answered. I still haven't replied to his message from Saturday night. The one where he said he enjoyed himself.

I meant to. But every time I start typing, I overthink it. Too casual? Too serious? Too soon? And now he's checking in again, which I appreciate. I do. I just don't know what to do with it.

I like him. Too much, maybe.

My fingers hover over my phone.

I type.

I delete.

I try again.

God.

Why is this so hard?

It's nine years since I last dated. Really dated. I don't count the few men I've gone to dinner with since my divorce. And I haven't had sex with anyone since my divorce, so that means it's nine years since I've had sex for the first time with someone. And oh boy, has my body changed since then.

I have no idea what the dating etiquette is anymore. Like, do people even date to get to know each other? Or do they just send each other cryptic texts, trade memes, and trauma dump at 1 a.m.?

And the whole app thing. *Apps*. Like ordering takeout, but with more disappointment. Sure, they existed when I was dating, but they weren't everything. I never used them. Now? They *are* dating culture.

Swipe right if they don't lead with gym selfies and "looking for a partner in crime." Swipe left if their bio gives you the ick. Hope they don't ghost you. Pray you don't get murdered.

Honestly, the whole thing feels like a series of red flags held together by unhealed childhood wounds and curated playlists.

Everyone's hiding behind vibes and vibes only.

I've forgotten how to flirt. I don't know how to be

casual. I mean, I had my first kiss at seventeen and lost my virginity to James when I was twenty. I learned how to have sex in the context of a committed relationship, not one where you have to pretend not to care afterward.

And now I'm trying to text a man who has cheekbones carved by gods, a tuxedo that gave me an actual hormonal imbalance, and probably his very own fan club, while I can't even type a text without second-guessing my entire personality.

ME:
I'm okay.

As soon as I hit send, I drop my phone to the kitchen counter like it's too hot to be in my hands a second longer.

My reply was fine. Totally fine. If fine means awkward and underwhelming and wildly late considering I still haven't replied to his message from *two nights ago*.

Somewhere out there, women are breezing through conversations with ease. Effortless. Flirty. Meanwhile, I'm over here catastrophizing two words and flirting with a stress rash.

Of course, Gage being Gage, he calls.

My phone lights up with his name, and I stare at it like touching it might trigger a full-blown crisis. Who even calls anymore?

I just sent a two-word text and had to emotionally recover like I was sixteen again, stomach in knots, palms clammy, and one notification away from either euphoric bliss or emotional collapse. And now he wants to talk? This man is trying to kill me.

I take a breath and then do my best not to sound like

the hot mess I am on the inside. "Hey." My voice comes out smoother than I expected, which is both a win and a mystery, because nothing else in my body is operating like it should.

And then he speaks, and I find myself again. "Amelia." Just his voice. That's all it takes. Low, unwavering, and threaded with quiet concern. "Talk to me. Do you need anything?"

"I don't know." It slips out before I can stop it.

"Do you want to talk it out?"

A laugh escapes me. "God, we could be here forever if we do that."

"It's that rough, huh?"

Such a simple question, but it cracks me open because I'm tired, and confused, and worried. And somehow, he's taken the pressure off. I'm no longer overthinking dating etiquette; I'm simply having a conversation with someone who cares how I am.

"Yeah," I admit quietly. "It's that rough." Just saying it makes me feel a fraction lighter.

"I'm here if you need anything. Even if that's just a shoulder to lean on."

"Thank you. I truly appreciate that."

He's silent for a beat. When he speaks again, there's an edge to his voice. "I mean it. You call if you need me. And we can push the meeting we'd planned for tomorrow. Or just cancel it altogether. I can take care of everything."

Shit. The science fair. It completely slipped my mind today.

Gage and I had agreed to meet at his office at noon tomorrow. There's a lot to cover, so I don't want to let him down. I quickly do the mental math on my ability to make it to his office from the hotel by noon.

"No, I'll be there."

"Okay. But let me know if things change."

"I will." I pause, feeling the significance of this call. "This means a lot to me, Gage."

"I'm here. You know where to find me."

After his call, I sit in the stillness he left behind. My shoulders drop. My breath comes easier. Nothing is solved. Nothing is certain. But my panic has softened. And I don't feel quite as alone as I did.

CHAPTER 11
GAGE

NOON COMES and goes on Tuesday, and Amelia doesn't show for our meeting. I give her fifteen minutes before deciding something's happened. I checked social media this morning, something I don't do often, and saw the updates on her. A lot of nasty shit has been posted, but most concerning is the speculation over her contract for *Velocity Reign*.

I call her at 12:15 p.m.

She doesn't answer, but within a minute, she calls me back.

"Oh my god, Gage, I am sooooo sorry!" She's a burst of frantic energy and words that are slightly slurred. "Shit! Shit, shit."

I frown. "Have you been drinking?" It certainly sounds like it.

I'm met with silence, and in it, I hear the distinct sounds of low music, laughter, and the soft hum of a midday crowd.

"Where are you?" I ask, already out of my seat.

"I am so embarrassed."

"Amelia. Where are you?"

"I never do this. I've never missed anything in my life. I can't believe I forgot." Her words trip over each other, unfiltered.

"Amelia." My tone is firm. The kind I use when I need answers. "Tell me where you are."

She takes a moment. "At The Langham. I'm sorry I missed our meeting."

"Wait there. I'll come to you."

She says something that's muffled, as if she's got her mouth covered. It sounded a lot like, "For the love of God, don't wear a tuxedo."

I grab my jacket and walk out of my office. "Did you just tell me not to wear a tux?"

"Shit. Did I say that out loud?" Before I can answer, she adds, "I'm not taking it back."

My lips twitch. "Amelia, are you day drinking?" I'm both amused and concerned by that idea.

"In my defense, I have reasons."

I chuckle. "Good to know this isn't just something you do for fun." We end the call, and I eye my assistant who I'm now standing in front of. "Cancel my afternoon."

Lucy's eyebrows hit her forehead. "No way. Don't do this to me, Gage," she whisper-yells. "You've got John at three."

John's one of the most powerful men in global finance. He hired me to assess cross-market risks tied to rising geopolitical tensions. It's the kind of work that shifts forecasts and rattles portfolios.

I don't cancel on men like John. Ever. Not when the

work we do reshapes markets and moves governments. But I'm already walking.

I meet Lucy's panic with a firm, "Reschedule it."

She mutters something about updating her résumé, but I block it out and head for the elevator. Lucy has worked for me for five years, and this isn't the first time she's threatened to quit. We've seen some shit together in those five years and she has my back just as much as I have hers. She's not going anywhere.

It's a ten-minute walk from my office to The Langham. Less if I'm walking with intent, which I am today.

I spot her the moment I walk in. She's alone at a table near the bar. Dressed in a black sleeveless jumpsuit that's belted at the waist. Her blazer hangs on the back of her chair. Her heels have been kicked off under the table.

A cocktail glass sits in front of her, half-empty, the stem caught between her fingers while she stares at it like she's considering all her life choices to date.

She doesn't see me until I reach her. When she glances up, I catch the look of someone who's past the point of pretending. Her eyes are a little glassy, her smile wobbly.

"Oh, thank god," she says. "No tuxedo."

I take the seat across from her. "You really hate the tux, huh?"

She rolls her eyes, and this isn't just any eye roll. This is dramatic and so un-Amelia. "You really have no idea, do you?"

Fuck, I'm invested in this conversation to the point I'd blow off a thousand Johns for it. "I really don't. You're going to have to enlighten me."

She lifts her glass to her lips and takes a sip, all while

keeping her eyes very much locked on mine. "You wear a tux like nobody's business. It's actually rude how good you look in it."

I bite back a grin. "Got it. A tuxedo is required the next time we blow off work together."

"If I ever see you in one again, there will be hell to pay."

"That'd be the kind of hell I think I'd enjoy."

The flare of heat in her eyes tells me that landed. And then the alcohol she's consumed does all the talking, telling me things Amelia would never say sober.

"Honestly, I'm convinced God put you on earth to drive me wild. Between your eyes, your mouth, your voice, your hands, your muscles"—she makes wide eyes at me—"that cologne you wear. Not to mention the way you just"—she waves her hand in the air, searching for the right word—"I don't know, exist. It's too much."

I let out a low laugh. "The way I exist."

"Yes!"

"I think you may need to explain that to me too."

"I thought you were just like James. The kind of guy who thinks he owns everything in his life, including the people. But no, you had to go and show me you're not like that at all. You're a good dad, *a really good dad*, and you care about people. Although, it *was* mean that you wanted to scrap all those science fair plans without taking Stephanie's feelings into account. So, you could work on that." She pauses, giving me those dramatic eyes again. "It's a lot, Gage. Like, I'm just over here trying to live my life and get through my days. Which, can I just tell you, are already *busy*. And now I have to add thinking about you to my schedule."

I open my mouth to speak, but she's not finished.

"And dating. Good. God," she carries on. "I don't know how to date anymore. I don't know how soon men expect sex. I don't know what 'soft launching' really means. I don't know if emojis are flirting or just punctuation now. I don't know how you're supposed to be chill and honest at the same time. I don't even know if it's okay to ask if you're the only person someone's seeing anymore. Is that desperate? Or, God forbid, cringe?"

Fuck me.

Amelia just placed her heart down between us. Handed me her truth, piece by unfiltered piece like she didn't even realize what she was giving me. And I have never seen anything more beautiful.

"It's not desperate or cringe."

That slows her down. She narrows her eyes at me like she's not sure if I actually know the answer to her question. "Really?"

"It's real. And fucking refreshing. As for emojis, they should be banned from dating. They leave too much room for misunderstandings. Soft launching? No fucking idea what that is either. And sex? You decide that for yourself, Amelia, and you don't ever let any man tell you your decision is wrong. Dating is your choice. All the way around."

It's like I've knocked the wind out of her with that. Gone is the wildly expressive woman of a moment ago, and in her place sits a woman stunned by my response.

"I think I need another drink to process all of that," she finally declares.

I'm not convinced that's her best course of action but

far be it from me to tell a woman what she should do. Instead, I ask, "What happened today?"

Her gaze drops to her empty cocktail glass, and she runs a finger back and forth over the base of it. She does that for a long moment before glancing back up at me. "I lost the *Velocity Reign* contract. I came here for a meeting, but the studio canceled at the last minute and didn't show. They said they're moving in a different creative direction now, which is studio-speak for 'I'm a liability now.'"

"I'm sorry."

She nods. "Yeah. Me too." She goes back to the base of the glass, but only for a few seconds before looking up again. "No, I'm pissed off, actually." Her expression turns fierce. "I'm fucking angry that Sofia Raye can spread lies about me and ruin my career. I'm fucking angry that strangers who don't even know me get to say shit about me on social media. I'm fucking angry that I have to stay silent. That the lawyers I'm paying a fortune to won't let me defend myself in public. I'm fucking angry that I now don't get to work on a film I really wanted to. *And*"—she inhales a sharp breath—"I'm fucking angry that I lost one of my favorite earrings today."

She exhales a long breath after unloading all of that. I can't tell if she feels better or not now. I watch her silently, giving her space. She doesn't look away. Just takes all the time I give her to direct the conversation.

"I didn't do it." Her voice is raw, stripped of the anger now. "I didn't steal Sofia's work."

She watches me like she's bracing for my response.

"Amelia, if there's one thing I know about you, it's that you would *never* do that."

"You don't even know me," she says softly. "How can you be so sure?"

I lean forward. "Because I've been watching you for a year. I've seen the way you carry yourself, what's important to you. You show up, even when it's hard. You speak the truth, even when it's uncomfortable. You own your shit. I've never once seen you pass the blame or spin a story to make yourself look better." I let that sit before continuing. "You don't perform for the world. You don't play the game. Fuck, I don't think you even know what the game is. You're too real for that. And your work? You're fucking talented. And you've got pride in what you do. But more than that, you've got pride in who you are. That's how I know. I see your standards. I see your integrity. People like you don't steal. You don't need to."

I sit back, watching her process everything I just said. I don't think she was expecting any of it when she asked how I could be so sure. And once again, I'm hit by how wrong I've been about her this past year. She's absolutely all the things I just said, but where I saw cool confidence before, I misread what was underneath. I assumed that meant she was in control. Content. Had her shit sorted.

Amelia is confident. I've seen it. But I think she's been taught to keep herself small. Manageable. I think if the world would just get the fuck out of her way, she'd stop playing by its rules and rewrite every damn one of them.

"So," she says after a lot of processing, "it turns out you're not an asshole after all."

I laugh. I couldn't stop it even if I wanted to. Amelia unfiltered is fucking disarming. "That's the second compliment you've given me. I thought the first one was an outlier and there would be no more."

"Well, you just gave me some, so I thought I'd return the favor."

"By my calculations, I'm still due a few if you're returning the favor."

She lifts her brows. "Did I, or did I not, tell you that your ass is hot when you first got here? I think that makes us even."

Christ, I could do this with her all day.

"No, my ass wasn't mentioned. But I've just made a mental update to your list."

Her own enjoyment of this conversation is written across her face and I fucking like seeing that in her.

"Honestly, I don't think you need me to help you out with compliments. I'm pretty sure you've got a long line of women ready to throw them at you."

"Yours are the only ones I'm interested in hearing, Amelia."

That causes heat in her eyes again. Then, a long stare before she stands abruptly. "I need to use the bathroom," she announces. "And you need to stop saying things like that." She grabs her heels from under the table. "When I get back, we should have our science fair planning meeting."

She's slipping her shoes on when the server approaches to ask if we'd like food or drinks.

"Sure," Amelia says. "I'll have another cocktail. An Everything All At Once, please."

"Jesus," I say. "What's in that?" It sounds like something I would have chosen in my early twenties. Something to really fuck me up.

She shrugs. "I can't remember, but it's good." She looks at the server. "Do you know?"

He nods and rattles off the list of ingredients. "Whisky, rum, pear spice, and walnut liqueur."

Fuck. That's not a drink. That's trauma waiting to happen.

"And you, Sir?" he asks.

"I'll take a bourbon. Neat. Someone here has to remember their name tomorrow."

He gives me a quick grin before leaving.

"How many have you had?" I ask Amelia who's now hunting around in her purse for something.

"Three. I think." She locates what she's looking for and then glances at me. "I'm going to the bathroom now. Don't steal my drink if it arrives before I come back."

She says that like it's a real possibility, which I find highly amusing. My amusement vanishes the second she heads for the bathroom and I see what those three drinks have done to her.

I should have discouraged another drink. She's walking like the floor's shifting beneath her.

I signal for the check and push my chair back, ready to get us out of here. By the time Amelia returns, the bill has been settled, and the drinks returned.

She gives me a questioning look. "Are you leaving?"

I button my jacket. "No, *we're* leaving."

Her expression shifts into a frown. "I thought we were going to do some science fair planning over drinks."

"Amelia, I'll never tell you what to do, but from where I'm standing, you're looking at a bad headache in the morning if we stay for drinks. If you really want to have another one, just say the word and I'll make it happen, but I'd rather take you home and help prevent a hangover."

She's silent for a long beat and I can't tell which way she'll go. Finally, she says, "God. You really are a whole-ass situation, even when you're not wearing a tuxedo."

And then she's reaching for her blazer, turning, and walking out of the bar while I'm left wondering what the hell she means by that.

The thing I'm not in the dark about?

Amelia's been thinking about me just as much as I've been thinking about her.

CHAPTER 12
AMELIA

MY WEEK DOESN'T GO from bad to worse as it wears on, but it certainly doesn't go from bad to good.

On Wednesday afternoon, the day after my day drinking episode, I get stuck in a long meeting with my lawyer and agent. Just after two p.m., I realize I'm nowhere near close to being finished and that I won't make it to school on time to collect Sarah. Since I don't want to ask James for help, I open my phone to text Shayla and Gage to see which of them has Luna tonight and whether they can help me out.

The second I open my messages, I'm reminded that Gage texted me this morning and that his text remains unanswered. The mortification I feel over my behavior yesterday flares again, just like it did when I woke up and found his text.

Not only did I mess up his schedule by forgetting our meeting, but I also said a lot of things to him. A *lot*. And although some of it's hazy, I remember most of it.

He was a gentleman about it all and got me home safely. But God knows what he thinks of me now.

I push my embarrassment down so I can find someone to pick Sarah up.

GAGE:

How are you feeling after yesterday?

ME:

Hey, sorry I haven't had a chance to reply. I wasn't too bad this morning. Just a slight headache. I actually have a favor to ask. I can't get to Sarah in time for pickup. Do you have Luna tonight?

GAGE:

Yeah. I can grab Sarah too.

ME:

You're a lifesaver! Thank you.

I go back and forth in my mind over sending him another text with an apology for yesterday, but in the end, I have to put my phone away and get back to my meeting.

It's almost four by the time I get to Gage's building, and by then I'm a walking ad for overwhelm, poor life management, and total disarray.

I walk into the lobby, the tall glass doors whispering shut behind me. The space is all muted luxury with its sleek stone, matte black accents, and low lighting that makes it feel more like a private gallery than a residential building.

The doorman spots me from behind the curved marble desk and smiles in recognition. He taps something on the embedded touch panel in the desk and greets me. "Good afternoon, Ms Sinclair. Mr. Black's on his way up. I'll let him know you're joining him."

"On his way up?" I thought he was already home.

He nods and gestures toward the elevators. "Yes."

Right. That explained everything.

His arm stays extended, a quiet prompt to head for the elevator bank.

"Thank you," I say and make my way over.

A moment later, Gage's private elevator opens, and he's standing inside. His intense gaze settles on me, and it feels like his eyes hold a thousand questions. But that could just be me. Maybe I'm overthinking all of this.

"Hey," I say a little breathlessly as I join him. My fingers are instantly in my hair, running through it the way they do when I'm nervous. "I thought you would already be home." *I thought I'd have this elevator ride to gather myself before having to see him and face my embarrassment over yesterday.*

The elevator doors close as he says, "I got caught at work. Shirley collected the girls." His nanny.

I nod, still feeling like my lungs hold barely any oxygen. "Right."

God, this is awkward.

When he doesn't say anything, I rush to fill the silence. "Thank you." My words come out too fast. And go nowhere. And there's still not enough oxygen inside me. My gaze darts to the doors in front of me as I listen to the quiet hum of the elevator going up. Only for a second, and then I force my eyes back to Gage. "For helping me out, I mean. Today, that is."

He's watching me intently. Too intently. It makes me feel naked. This man sees far too much, and I want to pull a thousand curtains between us so he can't see anything.

"Amelia," he starts, but the elevator lurches, stopping all conversation.

There's a hard, mechanical thud, and then a sudden stop that throws me off balance.

I reach a hand to the wall to steady myself. "Did it just . . ."

"Yeah," Gage says, already stepping forward and pressing the panel. He taps a few buttons. Nothing lights up. I hear him curse softly before hitting the call button.

A moment later, a robotic voice says, "Emergency call initiated. Assistance will arrive shortly."

Shit.

I'm not claustrophobic, but I suddenly feel like I am as my anxiety rises.

"You okay?" Gage asks.

I nod, trying to ignore my inner spiral. "Totally fine."

His eyes narrow slightly. "Liar."

I let out a breath that's also half a laugh. "Okay, not *fine*. But I'm trying not to panic."

A soft chime sounds and then a crisp voice comes through the speaker.

"Mr. Black? Tony here. Just letting you know we've flagged the elevator issue. Maintenance is en route. They're saying twenty minutes."

Gage steps closer to the panel. "Thanks, Tony."

"I'll keep you updated, Sir."

The line clicks off with a soft beep.

I exhale through my nose. "Twenty minutes."

"That's worst case."

"Yeah, well, worst case is me dying in here and them finding my body in twenty minutes."

His lips twitch. "I think you'll survive."

I press my back against the wall. "You clearly underestimate my talent for internal collapse."

All traces of humor disappear from his face, and he holds my gaze with quiet assurance. "Amelia. You're safe. I've got you."

I nod, but don't answer. Instead, I focus on my breath.

Inhale.

Exhale.

Again.

My palms are damp, so I press them against the cool wall behind me. Close my eyes for a moment.

Four counts in.

Hold.

Four counts out.

My heart's still jumpy, but the buzzing under my skin starts to fade. Not gone, but manageable.

I open my eyes and look at Gage. He's back to watching with that intense focus. "I'm okay."

"Maybe we should sit," he suggests as he shrugs out of his suit jacket and undoes the top couple of buttons of his shirt. He doesn't appear rattled by any of this.

I, on the other hand, have stress heat crawling over my skin, and can't get my coat off fast enough.

Gage lowers himself to the floor, and God help me; even in my anxious state, I notice the way his shirt pulls tightly across his chest as he sits.

I follow, sliding down the wall into a seated position. My pencil skirt shifts with the motion, riding up enough to expose some of my thighs. I stretch my legs out, crossing one ankle over the other. When I glance up, I catch sight of Gage's gaze on my legs right before he shifts his attention to his phone.

He taps out a text. "I've just let Shirley know we're here. She said the girls are busy with their science project." Amusement fills his face. "Apparently, Luna's dramatics are getting too much for Sarah."

"I imagine Sarah's annoying Luna too. She's like me and tends to zero in on details that don't really matter."

"They all matter. It's a good skill to have. Luna will hopefully learn that from her."

His compliment throws me back to yesterday. To all the kind things he said to me. *And* the hot mess I was. "Gage, I'm sorry about yesterday."

"You don't have anything to be sorry about."

I smooth my hands down my skirt. Another nervous habit. There are too many words in my head. Too much wild uncertainty in my life. And I'm struggling to sort through it. To keep it all firmly under control like I usually do. And then there's Gage. And my attraction to him. It makes thinking about all the things I need to think about hard.

"Amelia," he says, and I realize I got lost in my thoughts.

I bring my gaze back to him. "I really do. Mostly because I missed our meeting, and it dragged you away from work."

"That was my choice. I was worried about you."

I rest my head back against the wall and look up at the ceiling of the elevator. "I hate that."

"What? Someone worrying over you?"

"Yes." I turn my head to him. "It's a responsibility you don't need to add to your plate."

"I care about you, Amelia. And that's not a responsibility. It's a choice."

I'm not used to this kind of care. Not the kind that's simple or that doesn't come with expectations. I've been showing up for myself since I was a kid, long before I even understood that not everyone had to. My friends are lovely, but they orbit the surface. Dinner, book club, school events. They don't ask the deeper questions. They wouldn't know where to look for my fault lines, even if I handed them a map.

My brothers are the only ones who see through the "I'm fine" and call me on it. Everyone else? I keep them at arm's length. Not because I don't want closeness. But because letting someone in means chancing disappointment, and care—real care—has always felt like something that comes with a cost. Like the moment you accept it, you owe something back.

"So, no hangover this morning?" he asks while I sit with the unfamiliar feeling of being seen, and the reflex that still wants to pull back.

"I was okay." I smile. "Which I know I have you to thank for. I'm not certain I would have stopped after three cocktails yesterday if not for you."

"I've been there. It gets messy real fast. I wanted to save you from that."

"I appreciate it."

"How was today?"

"Long. Awful. And for anyone out there looking for fun things to add to their yearly bingo card, I ten out of ten do not recommend what was added to mine this week."

He studies me. "Are you holding up?"

I draw in a long breath. The truth is I'm not okay. Not even close.

I was raised to believe messes are shameful. That if something falls apart, you fix it fast. And quietly. But this mess I'm in? It's loud. It's public. And for the first time, I don't think I can clean it up on my own.

"No," I admit softly with a shake of my head. "No, I'm not okay. I am so far from okay it's almost laughable."

He doesn't say anything. Just sits with me, holding space for me. His gaze doesn't waver, and it makes me feel like he sees the whole mess of me and doesn't mind staying in it.

"All my life, I've held things together," I go on. "It wasn't hard. It was just what I did. Then, my marriage fell apart, and *everything* has become hard. Slowly, though. It crept up on me and I didn't see it happening. The last couple of months have felt like compound interest kicked in, speeding it all up, and now here I am. Drowning."

"I know that feeling well."

"Really? Because it sure doesn't look like it."

"What does it look like?"

"You always seem so calm. So unaffected by life."

"Spend a little time with me. You'll see the cracks."

I shift, angling my body his way. "Can you just tell me one thing that makes you feel like you're drowning so I can believe you?"

He doesn't even have to think about his answer. "Parenting. That makes me feel like I'm drowning every damn day."

His admission stuns me. Not because he finds parenting hard. We all do. But because he was willing to be vulnerable. I like that he doesn't pretend life hasn't touched him.

"Co-parenting is the hardest thing I've ever had to do," he continues. "The tightrope of managing past hurts, current frustrations, getting hit every now and again with reminders of what once was, and constantly reminding myself I have a child who has to come first . . . that shit is fucking hard. And some days, I'm not sure how I'll make it through."

My breath whooshes out of me. Gage just put all my thoughts and feelings about single parenting into words and I physically felt every one of them. "Yes," I agree quietly. "I feel all of that too."

"But the flipside of that is something special." The emotion in his voice isn't loud, but it's there in every word. "I'm not certain I'd have the relationship with Luna that I have now if not for being a single father."

"Because of all the time you spend alone with her?"

"That. But also, because I was forced to assess my priorities. I had to decide if my work was more important than time with my daughter. I could have hired a full-time nanny, but I chose not to." He stops talking and glances away for a beat, then turns to me again. His voice is rougher when he says, "I think if Shayla and I hadn't divorced, I wouldn't have chosen to spend as much time with Luna. And that's a hell of a confession, because it says a lot about me as a man."

"It says a lot about the man you chose to be, Gage."

"Yeah," he says slowly, almost hesitantly, like he's not sure he's earned that version of himself yet. "Point is, sometimes when things go to hell, it clears space for something else you didn't even know you needed."

As I think about that, I become aware that it's getting warm in here. When I reach up to undo the top couple buttons of my blouse, Gage's eyes are drawn to my chest. He doesn't even try to hide it. The way he watches unapologetically is mildly erotic. And when I say mildly, I mean it would count as foreplay if we were together.

His gaze slides back up to mine once I'm finished with my buttons. We don't speak. We just watch each other.

Having only ever been with one man, I don't consider myself experienced when it comes to sex. Not really. And well, I've established I'm out of my depth when it comes to flirting these days. Especially with a man like Gage who embodies sex like it's built into his DNA.

But here, in this moment with him, I don't feel shy. God, I *like* his eyes on me.

I give him a slow smile, leaning into the ease of being with him, and return to our conversation. "I'm not sure what better place this plagiarism accusation will lead to, but I hope you're right. Because right now, it's shit. And social media can fuck right off."

His mouth quirks. "Is that a new Ameliaism?"

My smile deepens, spreading through me. An *Amcli-aism*. It's such a small thing, but it affects me because it feels like he's been collecting pieces of me and naming them. He sees me not just as a woman, or as Sarah's mom, but as *me*. "What? The fuck right off?"

"Yeah. I've never heard you swear like that."

"I've probably been spending too much time with you. You're a bad influence."

He raises a brow. "I'm not the one who was day drinking yesterday."

Surprisingly, I feel none of the embarrassment I've been feeling all day. "I was having a bad day."

More of that amused look. "Yeah, you had reasons. I remember." The amusement reaches his eyes fully. "You lost a favorite earring. Hell of a week."

"Oh, god." I laugh. "Did I tell you that?"

"You told me a lot of things." And there's that heat. In his eyes. Across his face. Pulsing in between his words. "I now know just how much you like a tuxedo."

I don't pull my eyes from his. I don't deflect. I stay right in this with him even though the part of me that's scared of where this will all end is doing her best to signal danger.

"You do look good in one."

"Apparently I'm a whole-ass situation even when I'm not wearing one."

"You're enjoying this a little too much."

He gives me a sexy smile and goodness if I don't feel it low. "Guilty as charged. Though I'm not entirely sure what a whole-ass situation is."

"I think you know exactly what it is. And if you don't, I'm not explaining it to you."

He chuckles and then proceeds to roll up his sleeves as he says, "So, you're considering dating."

I'm staring at his forearms when he throws that out. They're a whole-ass situation all on their own. "Yes," I answer distractedly, then lift my gaze back to his and shake my head. "No. No, I'm not dating." *And put those arms away. Now.*

"I got the distinct impression yesterday that it's on your mind. Have you dated much since your divorce?"

"Just a few dinners here and there. Honestly, I don't have the time for it."

He takes a moment with that. "Right. And then there's the emojis and the soft launching and all the expectations."

"Did you memorize everything I said to you yesterday?"

"I think you know the answer to that."

Good lord, Gage is the most direct man I have ever met. And where he allowed my retreat when we danced at my parents' party, I don't think he's going to do that again.

"Dating feels hard. And messy. I need another year to overthink it."

"Or maybe, you just need someone who will give you the space to figure it out in your own way. On your own terms."

My heart starts beating faster. A little panicked at where he's pushing this. And at not being able to exit stage left out of this conversation right now.

I'm more attracted to Gage than I've been to anyone. However, I wasn't looking for a man, and just jumping into whatever this is with him? Absolutely not. I need to be more certain about it before taking that kind of risk.

"I've barely moved on from my marriage, Gage. I'm not rushing into another relationship. And I have Sarah to consider. I have to be very sure about whoever I choose to bring into our lives."

The elevator intercom buzzes, interrupting us. "Mr. Black," Tony's voice comes through the speaker, "maintenance is in the building. They should have the elevator running in the next five minutes."

"Thanks, Tony," Gage says as he stands.

The line clicks off and he turns to me and extends a hand.

I slip my fingers into his, and the moment he pulls me up, I'm closer to him than I anticipated. We're chest to chest, the air between us tight, and I'm staring into those dark eyes of his. Those absolutely lethal eyes of his.

He keeps hold of my hand, not letting me step away. "Stay for dinner."

My pulse slams into overdrive. "What are you cooking?"

"Does it matter? It's gotta beat going home after a long and awful day and having to cook for yourself."

"I don't like fish," I throw out, stalling.

"I'm not cooking fish."

"Or lamb. I'm not in the mood for that tonight."

"Got it. No lamb."

I swallow a tangle of emotions that have nothing to do with food. "It's not a bad idea. We could work on the science fair."

"We could," he agrees, but everything I'm looking at right now says that's the last thing on his mind.

"I saw the email you sent Stephanie." The one he sent her last night expressing his hope that she's okay and offering the opportunity to help us on the day of the fair if she still wants to be involved. He cc'd me on it. "That was a nice thing to do." *And yes. I. Am. Stalling*.

"Well, I *was* told to work on being nicer to people."

"'Told' seems a little strong. I feel like it was more of a suggestion."

"Amelia," he says, and *God*, this man knows how to boss a woman without even trying.

"Okay, yes," I blurt. "I'll stay for dinner. But it's just dinner. So you know."

"I wouldn't dream of assuming anything where you're concerned. I imagine that would get me into some hell."

And just like that, he settles my racing heart.

I can trust Gage to let me take my time. He's proven that already.

I unthread our fingers and bring my hand up to pat his chest. "You would do well to remember that."

His grin is the last thing I see before maintenance interrupts us.

CHAPTER 13

@THETEA_GASP

JUST WHEN WE THOUGHT THE @ameliasinclair situation couldn't get messier, she said "hold my cocktail." In a plot twist no one saw coming, she was spotted day drinking (yes, DAY. DRINKING.) this week with none other than @gageblack, aka CEO of BMS™, walking credit card slam, and collector of heiresses. ICYMI: Amelia is currently getting absolutely dragged on social media over plagiarism accusations from pop darling @sofiarayeofficial, and things are escalating FAST. Sources are saying she's officially been dropped from Velocity Reign. So, what's she doing sipping cocktails with Gage "Unattainable" Black? Bestie, look at that photo of them! Suddenly "unattainable" is looking very much booked and emotionally compromised. They're not even touching, but the way he's looking at her? It's giving "I'd ruin my whole reputation for you" energy. MFW the internet stopped dragging just long enough to zoom in on the intensity in that man's eyes. We're not saying he's obsessed, but if he isn't, someone better tell his face. Is this a soft launch? We don't know. But if it is? We. Are. Seated.

CHAPTER 14

AMELIA

TIM:

Happy Saturday.

ME:

Why must you be so cheery all the time?

TIM:

You checked Instagram today?

ME:

No. You know I hate that place.

TIM:

Okay.

ME:

OMG don't leave me hanging. What is it?

TIM:

Someone went day drinking with someone this week and didn't spill the goss.

ME:

What?

COLIN:

It's all over Instagram. Your date with Gage at The Langham.

TIM:

Can we get confirmation that this is no longer fake dating?

ME:

That wasn't a date.

ME:

That was me having a bad day. I told you about it. That was the day I lost the contract.

TIM:

And Gage just happened to pop by?

COLIN:

You told us you lost the contract. You didn't tell us Gage and day drinking were involved.

ME:

It was NOT a date.

TIM:

The lady doth protest too much, methinks.

COLIN:

Agreed.

ME:

I'm done with you two for today.

TIM:

And this is why I'm so cheery today. As
you were.

AGAINST ALL GOOD JUDGMENT, I do something I've
managed not to do for three days. I open Instagram. And
after reading some posts, I wish I hadn't.

Someone snapped a photo of me and Gage at the bar
on Tuesday and posted it last night. Why they waited
three days to post it is anyone's guess, but my brain takes
all of one second to twist the timing of it into being part
of some bigger plot. Because that's what this entire week
feels like: one big plot against me.

The three days since that photo was taken have felt
like a demolition of everything I've built in my career.
After the *Velocity Reign* contract was pulled, other projects
started slipping through my fingers. Suddenly, I'm
receiving emails with words like "we need more time
before moving forward", and "we need to pause the
current direction." No one's saying it, but it feels like I'm
being quietly blacklisted.

I'm five minutes into my Instagram scrolling when a
text comes through from my publicist.

MARIN:

Babes. What's the go with Gage Black?

My agent brought Marin in the morning the story
broke. She's young, terrifyingly upbeat, calls me *babes*,
ends half her sentences with sparkle emojis, and seems
alarmingly unfazed watching my life implode.

And great question, Marin. I'd like to know the
answer to it also.

Gage cooked me dinner on Wednesday night. Not fish. Not lamb. But steak with sautéed broccolini and roasted potatoes. It was, frankly, the best thing I've eaten all week. And I may or may not have cursed the Universe while eating it because apparently the man is not only hot and emotionally aware, but he can cook too.

The girls loved the four of us having dinner again and happily chatted about all the things that happened that day at school. After we ate, they played in Luna's bedroom while Gage and I cleaned up. He kept it light between us and didn't broach the subject of dating again. Instead, he asked me about my work and how I became a composer. We also went over some things for the science fair.

Since then, we've texted a few times. Mostly about the science fair, solving problems as they popped up. Nothing deep. Nothing that even came close to touching on the heat that's been simmering between us. The heat that *I* can't stop thinking about.

The fact he's now living rent free in my head is deeply inconvenient for my emotional stability and productivity levels. Every time my phone buzzes, I want it to be him. And when it's not, I reread his last text like it holds the answers to life, the universe, and whatever this is between us.

He pushed things between us three days ago and hasn't made a single move since. Which means I'm now obsessing over a man who's either giving me space or has quietly changed his mind. And I can't decide which option I prefer.

I tap out a text to Marin.

ME:

There's nothing happening between us.

MARIN:

That's not what that photo looked like. I need an angle.

I swear she talks in another language.

ME:

An angle?

MARIN:

Yeah, give me something to go on.

ME:

There's nothing to go on.

MARIN:

Okay, let me bring you up to speed, babes. Comment sections on Tiktok have turned into war zones. One half thinks you're the villain who stole music and seduced a billionaire to clean up the mess. The other half thinks you're a misunderstood artist who soft-launched a zaddy to distract from the scandal. I need to know which one to run with.

A zaddy? Does she not know I'm a single mom who spends her days packing school lunches, googling how to get slime out of a rug, trying to remember if I already RSVP'd to the school field trip, and barely has time to shave both legs at the same time? I know some slang. I'm not completely out of touch. But my brain only has space for about five pieces of Influencer Speak, and "zaddy" isn't one of them.

ME:

Gage is my daughter's best friend's father. We're friends. That's all.

MARIN:

Okay, so friends to lovers. I can work with that.

ME:

What??? No!!

MARIN:

Thanks, babes. Gotta run xx

I switch to texting my brothers in our group chat.

ME:

What's a zaddy?

TIM:

I see you've been on Insta.

ME:

Tim!

TIM:

Zaddy = hot older dude with $$$, style, and "I could ruin your life and buy you dinner after" energy. So, basically: Gage.

ME:

Gage isn't old.

TIM:

Okay, so zaddy status isn't just about age. It's about energy.

COLIN:

I think this is what they call a situationship.

ME:

> What the heck is a situationship? And why can't we all just talk in proper English?

TIM:

> Oh, babe.

TIM:

> A situationship = somewhere between "we're just friends" and "I'd burn down a small village if someone else touched you."

TIM:

> Undefined relationship that's confusing. Low-commitment, high emotional damage. Also known as: modern romance.

ME:

> I hate everything.

COLIN:

> Define "everything."

ME:

> This. You two. The internet. Modern dating. Words like zaddy.

TIM:

> She's spiraling. Place your bets now. I give it two hours before she bakes a dozen cakes and starts labeling her pantry.

I place my phone down and decide Tim doesn't know me at all. I then proceed to take a shower, shave both legs, exfoliate, moisturize, and put on actual clothes. I am calm. I am collected. I am absolutely not spiraling over whatever Marin has decided is our "angle", or the things being said on social media.

I even light a candle and read a chapter of a novel. That's how not *spiraling* I am.

And then, an hour and fifty-one minutes later, I receive a text from James about how he just knew I was giving it to Gage, and my spiral is on. I'm in the kitchen, lining up ingredients like I'm prepping for *The Great British Bake Off* and muttering things like "It's just one cake, Tim can calm down."

Five hours later, I'm still in my kitchen. I've baked my little heart out. I've rearranged my pantry. Cleaned my fridge. And successfully avoided both social media and my ex-husband all afternoon.

My kitchen is a mess, though.

I'm thinking about cleaning it up when my doorman calls to let me know Gage is here. I glance down at myself, at the oversized oatmeal knit sweater that hangs off one shoulder, black leggings dusted with flour, and fuzzy socks that used to be all white but now have cocoa sprinkled over them. My hair's in a messy bun that's doing more mess than bun, and I'm pretty sure there's flour in there too. Not exactly the picture of "come on in", but here we are.

"Thanks. Send him up, Dan," I say, then spin to assess the war zone that is my kitchen. If I had magical powers, now would be the time to summon them. One snap of my fingers, and poof—clean hair, spotless kitchen, and maybe clothes that don't look like I lost a baking battle. But no, no magic. Just me, knee-deep in domestic disarray, and Gage on his way up.

I'm back in the kitchen when the elevator dings and I

swear that sound just became as sexually charged as a text notification is for me these days.

He strides into my kitchen wearing black dress pants and a fitted, crisp black shirt with the sleeves rolled up just enough to end me.

"Seriously," I toss out, unable to stop myself, "do you own any clothes that don't scream 'sexy hostile takeover?'"

A slow, sexy smile fills his face as he comes to a stop on the other side of the island to me. "What are we talking here? Gray sweatpants that hang low? Running shorts? I've got some of those in my closet."

"I walked into that one," I mutter, now imagining Gage in sweatpants.

That sexy smile remains locked in place while he takes a long moment to look me over. Then, his gaze sweeps across the kitchen, and he comes back to me with a raised brow. "Is the school having a bake sale I forgot about?"

"No. I decided I'd bake ten cakes just for the fun of it. You're welcome to take them all home so I don't have to eat any of them."

"Right," he says, and I see him trying to make sense of me. "Is this because of social media? That photo of us that's circulating?"

"Maybe." I really don't want to have to tell him the angle that Marin's decided to run with.

"That's cleared things up for me."

I bite my lip. "Yes."

"Amelia." His voice drops into that tone he uses when he's trying to boss me into something. "Tell me what's going on."

I may be a highly intelligent woman, but Gage is a walking override button for all things logical, rational, or remotely self-preserving. And sometimes, I'm horrified by what escapes my mouth. Today is one of those times. Because when I open it to answer his question, what actually comes out is, "Do you know what a zaddy is?"

Good. God.

I shake my head like that'll delete the last three seconds. "No. Ignore that. Tell me why you're here and then I'll tell you why I'm baking."

"I do not know what a zaddy is," he says, entirely too entertained and not letting me off the hook. That smile of his makes a full comeback, shifting into a smirk as he adds, "Care to tell me?"

"No. You'll have to do your own research, just like I had to."

He pulls out his phone, taps for a second, reads, and then lifts that smirk right back up to me like it was made for this very moment. "I now know what a zaddy is. I'm still clueless on the whole-ass situation, though. Google says it's a problematic situation, but that doesn't seem accurate."

This man.

For real.

"Right," I say, calling on every ounce of bossiness I have. "That smirk needs to go. And you need to tell me why you're here. Then you need to pack up all these cakes and take them home. And I don't care if you don't want them, or have no room for them, they're leaving here in your arms."

"I should have come ten minutes earlier so you could issue more orders."

I don't know what it is about Gage, but he's got this maddening, irresistible pull that I can't deny. He knows exactly the effect he has on me, and even when I'm trying to hold my ground, he makes it so I can't.

I shake my head while a smile breaks through. "You're impossible."

His smirk gives way to a questioning look. "Are you going to tell me the reason I have so many cakes to take home?"

I sigh. "I have a publicist. She's annoyingly young and I don't understand half the things she says. Today, I may have given her the wrong idea about us."

He waits for me to elaborate.

"She texted looking for an angle for us. I had no idea what she meant. Apparently, the internet is coming to their own conclusions about us, and she was looking for which way to push them."

"What's the angle she chose?" He doesn't even look bothered by this.

"I told her you're the father of my daughter's best friend. She took that to mean friends to lovers." I wince. "I am so sorry to drag you into my mess, Gage."

If I thought he looked unbothered a second ago, whatever you call the level below unbothered . . . that's where he is now. With a side of heat.

"Right," he says, moving around the island to where I'm standing. "So you and I are a thing according to your publicist." It's not a question. It's a statement that he looks very pleased to be making.

"Uh, yes." I watch him come closer, zero idea of his intentions right now, while also feeling all kinds of bothered myself. I am far, far above Gage on that scale.

"And you thought I'd be upset about that angle?"

"Yes."

He stops just shy of the line between close and too close. "You have a lot to learn about me, Amelia."

My heart beats so loudly I'm sure he must be able to hear it. "You're okay if people think that about us?"

His eyes blaze with intensity, and I feel it *everywhere*. "I don't give a fuck what people think about me. And if I had to choose a woman for my name to be linked with, it would be you."

My fingers curl against the island as my body sways toward him. Heat blooms low in my stomach, and it spreads fast. Every nerve tuned to him now.

I want this man.

Goddamn, do I want him.

I have never felt this kind of pull.

It's raw need.

Desperate and undeniable.

My breath hitches when his gaze drops to my mouth, and I think I might beg him to kiss me if he doesn't.

"Fuck," he growls, reaching for me, his hand sliding into my hair.

My hands go to his hips when he moves into me, and then his mouth is claiming mine like he's waited too damn long for this moment. His other hand finds my waist, strong and sure, pulling me against him. Exactly where I want to be.

He's all hard muscle and restrained dominance. I feel every inch of him and want it all more than I've wanted anything.

My hands move to his abs, his chest, his neck, and I

press myself against him harder, chasing the pressure. Needing everything he can give.

When my fingers dig into his neck, he groans and deepens the kiss, his tongue sweeping over mine. His restraint slips and then he's demanding, taking what he wants.

There is absolutely nothing tentative about this kiss. No hesitation. Just heat and hunger and the rough edge of want that's been daring us to cross this line.

Gage slides his hand to my face, fingers pressing into my neck and jaw, firm and unrelenting. The way he holds me there, like he *needs* to, is more intimate than half the sex I've ever had.

It clears every thought from my mind and lets my body take over.

My hands are on his shirt.

My fingers are tearing at buttons.

My desire consuming me.

I've got his shirt open and halfway off when he drags his mouth from mine and grips my face with both hands. His eyes bore into me, wild with lust. "Tell me to stop."

My brain tries to catch up. "Why?" I'm breathless. Confused as to why he's saying that.

"Because I don't think this is what you want. Not yet."

"I don't want you to stop."

He lets go of my face. "Amelia." His voice is raw, like he's only just managing to hold himself back from what he wants. "I don't want to fuck this up."

"You're not." I reach for his belt with the kind of sexual confidence I don't really have. "I want you to fuck me."

"*Fuck*." He utters just one word, but the way he drops it between us undoes me.

I see his desire for me.

I hear it.

And I feel it.

God, do I feel it.

I could easily get addicted to this man if he keeps looking at me the way he is.

He lets me undo his belt buckle.

I keep my eyes on his every second that takes.

Then, I flick the button on his pants and am about to lower his zip when his hand comes to mine, stopping me.

"We do this," he says, "and everything changes."

"It doesn't have to."

"You just want me to fuck you." His eyes are absolutely refusing to let mine go. "And then you want to go back to just being parents who help each other out with childcare?"

"That works for me."

"It doesn't work for me."

The way he says that with such certainty causes me to slow myself down and pull my brain back into this conversation. "You don't want sex?"

"Oh, I want it. I also want what goes with it."

I stare at him, my heart beating loudly. "I'm not sure that's a good idea."

"Why?"

"Gage. You need to think about this. We've got the girls to consider."

"Trust me when I tell you I've thought about it. I've spent two weeks doing nothing *but* thinking about it. And as much as I've tried to get you out of my head, to put

Luna first, I can't. For the first time in a long fucking time, I want something for myself."

"You want a relationship?"

"I want to spend time with you. Get to know you. See where that takes us."

My mind spins, trying to unravel my feelings about this. Trying to think my way through something that has nothing to do with thinking. "Is that why you came here today?"

"No. I came here to make sure you were okay after that photo of us turned into an onslaught of strangers saying shit about you on social media. Kissing you was not in my plan."

I turn silent. Unsure of everything now. Unable to decide anything.

"I'll go," Gage says. "Give you some space to think about what you want."

"Okay." My thoughts are in such a mess that I have trouble stringing more words together, so I simply wait for what he does next.

His eyes search mine and I think he's fighting with himself. He looks conflicted. Reluctant to leave. In the end, he says, "I'll take care of the photo," before turning and walking out of the kitchen. The sound of the elevator lets me know when he's gone, leaving me alone to make sense of everything that just happened.

I have no idea what he meant about taking care of the photo, but I don't think too much about that. I'm too busy wondering what "space" means to a man like Gage?

This is the third time he's retreated. Something tells me that next time, he won't step back. He'll push.

CHAPTER 15
GAGE

SHAYLA:

I'm going to drop Luna's stuff to you tonight after I have dinner with friends. Is that okay? Or would you prefer I bring it over tomorrow?

ME:

Either works. Whichever is best for you.

SHAYLA:

I'll bring it tonight in case she needs any of it before tomorrow.

IT SEEMS Blair's letter to Shayla a week ago did its job. Or maybe it was the argument I had with her. I braced for backlash, but instead, she's been different. More present with Luna. She had her four nights this week and even called on the others. I don't remember the last time I saw my little girl smile as much as she has this week.

Just before four on Sunday afternoon, I arrive to collect Luna from the birthday party Shayla dropped her at a couple of hours ago. The private room in this residential tower where the party's being held has been transformed into a mini art studio. Easels and canvases are scattered around, half-finished masterpieces bursting with color. A table in the corner holds pastel cupcakes, juice in plastic cups, and a spread of kid-friendly snacks.

Luna's grinning like she's never been happier. And when I spot Sarah calmly dabbing at her canvas, I scan the room. Because where Sarah is, Amelia's never far behind.

I spot her standing alone in the corner opposite the food, engrossed with her phone. Quietly keeping to herself while most of the parents are talking in groups. I run my gaze over her, taking in the blue jeans and simple white top she's wearing. Her hair is pulled back in a ponytail and fuck if I don't imagine getting my hands on it.

Saying no to her yesterday was fucking difficult. I want Amelia more than I've wanted any woman. And it's getting harder to focus on the shit I need to, because my mind is constantly pulled back to her. I told her I'd give her space, but I'm not convinced I won't start pushing.

She looks up just as I reach her. Our eyes lock. And right there, in that split second, I see it. The interest, the heat, the longing for something she's not allowing herself to have.

"Hey," she greets me, her cheeks flushing in that way I've started craving.

"How's the party going? Any feedback from the girls yet?"

"Well," she starts, shifting her weight onto the foot closest to me, her body leaning toward mine in the tiniest of ways that I don't think she's even aware of. "As you can imagine"—she says with a grin—"Luna has painted the masterpiece of all masterpieces. When I arrived, she was holding court, showing it to all the girls. And then she tried to help Sarah, but they had a differing of opinion over the bright colors Luna suggested she use. I do love watching those two together. Even when they're disagreeing, they're still the best of friends."

I'm listening to every word she's saying, but I'm having trouble not thinking about what she said to me yesterday. *I want you to fuck me.* Words that are now burned into my memory, right alongside the way Amelia's voice sounds when she's turned on.

"So, the party was a success."

"Yes, thank God." Her relief is real, and I get it. These things can go either way. Luna and Sarah have both had meltdowns at parties before, feeling left out, left behind, or just feeling miserable.

She lets out a soft breath and runs her fingers through her hair. As she does that, her perfume hits me. Something soft and floral. Not overwhelming, but enough to fuck with my focus. The kind of scent that makes a man want to lean in and find the exact spot it lingers strongest.

I'm distracted as hell by how close she is, how good she smells, and how much I want her when Luna barrels into my side like a missile, jolting me back into reality. "Daddy! Come see my masterpiece!" She takes hold of my hand and drags me to her painting.

She's painted flowers in a field, all vivid pinks, reds, yellows, and greens. Luna has been blessed with creativity, and art is something she has a flair for. This painting is her best yet.

I crouch down to her level and listen while she details all her color choices. When she's finished, I put my hand around her waist and say, "It's beautiful, Luna."

She beams and then turns to gesture at Sarah's painting. "Look what Sarah painted! It's beautiful, too."

"It is." I look at Sarah who's uncomfortable with the kind of gushing praise my daughter enjoys. "You've done a great job, Sarah. Will you hang it on your wall?"

She nods, a shy smile filling her face. "If Mom lets me."

"I'm sure she will." I can't imagine Amelia not encouraging her daughter in this way.

"Daddy." Luna tugs on my arm, drawing my attention back. "Sarah and I were thinking, and we thought it would be fun if you took us to the science museum next weekend."

"Sure. We'll have to ask Sarah's mom if she's okay with that."

Luna takes a deep breath, the kind she always does right before saying something important. "Well," she says carefully, "her mom would *have* to come too. Because, you know, Daddy, she *loves* science. And it wouldn't be fair if she didn't get to go."

Their expectant stares pin me in place as I glance between the two of them. And yeah, this has all the markings of a carefully orchestrated setup. I think I'm being matchmade by six-year-olds.

"Okay," I agree, standing. "I'll ask her."

"Now?" Luna pushes.

"No, she's busy. I'll ask her later." The last thing I want to do is put Amelia on the spot.

Luna glances over to Amelia before frowning at me. "She's not busy, Dad."

"Sweetheart," I use my sterner voice, the one she knows to listen to. "I'll ask her later."

She doesn't force the issue, but the firm press of her lips together says she's not happy about it.

The girls get swept up in photos with the birthday girl after that. I go back to Amelia and try to find a moment to let her know our daughters are on a matchmaking quest, but don't get the chance. We're surrounded by other parents by that point. Then the girls join us, we say our goodbyes, and the opportunity is missed.

Later that night, once Luna is asleep, I text her.

ME:

> I wanted to give you a heads-up that our daughters are in a matchmaking mood. They hit me with a request for us to take them to the science museum next weekend.

She replies almost instantly.

AMELIA:

> Okay, this suddenly makes so much more sense now! They brought up the science museum earlier and vaguely mentioned you coming too, but I thought they meant like transport logistics. Not matchmaking logistics.

ME:

> I suspect it was all Luna.

AMELIA:

> I wonder who she learned that from?

ME:

I'm wounded.

AMELIA:

You'll survive.

Fuck, I like doing this with her.

ME:

I'm still giving you space, Amelia, but you should know it's not easy.

She doesn't come straight back this time.

AMELIA:

Let's go to the science museum with the girls and take it from there.

ME:

I never imagined the day would come when I'd need my kid to help me score a date.

AMELIA:

Goodnight, Gage.

And now I know just how much of an obsession Amelia is becoming.

I'm accepting a date that involves children, the science museum, and no chance of sex. And looking forward to it like it'll be the greatest fucking day of my year.

CHAPTER 16

AMELIA

MONDAY

MARIN:

Great news, babes. Socials are doing a
full 180.

ME:

In what way?

MARIN:

That OG thirst trap of you and Gage?
Gone. Poof. Vanished. And the
comments are finally vibing. Amelia stans
are loud rn.

ME:

Amelia stans?

MARIN:

Yuh. As in, the girlies are here for you.
Like full ride-or-die status.

ME:

Okay. Great. And when you say thirst trap, do you mean the photo of us?

MARIN:

Yep.

ME:

Thanks for getting it pulled.

MARIN:

I'd love to say it was me, but I think it was Gage's main character energy working overtime.

ME:

Right...

MARIN:

Anyway, you're trending chill rn. Don't do anything chaotic. Talk soon, babes x

I FROWN, wondering why that account would delete the photo just like that. It doesn't make sense, but I don't have time to dwell on it. I'm in the middle of emailing a friend back who reached out about a job he wants me to do. A short indie film with a three-week-turnaround. We've worked together before, and I love collaborating with him.

I'm also relieved to know not everyone's blacklisting me.

~

TUESDAY

ME:

We need to finalize the prize categories for the science fair.

GAGE:

I thought we had.

ME:

I'd like to see more prizes.

GAGE:

You want a prize for everyone?

ME:

I want more encouragement, yes.

GAGE:

We don't need to give every kid a prize. It waters it down.

ME:

It's not watering it down. It's celebrating different strengths.

GAGE:

So we're rewarding them just for showing up?

ME:

No. We're making sure no one walks away feeling like they failed. There's a difference.

GAGE:

Kids survive not winning, Amelia. Let them learn to be proud of the work, not the ribbon.

ME:

They're little kids, Gage. One kind word on a certificate could be the reason they keep loving science. I'm thinking awards like "Most Curious Concept" and "Most Passionate Presentation" and "The Einstein Enthusiasm Award."

GAGE:

Those aren't real metrics.

ME:

They could be.

GAGE:

Let the record show you talked me into this with absolutely no logic and a lot of charm.

WEDNESDAY

TIM:

So now that we know you've officially entered your dating era, I have names.

ME:

Names? And I never said I was in my dating era.

COLIN:

You really did.

TIM:

Names of guys I could set you up with. Solid options. My Dating Era Dream Men List has a firefighter, a dog bakery owner, a lumberjack-themed influencer, and a librarian who reviews romance novels on TikTok on it so far. I'm handing you flavor. Don't waste it.

ME:

Absolutely not.

TIM:

This is curated thirst, sis. A buffet of potential.

COLIN:

She doesn't need names, bro.

TIM:

True.

ME:

Wait. What?

COLIN:

You've already found him.

TIM:

Tall. Hot. Intense. He's got that feral-but-contained look. Like he's polite until he's not. No one on my list even comes close.

COLIN:

I can't figure out why he hasn't made his move yet.

ME:

Oh, he has. Trust me.

TIM:

EXCUSE ME? Run that back.
Immediately. You just casually said "he
made a move" like we weren't out here
STARVING for content.

ME:

We're taking the girls to the science
museum together on Saturday.

COLIN:

Why am I sensing there's more here that
you're not telling us?

TIM:

Agreed. She dropped "trust me" like it's
not a whole confession. Back it up,
Queen, and spill.

ME:

He kissed me.

TIM:

See, this is why I don't trust you. You
hold onto the good gossip like it's state
secrets.

COLIN:

How are you feeling about it?

ME:

Honestly? I don't think I'm ready for this.

COLIN:

I think you are. I think you're just scared.

ME:

Yes! If we start something and it crashes and burns, Sarah will be affected. God, I can't even imagine navigating her friendship with Luna if things got messy with Gage.

TIM:

Know what I think?

ME:

I'm sure you'll tell me even if I say no.

TIM:

I think you're using Sarah as a shield because you're terrified of getting hurt again. Not every guy is like James, Amelia. The other thing? You're not just someone's mom. You're still you. A woman who deserves more than just surviving the day. You deserve something that lights you up.

THURSDAY

ME:

We need to talk color scheme for the science fair.

GAGE:

We need a color scheme?

ME:

Absolutely. I'm thinking navy and silver with galaxy-themed table runners and maybe string lights if we can swing it.

GAGE:

String lights?

ME:

Yes. Just because it's educational doesn't mean it can't be magical.

GAGE:

I was going to suggest using the school banners.

ME:

Let me have my stars and shimmer, Gage.

GAGE:

Not arguing. Just imagining you bossing me into hanging string lights.

FRIDAY

BY THE TIME Friday afternoon rolls around, I feel like I've crammed a month's worth of stress into five days. It's been one thing after another. Work deadlines. Science fair planning. School emails. Life admin piling up. The house refusing to clean itself. And in between it all, I've been helping my lawyer pull together evidence for the plagiarism case.

Then, there's Gage.

He's been politely distant this week. Giving me space like he said he would. And I can't decide what I think about that. Which probably says a lot about where my mental state's at.

The only thing I know for sure?

He's woken my body the hell up.

I'm officially sexually frustrated, and the fact I wasn't during my long celibate era but *am now*, after *one kiss* from that man, says everything.

We've seen each other only once this week, at school pickup. Five minutes of conversation while the girls buzzed around us, all science fair logistics and surface-level parenting talk. But his eyes? They said *plenty*.

That was three days ago, and when I run into him at school on Friday afternoon, literally run into him, his hands are firmly on my hips before I have a second to catch up with what's happening.

"Shit," I say, gripping the first thing I can find, which happens to be his suit jacket. "Sorry."

"No." His fingers curve around me tighter rather than letting me go. His eyes settle intently on me. "Busy day?"

"Huh?" My brain lets me down yet again because his cologne is currently ruining me.

"You look like you ran here."

I let go of his jacket and take a step back. "Oh. Right. Yes." Then I realize not one of those words actually constitutes an answer to his question. "It's been a busy week. And yeah, I was running late today."

"How's everything going with work?"

"My lawyer's busy compiling evidence, so that's keeping me busy. And I've got some other projects I'm working on." I smile as I run my fingers through my hair.

"Things on social media seem to have calmed down, though, so that's a relief."

"Good to hear."

We're standing in the school playground, surrounded by parents and noise, having a conversation about work, and all I'm thinking about is his mouth on mine, and how good that felt.

I've replayed that kiss a thousand times.

I've remembered the feel of his hands on my body and the way his growly voice made its way into my veins.

And I've gone over and over the moment when he said, "I don't want to fuck this up."

Tim's right: I am terrified of bringing another James into my life.

He was as charismatic and magnetic as Gage is when I met him. There was none of the manipulation back then, only love and tenderness. I had no idea who I was marrying the day I said, "I do" to James.

When I search my memory for the signs I missed, I struggle to find them. But if I were to search for the signs that reveal a good man, I know I wouldn't find a time when James showed me his fear of fucking things up with me. When he put me first in the way Gage did the other day.

Looking at Gage now, I see a man watching me like he's hoping I'll let him in. And I'm reminded of the other thing Tim said: I'm a woman who deserves more than just surviving my days.

I move back a little closer to him, enjoying the way I surprise him. "I'm looking forward to tomorrow."

He turns slightly, angling his body into mine. "I am too."

The sounds of children coming our way filter into my awareness, but I'm lost in Gage for this one last moment before our daughters arrive and demand our attention. He's lost in me too.

The tension thrumming between us is intense.

I desperately want to reach out and trace a line from his throat down to the third button on his shirt that's still done up. I want to press my body into his and undo that button. Undo them all. Get that shirt off him.

Holy god.

This is not a thought to be having while standing in a school playground.

"Mommy!"

Sarah's voice pulls me from my thoughts. The last thing I see before turning to look at her is the heat in Gage's eyes.

I'm still thinking about that heat later, while helping Sarah with a project, then during dinner, and after Sarah goes to bed. That is, until James texts me, knocking the air from my lungs.

JAMES:

I barely recognize you lately, Amelia. Stealing someone else's work. Drinking during the day. Practically fucking a man in public. Just make sure you're not dragging Sarah into your mess while you figure out who you are now.

Anger flares hard in my chest as I read his bullshit. And instead of not taking his bait, I tap out a furious response.

ME:

> The only thing I did from that list was the day drinking. And what the hell makes you think you have the right to judge me for that?

JAMES:

The fact I'm the father of your daughter.

ME:

> Being Sarah's father gives you NO RIGHT to say anything to me like you just did.

JAMES:

Oh, sweetheart, it does. One of these days, you'll find out just how much of a right it gives me.

ME:

> I don't know what you mean by that. Are you threatening me?

JAMES:

You always were easy to impress. A few kind words, a smile, a quick fuck, and you'd believe anything I wanted you to. Seeing what you've become is embarrassing.

My throat closes. My stomach flips. My fingers freeze.

And then my brain, *God, my brain*, starts twisting everything.

I *was* that woman.

The one who fell too fast for the wrong kind of man.

What if I'm her all over again now?

With Gage.

What if I'm walking straight back into the fire, holding my daughter's hand?

I need to slow this down.

Figure myself out some more.

Wait until I know for sure I'm not letting a man talk me into things with a few kind words.

I tap out a text to my brother.

ME:

> Hey, are you free tomorrow? I'm supposed to be taking Sarah to the science museum at 2 p.m., but something's come up.

COLIN:

> Yeah, I'm free. I can take her.

ME:

> I owe you. But also, she'll love spending some time with her favorite uncle.

COLIN:

> I am under no illusions I'm the favorite.

ME:

> You underestimate yourself, big brother. Love you xx

I don't send Gage a text letting him know of the change of plans. Instead, I tell myself he'll understand. He'll be okay that I just need a little more space.

What I conveniently ignore is the way that man looks at me, the way he's made it abundantly clear he wants so much more from me than a quick fuck, and that he's not the kind of man who would ever tolerate being ghosted.

CHAPTER 17
GAGE

She didn't show.

She sent her fucking brother.

No text. No call. Nothing.

She has a hell of a lot to learn about me because I am not a man who walks away from what I want. Amelia does not get to look at me the way she does, kiss me like that, and then run. Not without facing me.

After I put Luna to bed on Saturday night, I leave Shirley with her, and I go to Amelia. It's late. Nine thirty. But I don't care if she's already asleep, we're having a conversation.

Her doorman calls her when I arrive, and I'm already prepared to fight my fucking way up there if she says no. But she doesn't. She lets me in. And when the elevator doors slide open into her condo, she's standing there barefoot, wide-eyed, and looking at me like she had no idea I'd show up here tonight. Like she thought I'd just let this slide.

I step out of the elevator, every muscle in my body pulled tight, every part of me on edge.

"Gage," she starts, but I cut her off.

"You blew me off." I move into her, invade her space. "Without so much as a text."

Her long lashes blink up at me and I see her brain spinning. I'm too close for her comfort, but she's going to have to deal with that tonight. I'm done giving her space.

Her hands come to my stomach and I fucking wish they were doing that for a different reason, but I rein my focus in, keeping it fixed on why I came here.

"I'm sorry. I—"

"No. Don't be sorry, Amelia. Be fucking anything but that. Be honest with me. Tell me why."

She flinches at my hard edge and I'm not sure if I'm going to get the realness from her that I'm desperate for, that I've fallen hard for. Because it looks a hell of a lot like she's about to cut and run, and try like fuck to never come back.

"You kissed me last weekend like you wanted me to ruin you," I say, pushing harder than I intend, but *fuck*, I'm barely keeping my shit together right now. "You want this. You want *me*. But I could see you were running scared, so I gave you space. Didn't force anything. Hell, I refused to fuck you because I knew you weren't ready." My shoulders tense as I try to find the edge of whatever the fuck this feeling is. "Tell me what you need from me that'll help you give this a chance."

Her breaths are coming faster now, and when she speaks, I hear her breathlessness. "I told you my fears, Gage. I've been honest with you."

I clench my jaw. "No. You've given me your reason, not

your honesty. You're using Sarah to keep yourself safe. But you look at me like you're thinking about me just as much as I'm thinking about you. I want you to admit you're lying to yourself."

Her eyes flare wide, and she steps back. "If you're going to come here and—"

My hand's around her waist and I'm backing her up against the wall before she can finish that sentence. My other hand slides along her jaw. "I'm not giving you an easy out. Not anymore. Tell me you want me. Just say the words. That's all I need."

I've bewildered her, which wasn't my intention when I came here, but fuck if it doesn't get her talking.

She grips my shirt, her entire being so fucking beautifully alive, her eyes blazing with heat like never before. "Yes, I want you! I've never wanted a man so fucking much. I think about you all day, every day. I can't get you out of my head. When you text me, I can't read it fast enough. When I see you, I can't take my eyes off you. When I talk to you, I hang off every word. Even when I want to tear a smirk from your face, I want so many more of them from you."

Fuck.

My mouth crashes down onto hers, my hands tighten their hold on her, and I kiss her so fucking thoroughly, losing my mind, my good sense, my fucking everything. Amelia has me caught in her web and no idea of just what I'd do to make her mine.

I tear my mouth from hers. "The next time you get scared, you come to me. You give me that. Your honesty. Give me anything but your absence. *Anything.* Tell me emojis make no fucking sense to you. Tell me you need another year to think about having dinner with me. Tell me about your goddamn laundry piling up. Just don't ever not show up again."

She lets me get all of that out, listening to every word I say. Then she's got her hands up around my neck, and she's pulling my mouth back to hers. She grips my face with both hands while she kisses me again, and I realize I may not survive this woman.

I want to be the man who gets past all her defenses. Who knows what makes her laugh when no one's around. Who gets the unfiltered version of her no one else gets.

And fuck me, I want her to kiss me like this forever.

Her hands come to my coat, shoving it off my shoulders. Then she's tugging at my sweater, desperate to get it over my head.

When she starts on my belt, I break the kiss, my breath ragged, and lock eyes with her. "We're only doing this if you're going to give me more."

There's not one ounce of hesitation from her when she says, "Yes." Then, she slows herself down and gives me what I need. That realness I've known from no other woman. "I'm terrified, Gage. Terrified of you hurting me. Of us screwing this up and harming our kids' friendship. Of so many things I've lost track. But I'm tired of living in that fear. I want more than just getting through the day. I want to live. *Really* live. I want to let things get messy." She bites her lip, and it hits my veins like a goddamn drug. "And I want to do that with you."

"Fuck," I growl, lifting her into my arms. "Where's your bedroom?"

She directs me down the hall, and the second I step

into her room, I feel it. Her. Everywhere. It's elegant and feminine, but not pristine like I expected. There's a sweater tossed over a chair, heels kicked half under the bed, books piled in uneven stacks beside it like she was halfway through five of them at once.

I'm immediately back in her hotel suite in Nashville, remembering the mess of it. This is the same woman. The one who keeps everything together until it all spills out.

I set her down, and in the short walk here, some-thing's shifted. Amelia's still with me. All in. But there's a flicker of hesitation in her eyes now. Not shyness. Just that first-time pause. Like it's hit her this is really happening.

I move in, gently smoothing her hair back from her face. My other hand finds her neck, and I bend to kiss her, slow at first, then deeper as I feel her body curve into mine.

When I pull back, I murmur, "We can go slower."

"I don't want to," she says, softly. "I just haven't had sex in over a year."

I nod, brushing my thumb across her skin. "Then we take our time."

She loops her arms around my neck and moves in with the kind of hungry certainty that sets my blood on fire. "I don't think that's possible with you," she says, her mouth ghosting over mine. "I want you too much."

"Jesus," I rasp. "You have no idea what you do to me." I kiss her neck just below her ear. When I catch the scent of her perfume, I graze my nose along her skin, scenting her, and it fucks with my restraint. "I'm trying to go slow, Amelia, but you're gonna have to help me do that."

She's already back at my belt. "I don't want you to go slow." She pops the button of my pants, lowers the zipper. "I want you to absolutely *ruin* me."

And that's it.

I finally lose my mind completely.

Every bit of restraint I was clinging to. Gone.

I've got her in my arms and then on the bed, and I'm prowling over her, my eyes on her body. That pink tank she's wearing that clings to every curve and dips low at the neckline has been testing my patience since the second I saw it. I reach for the hem and slide it up, revealing bare skin. No bra. And fuck, her breasts are full, soft, and I'm going to need a long fucking time with them.

Once I've got her top off, I suck one of her nipples into my mouth, groaning against her skin as my hands finally close over her tits.

"*Gage*," she breathes, her hands coming straight to my biceps.

"You like that?" I rasp, licking slowly over her nipple, then sucking it back between my teeth.

"Yes."

Fuck.

Her voice.

The moan in that one word.

It takes me to my edge.

I want to spend hours learning Amelia's body, but I'm not sure I have it in me to be anything but selfish and just take what I want first.

Not when she speaks to me like that.

I make myself slow down, but it's a fight the whole way.

I shift to her other nipple while palming her breast,

giving her just enough teeth to make her rock her hips against me in a shameless way I really fucking like.

Her fingers tangle in my hair. They pull hard when I bite her, and it goes straight to my dick. I lift my head and find her eyes, needing that connection. Needing to see what I do to her.

Holding her gaze, I move down her body, my hands reaching for her pajama pants. I remove them, still watching her. And then, I drop my gaze, and am met with the sexiest, lacy panties. Pink. Just like her pajamas.

I run a finger over the fabric, finding her clit. I look at her again as I rub it. "You're fucking soaked."

She pulls her bottom lip between her teeth as she grinds herself against my hand. "You do have that effect on a woman."

Christ.

I thought she'd already made me lose my mind. I was nowhere near close. And when she drops her gaze to watch my fingers, all slow and hungry, I know she's got more in her arsenal. That mouth might beg pretty, but her body? It came here to wreck me.

I slide her panties down her legs and then I spread those legs. My eyes go back to hers as I settle in to make a goddamn mess. Ruin her pretty little mind. Drag every filthy sound she's got from that sinful mouth.

We watch each other as I lick her pussy one end to the other. I circle my tongue over her clit, sucking it in, and fucking worshipping it.

Over and over.

I bury my face in her and eat her out until she's riding my mouth and using me like she owns me. Her thighs clamp around my head and she fists the sheet with one hand while the other grabs the back of my head and keeps me there.

"Right there . . . right fucking *there,*" she pants.

Jesus Christ, I'd live between her legs if she let me.

I groan against her, sucking harder, and do my best to send her over the edge.

She moans louder, her hips jerking up, her grip in my hair turning desperate. "Gage . . . oh my god . . ."

She comes apart, thighs shaking, breath catching. She soaks my beard, crying out my name.

I don't stop. Not until she's completely undone. Not until I've licked her clean. Not until I've made damn sure she knows exactly who did this to her.

When I finally lift my head, her chest is rising and falling fast. She's breathless. Her fingers are still tangled in my hair. Her eyes are wild. And fuck me, she's the most beautiful thing I've ever seen.

She smiles and brings her hands around to my face as she murmurs, "A whole-ass situation."

I like her hands on my face. A fucking lot. Especially when it feels like she's getting to know me with those hands.

"A situation you like." I make my way up her body, kissing as I go, enjoying this slower pace for a moment.

"Probably too much," she says when I reach her mouth, bruising her with a kiss.

"Good," I growl, cupping her breast and tweaking the nipple. "We're going to keep it that way."

Her hands leave my face, moving around to the back of my neck, and then she's pulling me in for another kiss. One that consumes me body and soul.

I'm losing myself to it when I feel her hands turn

needy. One clutches my shoulder. The other slides down my back like she needs something to anchor her. And then she's searching for friction, grinding herself up against me, wrapping a leg around me to get even closer.

She moans into my mouth and it's one of the filthiest sounds I've heard. It's so fucking impure it hits me square in the gut. And my need to be inside her turns feral.

She feels it too, the shift in me, and greedily shoves my pants down, just enough to get her hand on my dick. Still kissing me, she wraps her hand around me and strokes, and *fuck*.

My hips jerk and I break our kiss, breathing hard against her jaw, trying to hold the fuck on.

She grasps my face and angles my gaze up to meet hers. Then she fucking kills me when she deliberately looks down at my cock in her hand and uses my pre-cum as lube. The final nail in my coffin is when she slowly licks her bottom lip while keeping her eyes on my dick.

I'm seconds away from pinning her down and fucking the breath out of her when she says, "We need a condom."

Yeah, we fucking do.

But first, I need my mouth on hers.

I grip her jaw roughly, my thumb dragging across her bottom lip before pulling her into a kiss that has zero mercy.

This mouth that just said we need a condom? I want it saying my name.

I want it gasping, begging, cursing me when I don't stop.

I want it screaming when I finally fuck her hard enough to leave a mark.

She lets go of my cock, grabbing my neck with one hand and burying the other in my hair, kissing me like she's falling apart from the inside out.

I keep hold of her jaw while I run my other hand down her body, in-fucking-delicately, until I'm palming her ass and pulling her leg around me.

I grind into her as I kiss her harder, deeper, dirtier. And all I can think is, *this isn't gonna be soft*. And I'm not stopping until she forgets every man who came before me.

I break contact just long enough to find a condom in my wallet.

"I hope you're ready," I growl when I return. "You're gonna take all of me, so fucking deep you'll feel it for days."

The look she gives me is all fuck-me eyes and I don't bother with another warning. I slam my cock inside her. And *goddamn*. She's tight, wet, and choking my dick like she's trying to wring every last drop out of me.

She cries out the second I thrust inside her, back arching, nails digging into my shoulders. Her legs wrap around me, locking me in like her body's decided I'm not fucking leaving.

I fuck into her as hard and deep as I promised, and Jesus, she's not just taking it. She's giving it right back. I find her eyes, and it's right there, that look that says she wants this just as dirty as I'm giving it.

I don't look away. If I'm going to fuck her like I own her, she's going to look at me while I do it.

"You feel that?" I grit, slamming in to the base. "This cock's yours, Amelia. I'll fuck you like this every damn night."

Her hands come to my face. Wild and rough. Claiming me. Demanding I kiss her, and heaven help me, I would give this woman whatever the fuck she wanted right now.

We find our rhythm and chase our release together, her hips rolling, matching every thrust I give. Her sounds get swallowed by my mouth, every moan mine to take. I can feel her getting close by the way she clamps around my cock like she's trying to drag me down with her.

"You gonna come on my cock?" I rasp against her lips. "Because I'm right fucking there."

She grips my biceps, her body goes taut beneath me, legs tightening, breath catching as her climax hits hard.

I thrust once more, driving all the way in, and the sound that tears from me as I come is raw and ragged, ripped out of me like it's hers to take. Then, every muscle goes slack. I'm done. Emptied. Mind blank. It's the kind of release that leaves nothing behind. Just heat, sweat, and the lingering ache of everything I just gave.

I stay inside her for a beat, catching my breath, not ready to let go of the feel of her around me. Then I force myself to move, bracing one hand beside her and slowly pulling out. I leave the bed to dispose of the condom in her bathroom and then come back to the bed, bringing her in close again.

We lie in silence, her skin warm and slick against mine, our breaths evening out.

Amelia's the one to speak first. She slides her arm across my chest and presses herself into me. There's a sexy smile in her voice when she says, "If I knew you fucked like that, I'd have begged for it sooner."

Fuck.

My hand's on her jaw and my mouth's on hers before she takes another breath. This kiss is possessive and slow, all tongue and intent. One more claim on her, one more way to say *mine* without the word.

"If I'd known you had that much filth in your veins, I would've bossed you into bed the minute we met."

Her smile grows, and when she tries to bring her body in closer to mine even though that's impossible, I tighten my arm around her, and say, "I don't think you can get any closer, but I fucking love that you're trying."

She curves a leg over mine and turns serious. "I know you don't want my apologies for blowing you off today, but I am sorry. I've never done anything like that before."

"What happened between you telling me you were looking forward to it and you not showing?"

She takes a moment before quietly saying, "James."

I internally curse but keep my shit to myself.

"He texted me some nasty stuff last night and tried to shame me. I would have been okay if that was all he said, but he told me I was always easy to impress. And I was. He was right." She swallows hard. "It messed with me. I started to worry I was doing the same thing all over again with you."

If I ever get my hands on that fucking guy.

"You think I've easily impressed you?"

I see her brain working, then the second she gets it, then the blink of realization. "No," she says softly.

"No is fucking right, Amelia," I say a little more intensely than I mean to, but I need her to hear this. To know it deeply. "You spent a year thinking I was an asshole. Then, I helped you survive your period at the wedding. You still thought I was an asshole. Then, you showed up to our first science fair meeting and schooled me over hurting people's feelings. You've challenged me every step of the way. You don't let me get away with a thing." I work my jaw, thinking about the way her ex manipulates her. "I had to push my way in and practically beg for a chance with you. James doesn't know shit, and the next time he says stuff like that to you, I hope you tell him to fuck right off."

She lets that all sink in for a long moment before saying, "I didn't think you were an asshole."

I arch a brow. "I distinctly recall the day you changed your mind on that."

Her mouth quirks as she recalls the memory. "Okay, so maybe a little."

"Right. So, can we agree that he's wrong about you, and that you are not the kind of woman who easily lets a man in?"

"Yes, okay, you have a point."

My mouth curves up at the way she's struggling to give me this. "You're fucking cute when you're trying not to agree that I'm right."

She rolls her eyes but lets me move in with a kiss.

"I want dinner tomorrow night," I say once I'm finished with her mouth.

"So, this is the part where I get to see your idea of bossy, is it?"

"This is the part where I help you figure out dating again."

"You are enjoying yourself far too much, I think. Just because I got drunk, and word vomited all my feelings about—"

"Amelia."

She blinks at my firm tone. Then says, "I can't do dinner tomorrow night. I have Sarah."

"Monday then."

"I can do Monday." A smile tugs at her lips. "I'd like that." Her smile turns wicked. "Will you wear one of your sexy, hostile takeover outfits? I have preferences if you're open to them."

My lips twitch. "Am I to take it that tuxes are back on the list?"

She slides on top of me and straddles me, fucking slaying me all over again. "I mean, a tux for dinner might be overkill." Her mouth grazes mine. "But if you wanna put one on and roleplay CEO, I'm your girl."

CHAPTER 18
AMELIA

MONDAY IS the longest day there ever was and the only thing that keeps me going is knowing I have a date with Gage tonight. Dinner at some unknown-to-me restaurant because apparently, he enjoys torturing women who require at least twelve hours' notice to emotionally prepare and mentally rehearse every possible conversation scenario.

He didn't stay at my place after we had sex on Saturday night because he had to get home to Luna. But he did make sure to fuck me again in the shower before he left. I think I've already replayed every second of the sex we had that night 10,735,307 times.

Last night, he called after Sarah went to bed, and we talked for nearly three hours. He spent a lot of the conversation finding out everything he could about me. I managed to discover only a few things about him. He practices MMA to keep his head clear, hikes mountains like it's no big deal, golfs for fun, loves fishing and skiing, and probably chops wood shirtless. I'm honestly starting to think he's a wilderness sex fantasy in billionaire clothing. And considering I think rage-cleaning my kitchen counts as cardio, this is going to be a very balanced relationship.

Monday's a blur of legal drama, PR strategizing with Marin, and a half-hearted attempt at the indie film score. My brothers blow up the group chat about Gage, and I refuse to open the texts. Mostly, I try not to obsess all day over my date tonight.

I'm running on fumes by the time I pick Sarah up from school, and God help me, she's channeling peak teen drama energy. Argumentative. Dramatic sighs for days. Exactly what I don't have the capacity for.

All I wanted was an easy afternoon. To help her with her homework, drop her at James's by five, and then come home and get ready. Light a candle. Overthink my lipstick choice. Rehearse exactly how to say, "Hi" like a normal person. But no. Of course not. That would've been too easy for the Monday gods.

We survive the homework. Just.

Then, we pack her bag for the night. She loses it over glitter shoes we can't locate and throws herself on the bed, refusing to move until I find them. Cue a frantic condo-wide search that eats fifteen minutes of my already-limited date prep time.

James texts during the search, bailing on me. He now has to work tonight. Cue a fresh wave of panic, because I have to find a babysitter on zero notice while my daughter sobs over not seeing her father.

Which means I have to do the thing I've been avoiding all day: enter the group chat with my brothers.

ME:

Okay fine. I need one of you to take Sarah tonight.

TIM:

WELL WELL WELL

TIM:

Look who remembered she has siblings.

COLIN:

Is everything okay?

ME:

James bailed. I'm running behind. I haven't showered. Sarah just staged a protest over footwear. I'm dying.

TIM:

She's spiraling. I knew it. I said three hours ago she was on the edge.

ME:

Are you free or not??

TIM:

I mean, I was going on a date. But...

COLIN:

Sorry, I've got work I've gotta do tonight.

ME:

Tim.

TIM:

Say it.

ME:

You're the best brother alive and I owe you my soul.

TIM:

There it is. I'll be there in an hour.

COLIN:

I'll do school drop-off tomorrow.

ME:

Colin, you are a gift from the heavens.

TIM:

Okay, rude. I'm the one canceling on hot
girl summer over here.

ME:

You were going to the same bar you
always go to on a Monday and ordering
the same beer you always order.

TIM:

Unnecessary.

After I tell Sarah that she's going to stay with her
uncle tonight, I get exactly ninety seconds of peace before
she walks out in her "Future Career Day" costume. The
one she's supposed to wear tomorrow. The one I've kept
in perfect condition, bagged, and labeled so nothing
could go wrong.

She's dressed as a vet-slash-pop-star, which,
according to her, required a white lab coat covered in glitter, a microphone, and a stethoscope.

She twirls like she's in a Broadway audition. "I want to
show Uncle Tim!"

"No," I say calmly, like I have energy for calm. "Take it
off. We'll pack it and you can show him tomorrow
morning when you get dressed for school."

She refuses. I argue. She argues louder. And then—
RIP.

She yanks the costume off like a feral little tornado and tears the sleeve clean down the seam.

I let out a sound that might actually have been a growl. Or a scream. Or maybe just my soul trying to exit my body through my throat.

And then I do what any emotionally regulated, high-functioning woman would do: I dig out the sewing kit with shaking hands and start stitching like I'm defusing a glitter-covered bomb.

At six o'clock, Sarah's finally watching cartoons, the costume is patched, and I'm in the shower trying to wash the day off. I've got exactly one hour until Gage arrives.

It's fine. Everything's fine. I definitely didn't need time to light a candle or sit cross-legged on my bed and visualize my best-case dinner scenario like a lunatic. I'm totally chill. Very zen. Practically floating.

By 6:30, I'm wrapped in a towel, staring at myself in the mirror like I've never had a face before.

Red lipstick? Too much.

Gloss? Too casual.

Red? Sexy. Confident. Dangerously close to trying too hard.

Gloss? Effortless. Barely-trying. Possibly boring.

I hold both up like I'm consulting a jury. "What do you think?"

Sarah appears in my bedroom doorway and walks into the room holding her stomach. "I don't feel—"

And then she vomits.

All over my bed.

All over the dress I just laid out.

All over the last shred of sanity I was clinging to.

I stand there for a solid five seconds, staring at the

dress that is now aggressively dead. Sarah's crying. My hair is still wet. I'm somehow freezing and sweating. And I'm supposed to be seducing a man in less than an hour.

I contemplate grabbing a towel and blotting at the crime scene like that would fix the situation, but Sarah needs me, so I shift gears.

I clean her up, tuck her into a blanket on the couch with a bowl in case round two happens, and give her mommy hugs until she's okay. She snuggles in like it's just another Monday and not the final act of my personal apocalypse.

I walk back into the bedroom, stare at the vomit-covered dress again, and release a breath I've apparently been holding for six years.

That's when my phone buzzes with a text.

I hesitate.

I haven't checked my messages since I sent out the sibling distress signal, and frankly, I'm not sure I'm emotionally stable enough to witness whatever Tim has decided to contribute to the situation. But at this point, what else could possibly go wrong?

The dress is dead. The child is sticky. My grip on life is holding by a thread.

I check the screen, hoping, *praying*, for something mildly helpful.

I get Marin.

MARIN:

> Babes. Gentle reminder that I cleared my entire schedule for tonight's DATE LIVESTREAM.

ME:

Livestream???

MARIN:

Ummmm the verbal soft launch you did this morning when you casually mentioned mid-PR meeting that GAGE MOTHEREFFING BLACK is taking you to dinner??

ME:

Oh no.

MARIN:

Oh YES. I am now spiritually handcuffed to this storyline. If you don't live-text-me, I will dissolve into particles.

MARIN:

I need: fit check. vibe report. pre-date emotional temp. makeup mood board. tension rating. All of it.

ME:

This feels like a lot of energy for someone not going on the date.

MARIN:

Excuse you, I am going on this date. Spiritually. Emotionally. Existentially. Cosmically.

MARIN:

Also? Venus is sextiling Mars, so if you don't at least make out tonight, the planets will literally be offended. Don't piss off the cosmos, babes.

Somewhere between my brothers live-commenting their way through my love life, James flaking, the glitter shoe crisis, the costume armageddon, the frantic sewing session that almost cost me a finger, my child barfing on my dress, and now Marin assigning herself a spiritual plus-one to my date, I lose the will to keep pretending I'm not one minor disaster away from complete psychological collapse.

My elevator dings. Assuming it's Tim, I head out to greet him, still wrapped in a towel, hair wet, dignity fully MIA.

Only it's not Tim.

It's Gage.

Wearing all black.

Black suit, black dress shirt, black shoes.

Looking like the solution to every fantasy I've ever denied having.

I freeze.

He keeps coming toward me.

All the way to me.

I forget how to exist.

Then, I speak.

Oh god, I *speak*.

"I'm so sorry. I swear I was going to be ready, but then James bailed and Sarah had a glitter shoe meltdown, and she tore her school costume for tomorrow because she had to show it to Tim tonight, and I had to sew it like I was auditioning for *Project Runway*, the breakdown edition, and then she threw up *on my dress*, which was *the* dress, like capital-D dress that I was going to seduce you in, and then Marin assigned herself as my spiritual chaperone after telling me Venus is sextiling Mars, which apparently means that if I don't seduce you tonight, I will piss off the cosmos." I stop talking long enough to breathe, and because my brain doesn't get the memo that silence might be the smarter choice here, I just keep on babbling. "And now I'm still in a towel, my hair is wet, I haven't chosen a lipstick, and I'm honestly starting to wonder if Marin was right, and I've pissed off Venus by not shaving my legs or spiritually preparing enough for this date."

Gage's eyes flash with amusement right before his hand curls around the back of my neck and he pulls me in for a kiss. Not a short kiss, not a long one, but just enough to wreck any ability I have left to think straight. That could also be thanks to his scent. Who knows at this point? Certainly not me.

When he lets me go, he says, "You're a whole-ass situation, you know that?"

I was not expecting that. Nowhere close to that.

He grins when all I give him is nothing.

Then, he takes charge.

"Why don't you go and get dressed, and I'll go sit with Sarah and make sure she's okay."

"My dress is ruined, Gage, and I'm not sure I'm up to seducing you tonight."

"Consider me seduced. A long fucking time ago. Put on whatever's comfortable."

I grip his suit jacket, needing to stay in this moment right here with him for longer than a second. "Thank you." It's a whisper, and only two words, but they carry the weight of an entire day, and the way he held it like it wasn't too much.

A few minutes later, I'm in my bedroom finding something to wear when my elevator dings and I hear Tim talking with Gage. Leaving them to each other, I decide to follow Gage's suggestion and opt for comfort. I put on my favorite soft black cashmere sweater and high-waisted jeans. No shapewear. No effort to smooth or sculpt. I towel-dry my hair one last time, then grab the blow dryer and run it through quickly. I pull my hair into a messy bun, and swipe on a little concealer and mascara. Just enough to say I showed up.

I've just finished applying the mascara when I receive a text from Tim. From my living room.

TIM:

I swear to God, if you don't go on this date, I will ground you.

And for the first time today, I laugh.

CHAPTER 19
AMELIA

AFTER I CLEANED up the bedroom disaster scene and handed off my child to her uncle, Gage brought me to his place. He asked me what I wanted him to order in for dinner. All I could think was I needed carbs. Urgent carbs. Soul-repairing carbs. I may have said all those words to him. I may also have told him I needed to be emotionally held by parmesan. I didn't even care about the way he looked at me at that point. Like he was thoroughly amused by me. I told him to please find me real carbonara. The good kind. No cream, no lies.

He ordered dinner, opened a bottle of pinot noir (which I've now decided is my preferred emotional support beverage until further notice), and pulled me down onto his couch like we do this every Monday.

Oh, and he may have discarded all those black items of clothing and changed into a slate-grey henley and dark jeans in the middle of all that. Don't get me started on what that did to me.

Dinner was amazing. The absolute best carbonara in

New York. Gage obviously knows people. Lucky for me he's currently focused on dating me. I may insist on him arranging all my future meals. I'll tip with emotional vulnerability and general cuteness.

We've talked our way through the evening like we've done this a hundred times before. Like this is just . . . what we do.

Wine. Pasta. Low lighting. My parmesan-providing god in a henley that could end civilizations.

And somewhere in between the pinot and the pasta, I've moved past my earlier spiral. Gage hasn't pressed me to talk about it. He's just let me come down slowly. Which, honestly, is sexy. I might be catching feelings for a man because he handed me cheese and didn't ask follow-up questions.

After dinner, I'm basking in full post-pasta bliss when Gage sets his wine glass on the coffee table and reaches for me. He pulls me onto his lap, his hands sliding up my thighs around to my ass. One hand then comes up to my neck, and he brings my mouth down to his.

He kisses me like he's been thinking about it every second since we had sex. It's downright dirty the way he uses his tongue and the way his hand stays glued to my ass like he owns it. Like he's not planning to let go anytime soon.

Breathing is now more of a suggestion than a reality.

"Fuck," he growls when he finally breaks the kiss, his breath ragged like mine. "This mouth . . ." He drags his thumb across my lower lip, his eyes locked on it like he's memorizing the shape. He doesn't finish that thought. Just pulls my mouth back to his.

He's rough.

All tension and zero patience.

His hands are under my sweater, leaving fire in their wake as they find my breasts. When he reaches them, he groans so deeply into my mouth that I feel it in my core, in my toes, in parts of my body I'm not sure I even knew existed.

It drives me absolutely wild, to the point where everything is too much, and I need a minute.

Tearing my mouth from his, I put my hands to his chest and just *breathe*.

Gage's hands move to my waist, his eyes finding mine. He's just as affected as me. "You okay?" God, his *voice*. The gravel. The need I hear.

I nod, still searching for breath. "Yes. I just . . . you can't groan like that and expect a girl to be able to go on."

His eyes go dark, and a second later, his hand's on my back, hauling me into him like he's done playing soft. "I need you spread out under me. My cock so fucking deep inside you." He curls his hand around the back of my neck. "I'm going out of my fucking mind here, Amelia."

"I know," I agree, because *god*, I know. "But I've just eaten . . . like, a heroic amount of pasta, and I'm gonna need a hot minute before you claim my soul with your dick."

He stares at me for a second, still feral for me, but processing what I just said. Then he swears, "Fuck," his voice still rough with all that gravel and need, "you're fucking killing me."

There's something dangerously hot about hearing this man say he's dying because he can't have me right now.

"Seriously," I murmur against his lips, "how are you

even in the mood for sex? Do men get bloated, or are you just built different?"

His grip on my neck doesn't ease, and neither does his stare. "I didn't carb-load like you, Princess."

Princess.

And just like that, Gage gets me in the mood.

Not for sex, because no way am I up for that yet, but a blow job? I think I'd like to see what damage I can do to this man by getting on my knees.

I slide off his lap and down to the floor, my eyes never leaving his. When my fingers reach for the button on his jeans, his eyes flare hotter, and he spreads his legs like he's already picturing my mouth on his. Like he's a king about to be worshipped by his queen. And he fucking *knows* it.

His breathing slows, just for a moment, and I see the control he's fighting for. But the second I touch his jeans, everything shifts. His chest rises fast, shallow now, as if I've pulled the air right out of him.

He watches me like I'm about to undo him completely.

I lower his zipper, being sure to look at him while I do that. I've worked out that Gage gets off on eye contact. On me watching him while I wreck him.

I pull his jeans and underwear down enough to take hold of his cock. The hiss he makes as I wrap my hand around him sends lust racing through my entire body. Eyes still fixed on his, I lick the tip. Slow. Sure. And I increase the pressure of my hold on him just a little, just to madden him a bit more, before I lick the entire length of him.

He thrusts his dick into my hand as he growls low, "*Fuck*, Amelia."

I take him into my mouth, all the way to my throat, then I pull back enough to swirl my tongue along the underside. He groans again, louder this time, and his fingers slide into my hair. He's not holding me down, just searching for contact.

I work my mouth around him, taking my time with every inch, learning the way he responds when I hollow my cheeks just right.

"Jesus fucking Christ," he rasps, his fingers tightening in my hair.

His thigh tenses beneath my palm, and I dig my nails in enough to make him feel it while taking him deep again. I glance up, and he pins me with a stare that's so damn dirty, and then his hips jerk, hard.

A rush of desire crashes through me. That look of his that says he's barely holding on is all mine. I'm the one doing this to him. And the way that turns me on is obscene.

I pull back and drag my tongue from base to crown. Then swirl my tongue over the head, watching him begin to unravel as I lick the pre-cum. He finally loses all restraint, letting out a guttural sound so raw it vibrates through me.

And then, he's on his feet and taking his cock from me with one hand while the other fists in my hair, done letting me lead.

"Open your mouth for me, Princess."

Fuck.

I never thought I'd be so into a man ordering me

around like this, but here I am. On my knees, desperate to comply.

I part my lips, and he steps in, sliding himself back past my tongue. His hand in my hair shifts to the back of my head, not forcing, but I feel his need in the way he guides me.

He's slow at first. Controlled. Eyes demanding mine. Each thrust a little deeper.

I rest my hands on his thighs, but then, needing to really feel him, I slide them around to the backs of his legs, gripping him there.

His breath drags rough through his throat and his hips move with more intent.

"Fuck," he groans, voice raw. "Just like that." His eyes blaze with heat. "Let me use that mouth."

Holy. All. Things. Filthy.

I should not like that so much.

But Gage could say that to me anytime he wants, and I would give it to him.

He reaches down, his hand finding my jaw, guiding it even wider, and when I take him right back, a string of curse words falls from his lips. Words I've never had said to me.

He keeps thrusting. Keeps dirty talking. "Mouth so fucking tight, Princess. Take it all for me."

He's so crude.

So purely masculine.

And he's so fucking gone.

His hand tightens in my hair while his other one keeps hold of my jaw. "Where do you want it?" he grits out, close to the edge. "That pretty mouth, or do you want me to cover you in it?"

I don't answer. Just take him deeper, my lips sealed around him, my eyes locked on his.

That hand on my jaw flexes. "Fuck, your mouth it is."

His hips jerk, his control fractures, and then he comes, hard and deep, growling, "*Fuck*," while he spills down my throat.

I swallow all of it.

And lick my lips after.

While looking at him.

When he finally stills, spent, he doesn't let go. His hand stays right there at my jaw, thumb brushing my cheekbone. "You're gonna fucking destroy me."

I try to process that. I really do. But I'm also trying to process the way he's looking at me like I'm the only woman in the world, right alongside the fact I just became a woman obsessed with dirty talk.

Before I can make sense of any of it, he pulls me up, grips the back of my neck like it's his to do what he wants with, and kisses me.

He steals every thought of mine before he's done with my mouth, and then he says, "That mouth should come with a fucking warning. I'm gonna be hard every time I look at it."

Somehow, I manage to gather myself. "Good. Because I'm a hot mess whenever I have to deal with your existence. It's only fair that I fuck with you too."

He mutters a curse, brushes his lips over mine, and then gets bossy with me. "I hope your carbs have settled, because I'm taking you into my shower and doing every indecent thing you'll let me."

~

GAGE WAKES me early the next morning. With his hands to my body in a way I'd happily wake every day. Except not so freaking early.

"It's five a.m.," I grumble, horrified as I eye the time on his bedside clock. "I need at least one more hour of sleep if I'm going to survive today."

His mouth closes over my nipple, his finger pushes inside me where I'm already wet for him. And he just carries on like waking early should be part of my morning routine.

He fucked me in his shower last night, and then after giving me a couple of hours to recover—which he spent talking with me like I was the most interesting person he'd ever met—he laid me out on his bed and devoured me all over again.

My muscles need about five years to function properly again.

Gage's muscles, however? Apparently god-level.

I'm convinced he could go all day and still look like he just stepped out of a fitness ad.

I'm caught between "please don't stop but also I might die."

I push gently at his shoulders, trying to slow him down. "I need a minute."

He pulls back and I head into his bathroom where I lock myself in and take more than a minute. I pee and then freshen up, combing my fingers through my hair, splashing water on my face, and stealing some of Gage's toothpaste.

When I crawl back into the bed, he's watching me closely. "What's happening in that pretty brain of yours?"

"Nothing." I roll toward him and wrap my hand around his dick that's hard and ready to go.

He reaches down to remove my hand, looking like it's the last thing he wants to do.

At my frown, he says, "Talk to me. You don't like morning sex?"

"What? Why do you think that?"

"I realized I got carried away and didn't pay attention when you said no before." His eyes are searching mine so earnestly, trying to get a read on me, and *god*, I love that he's a man who is so aware, who cares this much.

"I was just grumbling about the time. I don't hate morning sex." I give him a pained look. "Having said that, I think I have to say no to you today. I don't think my legs or vagina can take you today."

He grins. Or more accurately, he smirks, and I don't even want to remove this one from his face. He's too damn sexy for my own good.

His hand goes to my hip and curves over my ass so he can drag me closer. "So, just today?"

I ignore the way my core screams, *Yes! Just today!*

"We'll have to see," I play with him. "Because it turns out that when you put your mind to making me take it all, you get the job done real well."

"Jesus," he says. "Has this mouth always been so filthy?"

I arch a brow. "Oh, that's not filthy. I'm learning what filth is from you, and that's nowhere near close."

"Right. So, I need to stop feeding you carbs, and I need to pace your pussy better. Got it." With that, he presses a quick kiss to my lips and then leaves the bed.

I stare at his naked ass all the way until I can't see him

anymore, and then I collapse onto my back and commence praying for divine intervention.

This man.

We don't have sex. We do shower together and he manages to restrain himself. Then, he makes coffee and breakfast. When he leaves for work at 7:30 a.m., he kisses me and tells me to take my time. No rush to leave.

I don't intend on taking my time, but I do spend a minute collecting myself after he's gone. I sit on his bed and check my messages in case Tim needs me for anything. It turns out my brother can take care of my daughter without any help. I find silly photos of them that he's sent through, and a photo of her in her costume for today, smiling and happy.

I let my head fall back and release a sigh of relief that all is okay with Sarah. That's when I see them. Three cameras. Discreet. But watching. Cameras I missed while Gage fucked me in here last night.

It doesn't surprise me. I mean, he owns a company built on intelligence and security, and he runs on control. On protection. Of course, he has cameras in his home.

What does surprise me is the question that hits next.

Did he record us?

And if so, is he going to watch it back?

Because that's exactly where my brain goes.

To *him watching*.

And instead of being creeped out, I'm not. I'm hot and bothered, like I just got caught enjoying something I shouldn't.

Which is fine. Totally fine.

I mean, it's not like I know for a fact he recorded us. He may have turned them off last night.

But also, maybe he didn't.

Oh god.

Maybe they're recording right now.

I glance at one of the cameras. It doesn't blink or do anything suspicious. Which somehow makes it worse. Because now I'm wondering if there's a motion alert.

I'm wondering if he's sitting somewhere, phone in hand, getting a ping that says, "Amelia's moving. Bedroom cam. You might want to tune in."

And good god, why does that thought make my thighs clench like I've just read a smutty one-bed trope romance with a six-foot-five lumberjack and a praise kink?

I fan myself. Literally. With my own hand. Like that will fix me.

And then, because of course, my inner bad girl decides to strut in like she owns the place, tosses her purse to the floor, and says, "Don't worry, babe. I got this."

Fully aware of where each camera is now, I stretch out and lie across the foot of the bed on my side. I rest my head in my hand and stare up at one of the cameras. Nothing too obvious. Just enough to say: *You watching? Good.*

And because apparently, I now have zero shame and a newfound taste for attention, I crawl up the bed like I just remembered I'm a lingerie model and forgot to mention it earlier.

By the time I settle back against the pillows and remove my sweater, I've fully decided that if he's watching . . . he's going to *enjoy the show.*

My sweater hits the bed and a second later, I'm cupping my breasts through my bra.

Soft, slow, and teasing.

I let my thumbs graze over the fabric, over my nipples, watching the camera like it's his eyes on me. The knowledge that this might be live, that he could be watching right now, causes a fresh wave of heat to pool in my belly.

I unhook my bra and slip it off, deliberate and sexy as if I've rehearsed this scene a hundred times. I haven't. But it turns out I'm a fast learner when properly motivated.

My hands trail down my body to my jeans. I undo them and shimmy out of them.

One hand returns to my breast. The other slips into my panties. And just as I drag a single finger along the slick heat between my thighs, my phone rings.

I glance at the name on the screen.

Gage.

I let a sexy smile make its way across my face, keeping my eyes on the camera. *On him*.

Then, I answer, breathless and just a little bit wicked. "Hi." My voice is pure innocence. My hand is still between my legs.

"Be a good girl and spread your legs for me."

My body hears that command and decides it's his now.

My inner bad girl practically purrs, "*Took you long enough*."

I obey him and wait.

"You're in *my* bed. Touching what's *mine*. Are you soaked?"

"Not as much as I would be if it was your fingers inside me."

"That mouth," he growls. "That fucking mouth."

A beat of silence that's all lust.

Then he says, "You'd be dripping down your thighs if I was there. You'd make a fucking mess all over my hand, and I'd keep going until you did it again."

"Oh god," I moan, my back arching, heat flooding between my legs like his fingers are actually there.

"Take those panties off, Princess. I want to see that pretty pussy."

I don't even know who I am anymore.

His sharp hiss of approval once my panties are off only gets me hotter.

"Show me what I'm missing," he orders. "Use two fingers."

I slide two fingers in. And because I know exactly what it will do to him, I bite my lip and start fucking myself.

Gage goes quiet.

Not a breath. Not a word.

Just silence that somehow feels filthier than if he said anything.

I keep going.

Just to see how long I can keep this man speechless.

When he breaks the silence, his voice is rougher than I've heard it. "I've got a meeting, so you've got one minute, Amelia. Come for me. Make it fucking loud."

I keep my eyes on the camera.

My fingers work faster.

I lift my hips, angling myself so I can reach deeper.

Gage swears and my orgasm teases.

Deeper.

Faster.

Harder.

Fuck.

My eyes close and I imagine Gage between my legs, face buried, making a mess of me.

"Fuck!" I cry out as the orgasm starts to rush.

And then I come.

Hard and loud, exactly as he told me to.

Right here on his bed.

Right here in front of his cameras.

Right here with him listening.

"Jesus," he rasps. "I'm not going to get any fucking work done today."

I hear rustling and then a car door closing. And then he says, "The next time you want to put a show on for me, give me some notice. I'll clear my whole goddamn schedule."

And then he's gone.

I reach for my phone to send him a text.

ME:

I'm gonna need the recordings of you making a mess of me last night.

GAGE:

That mouth. I'm gonna make a fucking mess all over it the next time I see you.

CHAPTER 20
AMELIA

THE WEEK DISAPPEARS in a blur of glitter, glue guns, and me spiraling over whether we've forgotten anything vital for the science fair. It's on Friday. I spend approximately 78% of my time panicking. Gage spends that same amount trying to calm me down. All I can think is: *you wanted this. You wanted a relationship with me. Welcome to the circus, babe.*

Our kid-free nights are completely out of sync this week, which means no dates or sleepovers. And since we've agreed not to tell the girls yet, and we're both drowning in work and life, and his nanny is away, we're stuck with calls when we can fit them and far too much sexual tension. And yeah, it's been a long week.

The science fair ends up being way less of a train-wreck than I braced for. Mostly because Gage shows up like some overachieving dad superhero who thrives in glitter mayhem and can hang string lights without swearing. He takes charge of set-up like he's been training for this his whole life, and, miracle of miracles, he even manages to be nice to Stephanie when she arrives looking like she just crawled out of a Pinterest board that caught fire.

Yes, she throws our plans into mild disarray. Yes, Gage gives me a *look* when it happens. The "I told you her planning sucked" look. But he says nothing. Probably because I emotionally steamrolled him the other week about her. I choose to pretend I don't notice the look and remain firmly in my Gage Black Bliss Bubble.

He hangs my string lights. We hand out the science awards I created on a whim. Not a single complaint from him, even though I know he still thinks "Einstein Enthusiasm Award" isn't a real category. And the girls? They crush their presentation. Sarah's nervous at first, but Luna steps in and carries them both through it like a seasoned public-speaker-slash-baby-dictator. By the end, they're buzzing with adrenaline and practically begging us to take them out to dinner. Together. All four of us. Because the tiny matchmakers are back in action and probably already planning our wedding.

Gage somehow manages to get us into a restaurant you normally need to book six months in advance using both money and magic. I don't know how he does it. I just know one minute we're standing on a street corner with two sugar-high kids and no plan, and the next, a host is smiling like we're royalty and leading us to a table with a view. It's the kind of place with mood lighting, influencers everywhere, and guests who look like they spent the entire afternoon being styled for dinner. The kind of place you don't just go to, you make an entrance. And Gage gets us a table like he owns the whole damn building.

Ten minutes in, right after we've ordered and the girls are fully distracted by the glam surroundings and their coloring in, Gage finds a pocket of time just for us.

His hand brushes mine under the table and he leans in close. "Hey."

His touch lights me up immediately and I meet his gaze, my fingers threading with his. "Why is it still Friday? Why is it so noisy in here? And why is my food not here yet?"

His lips twitch. "This is grumbly Amelia?"

"This is tired Amelia," I say, resisting the urge to lay my head on his shoulder. "I need, like, a full week off life just to recover from this one."

"Yeah, I feel you there."

His gaze drops straight to my chest, and *holy god of filth*, he should not look at me like that in public. Especially not with our daughters sitting across from us. But he does. With no shame. Like he owns the view and has no intention of pretending otherwise.

Still staring at my chest, he says, "I need some time with you."

"You're having some time with me now. With my boobs, to be precise."

That earns me his eyes again. And where I expect a smirk, I get an intense look of heat and rough need instead. "When?"

Whoa.

A girl needs a warning before Gage Black throws a demand like that across white linen and mood lighting.

I shift, my thighs pressing together. And because I'm running on no sleep and too much sexual tension, I blurt out, "My period's due tomorrow. So, if you want me, you better kidnap me tonight or revise your expectations, because this girl does not let any man near her when it's period time. Not even when he's a whole-ass situation."

Gage goes the kind of still that makes it very clear he's doing mental math on how to get the girls fed and home, cancel his life, and get me alone.

"I was kidding when I said you should kidnap me."

"How about Sarah sleeps over tonight. Shirley's back. I could come over."

"No. James is picking her up at seven tomorrow morning."

"She's with him tomorrow night?"

I nod.

"I'll come over after Luna goes to bed tomorrow night."

"I hate to tell you, but that might be too late." My period will likely already have arrived.

"Yeah," he says like he's already figured that out. Then, leaning in close, he adds quietly enough that only I can hear, "I want you naked. But more than that? I want you alone." His hand comes to my thigh. Possessively. "Mine for a few hours."

This is the part no one teaches you about.

The making it all work part.

I'm out here juggling kid meltdowns, work fires I didn't start but somehow have to put out, an ex who's allergic to accountability, life admin that won't stop multiplying, brothers who think group chat = dating strategy talk, a school calendar that eats souls, and a man who thinks it's okay to eye-fuck my boobs in front of our children, and who should have come with a signed risk assessment, and a manual with red flags already high-lighted.

I'm tired.

I'm turned on.

I'm possibly losing my mind.

But also?

I think I like it here.

CHAPTER 21

@THETEA_GASP

SPOTTED: @ameliasinclair and @gageblack having DINNER TOGETHER, and yes, we have receipts. And no, not a private date. A family date. As in: their daughters were there too. Bestie . . . what do we even call this? A hard launch? A family soft launch? A co-parenting cosplay situation? Whatever it is, we are feral. They weren't even trying to be lowkey. Seated front and center at one of NYC's most exclusive restaurants. Mood lighting, cozy table, the kind of place where the waitlist is longer than Gage's last relationship. And speaking of . . . let's unpack that. Zaddy Gage has the kind of rizz that could get him a different snack every night *and* dessert on the way home. The man is BMS-certified. Never seen with the same meal twice since his divorce. Now? This looks like a canon event. He's not out there doing it for the plot. Because, with their kids there, this was: we're not just hooking up, we're building a whole vibe. Gage in this photo? Exact same obsessed and not hiding it energy as the last photo of them. It's giving CEO meets family reboot. And that man left no crumbs. We're not saying they're official. But we are saying if they're not, we're starting a group chat and our very own manifestation circle.

CHAPTER 22

GAGE

THE WEEK after the science fair is another long week of work, life, and nowhere near enough time with Amelia. Because I agreed to keep our relationship from the kids for now, I'm sneaking around like a goddamn teenager. And because she has her period, there's no sex in sight. Which I'm okay with. It's time with her I'm after. But when she sexts me during a meeting on Thursday, I'm unable to focus on anything but sex for the rest of the day.

> **AMELIA:**
>
> Can you come over tonight and make a mess in my pussy?

> **ME:**
>
> That fucking mouth.

> **AMELIA:**
>
> No, not in my mouth. In. My. Pussy.
>
> **AMELIA:**
>
> I'll take it all for you.

ME:

You fucking will. I'm going to fuck you so full of me and then I'll deal with that mouth.

AMELIA:

You can have my mouth but I'm not promising you'll survive it.

ME:

Princess, if you're gonna send texts like that, expect me to bend you over the first surface I see.

AMELIA:

My job here is done.

I fuck her every fucking way to Sunday that night, hoping all that sex will knock some focus back into me for Friday. It doesn't. At 11 a.m. Friday morning, I tell Lucy to cancel my afternoon and then boss Amelia into blowing off the rest of the day with me. After asking what her idea of the perfect afternoon would be, I take her to the Greenwich library. It turns out my woman's idea of bliss is cheap and easy to make happen.

I pack pastries and a blanket and grab coffee on the way, and we block out the world for a few hours. Amelia's perfect afternoon is reading in a library. We spend some time inside before heading out to the garden where she lies with her head on my stomach, reading one of her romance novels. I read too, but most of my time is spent watching her, thinking about all the things I want to do with her. Making future plans in a way I haven't done in years.

Neither of us have our girls Friday night, so we spend

it at my place. We cook dinner together. Rissotto. She schools me all the way.

When I want to clean as we go, she steps into her creative mess zone. "No. We cook first, clean later. That's the law."

I arch a brow. "Gordon Ramsay would not have your back on that."

When I reach for a thousand-dollar bottle of wine for the risotto, she gives me a horrified look. "Absolutely not. That's the wine you bring out when a royal comes for dinner. We're making carbs, not memories."

When I stir the risotto one time too many for her, she smacks my hand away. "This is risotto, not soup. Back away and let me whisper to it."

After we eat, I give her what I'm fast learning she needs: time for the carbs to settle. We watch a movie instead. I keep my hands to myself. Barely. But once the credits roll, I'm done waiting. I spend the rest of the night learning more ways to make her mine.

My only goal for Saturday is to spend as much of it inside her as I can. My family ruins that plan when they arrange a last-minute lunch at my parents' place. I say no. Liv and Kristen keep planning anyway. Ethan and Maddie just got back from their honeymoon, and apparently, it's now a tradition to hold the family hostage while they narrate footage of their holiday like it's a nature documentary.

Liv tells me to bring Amelia, and the fact that lands in my gut instead of my head is all I need to know I'm okay taking a woman I've been dating for less than a month to a family lunch.

"Okay," Amelia says, stepping out of my bathroom,

smoothing her hands down the dress she's put on for lunch. "I think I'm ready."

She's nervous. I caught that. And I'll deal with it in a second. But first, I need a minute to rearrange my entire brain, because that dress? That dress is a problem.

It's long. White. Tight. Knitted. Hits her calves. Comes all the way up to her throat. It's pretending to be modest as if it doesn't cling to every inch of her body like it was sewn on by sin. And now she's walking toward me looking like an elegant problem I want to solve with my mouth.

"Do you have any other dresses here?" No way am I making it through lunch if she's sitting next to me wearing this one.

Her brows pull together and then she glances down at the dress. "This isn't suitable for lunch?" She looks at me with worry and I see her nerves flaring.

"Fuck, sorry." I reach for her waist and pull her in. "That was me being selfish. This dress is good." I bring my mouth to her ear. "But next time I take you to a family thing, do me a favor and wear a fucking sack."

Her hands go to my hips and her body presses to mine. "Just so you know," she says all sex and tease, "I don't own any sacks. So, you'll have to spend some of your money and buy me one if that's what you want."

Fuck.

I'm claiming her smart mouth and getting my hands all over her before she can catch her breath, and fuck me, we're going to be late for lunch.

I glide one hand up her body and palm her breast while the other one curves around the back of her neck so I can keep her mouth right where it is. Not that she's trying to go anywhere. My dirty girl is already in the mood.

I kiss her like I'm trying to teach her a lesson, and when I'm done, I drag my mouth away and find her eyes. "You're walking out of here filthy," I growl. "If I have to survive that dress today, I'm doing it knowing my cum is inside you."

She grinds herself against me while her hands are taking fucking ownership of my ass, and *hell*. "You ruin my makeup, it's gonna make us late."

"I ruin your makeup, you can sit on my dick again while you fix it."

Her hands practically beg me to just hurry up and fuck her. So, I do.

I slam her up against the wall in my bedroom, yank that fuck-me dress up, unzip myself, and shove her panties aside so I can get the fuck inside her. Thank fuck we did away with condoms last night. I'm not convinced I would have had the patience for finding one right now.

She makes an unholy fucking sound on my first thrust and just keeps on making those noises as I pound into her. The second I realize she's got her hand to her pussy and is working her clit, my hips snap harder. Jesus fucking Christ, this woman was made for me. Sugar in her voice, sin in her bones.

"You feel that?" I grit out, my fingers gripping her hips so hard they'll leave marks. "That's all for you. You're not getting me out of you anytime soon."

Her pussy clenches hard, fucking owning my cock. She cries out my name, and that's fucking it. My name on her tongue like that? It undoes me. Has me emptying every lost drop inside her like I've got no choice in the matter. Like she just decided for me.

We stay right there, breathing hard. I'm not ready to pull out yet, and Amelia's got her head tipped forward and one hand flat to the wall like she needs a minute too.

I sweep her hair across her back and kiss her shoulder, taking in the dress she's still wearing that made me lose my damn mind.

She lifts her head. "I'm absolutely going to need to fix my makeup, my hair, everything."

I'm not ready to let her go, but we're working to a timeline I've just blown to hell, so I pull out. I watch my cum drip out of her, thick and wet, fucking made to spill down her thighs, and fight with myself over canceling lunch and making a mess on every inch of her.

When she turns and gives me a pointed look, I reach for the back of her neck and pull her in close. "You got something to say, Princess? You wanna complain after your pussy just choked the cum out of me?"

She fists my shirt, eyes flashing with so much heat, and kills me with a kiss that could end wars. Then, letting me go, she sasses, "I hope your mom doesn't spot the stain on my dress later. I'd hate to have to tell her how downright filthy her son is. The things he did to me before showing up for family lunch." Then, she walks that gorgeous ass of hers all the way to my bathroom. At the door, she glances back. "Do *not* bring that body of yours in here while I'm fixing the mess you just made. Go find your own damn bathroom. Your dick is dead to me for the rest of the day."

And fuck me, I asked for all of that.

And I'd do it again in a heartbeat just to keep that smart mouth running.

CHAPTER 23
AMELIA

Lunch with Gage's family is an experience unlike any meal I've had with my family. I'm used to polite conversation, no laughter, and three adults doing their best to get out of there as soon as possible. My brothers don't even bother bringing their personalities. My mother would make them put their fun away.

The Black family? Totally different. It's five sons, three daughters-in-law, and the kind of energy that feels like a family reunion crossed with a roast battle. The men rib each other like it's a competitive sport. The women hand out sass like party favors.

Gage's mom, Ingrid, clearly lives for it. She floats between conversations, the queen surveying her rowdy kingdom, refilling wine glasses, ensuring everyone has enough to eat, and occasionally joining the banter with a line that absolutely hits.

And then there's Gage's dad. Edmund is stoic, reserved, and watching from a distance. But every now and then, when the teasing gets particularly savage or the laughter too loud to ignore, I catch the flicker of amusement in his eyes.

And Gage? He's in his element. Settled back like he owns the whole table, casually tossing out dry one-liners that land harder than half the roast jokes flying across the room. He doesn't dominate the spotlight. He simply waits for the moment and delivers. It's smooth, low-effort hell-raising from him, and I kind of love that for him.

There's a calm confidence to the way he moves through it all, hand on my thigh under the table, whiskey glass in the other, looking like he was born to banter and breed alpha genes at the same time.

By the time dessert hits the table, I'm full. Like need-to-be-horizontal-and-reflect-on-my-life-choices full. But when Ingrid offers her lemon tart, I smile and say yes. Automatically. Instinctively. Like I was trained.

Because I was.

Both my mother and James's mother made it abundantly clear, repeatedly and aggressively, that refusing something offered to you, especially food, is rude. Not mildly impolite. *Character-definingly offensive*. The kind of social misstep that would land me in a lecture on grace and gratitude and "how it looks."

So, even now, in a warm, happy house with people laughing around the table, I still feel the prompt to "be good." I say yes without thought.

Which is how I end up sitting here, internally negotiating with my stomach while preparing to inhale a tart I do not have room for.

Gage's hand comes to my thigh while I'm in the middle of bargaining with my digestive system, and when

I glance at him, he's watching me with that look. The one that says he sees things I didn't realize I was revealing.

"You don't have to eat it," he murmurs so only I can hear. "My mom won't care."

My throat tightens. Just a little. Because of course he noticed.

I force a light smile, trying to keep my walls in place. Which is pointless when I've got Gage watching me so closely. He'll see right through it. And he'll push the point. This man doesn't do polite lies.

So, I give up and hand him my honesty. "Yeah, but if I don't eat it, I might internally combust. If I do eat it, I might also combust. Either way, we're dealing with an emotional lemon situation."

His mouth quirks, and then, *then*, he leans right in, and I know that look. That's not "pass the sugar", that's "I'm about to make you feral." His voice is full gravel when he says, "So you'll stuff yourself for my mother, but when I want to stuff you with my cock, you demand carb-recovery time?" His lips ghost over mine, smug. "Good to know where I rank, Princess."

I just shake my head at him as he leans back, throws his arm behind me like he pays rent there, and gives me that smug sex god look—full "I know your panty situation without asking" energy, and zero remorse.

"Fine," I mutter. "But if your mother comes at me with disappointed eyes, I'm making you fake a medical emergency. The dramatic kind."

He's amused, but he doesn't get to answer because Ethan, who's sitting on my other side, grins at me and says, "So, how did my brother convince such a smart woman to give him a shot? Did he charm you with that emotionally unavailable, brooding-bad-boy thing he does, or are you in an actual hostage situation here?"

I laugh, and my hand goes straight to Gage's thigh like it's got a mind of its own. What Ethan said is funny, and I know it's his way of breaking the ice some more with me, using the good-natured ribbing tactic these brothers have mastered, but I'm feeling all kinds of "he's mine, don't hurt him."

And suddenly, all eyes are on me.

So, naturally, my brain forgets how to exist as an intelligent woman and throws out, "I thought I was signing up for zaddy charm and some decent dinners. Instead, I got surprise feelings and a man who thinks my boobs are public domain."

A beat of silence follows.

I feel like I just said boobs in church.

Abort, abort.

I want to dissolve into particles like Marin.

Then Ethan groans. "Jesus, not slang. Anything but fucking slang." He looks at Gage like he's side-eyeing him with dramatic brotherly disappointment, but there's a grin in his eyes for me.

Kristen laughs into her wine.

Olivia's laughing and looking at me all "yes, girl."

Madeline thinks I'm hilarious.

Bradford, Hayden, and Callan? Also highly amused by the entire situation.

Ingrid's beaming at me like she just adopted me.

Edmund even appears to be smiling.

And Gage? His hand slides up my thigh, his mouth grazing my ear like the man doesn't care he's seated next to his mother, and says, loud enough for everyone to hear, "Not public. This is a very private collection."

I am deceased.

And now would be a great time for him to fake a seizure. Or spontaneous man flu, the kind that kills after one sneeze. Or literally any excuse to get us out of here before I really do dissolve into Marin particles.

Madeline saves the day. She leans forward to look around Ethan at me, and says, "Just ignore my husband. He's a grandpa and refuses to enter the twenty-first century. I personally try to send him as many texts that include as much slang as I can. And if you give me your phone number, you can too."

Ethan grins again and extends his arm behind her before swooping in for a quick brush of their lips.

"Yes," Olivia says, pulling out her cell. "We should add you to the group chat." She passes her phone across to me. "Add yourself and I'll put you in the chat."

I key my number in and as I hand her phone back, I look at Ethan. "I know less than ten slang terms. You're safe with me."

"Thank Christ," he says.

Ingrid stands and meets my gaze with a smile. "I'm so glad you came today, Amelia." Then, she just begins clearing the dining table like she didn't just give me something James's parents never gave me.

Gage, Callan, and Ethan get up to help their mom while Edmund, Bradford, and Hayden disappear down the hall like there's a secret portal that will take them somewhere very fun. Meanwhile, I'm pulled over to the couch with the girls, and within sixty seconds, I've learned two things: one, these women are emotionally invested in a dating reality show I've never heard of, and two, the latest episode sparked a very serious conversation about things you'd murder your man for.

You know, casual Saturday things we talk about.

"What would you kill Bradford for?" Oliva asks Kristen.

"Eating my strawberry jam."

She's not even joking, and I can't stop myself from laughing. I hold up my hands in defense. "I'm not laughing about the jam. I'm laughing at how serious you are."

"Oh, that's at the top of a very long list," she says, very straight-faced. "And he knows it."

"The key to a long marriage." Olivia nods, wisely, like they're passing down ancient secrets.

"How about you, Liv?" Madeline asks.

"Calling anything I do 'cute' when I'm mid-rage."

The girls all nod in solemn agreement like she just dropped gospel.

Olivia takes a sip of wine. "Callan does it all the time. And all I'm thinking is, 'my death glare is not a fucking *vibe*, Callan.'"

"Will there be violence to go along with that?" Kristen asks. "Because I've got ideas."

"I see you've thought about this topic a lot, Kris," Olivia says. "And I fully support that."

I settle into the couch. I think I'm going to like these girls.

Kristen looks at Madeline. "Okay, spill, and if you say anything about still being in your honeymoon phase, I *will* pick something off my violence list and harm you with it. Honeymoons are no excuse for forgetting your female rage."

Madeline laughs. "Oh, I have things. And I've just added 'waking me up to ask me where something is' to my list after he did that yesterday."

Kristen gasps. "He did *not*."

"Oh, he did," Madeline confirms, deadpan. "And I told him that if he has to interrupt my sleep again, to find *the salt*, he will forfeit his life."

"Oh my God," Olivia says, trying to sound serious but losing it as a grin takes over. "*The salt*?"

"The. Salt." Madeline gives us a slow headshake as if she's just remembered it and still isn't over it.

We're all laughing now, the wine is flowing, and all I can think is: how did I survive this long without a group like this? Why didn't I know this kind of friendship existed?

"Your turn, Amelia." Kristen points at me like I've just been chosen to testify in the court of justified girlfriend vengeance.

I don't even have to think about it. "Saying 'I don't really get why you need so many throw pillows.'"

Kristen gasps again, like I just spoke a universal truth. "Violence is required. There's no other option when a man says something that dumb to a woman."

"Right?" I throw my hands up. "It's like, 'oh I'm sorry, do you also not understand *joy*?'"

Olivia laughs and then raises her glass. "Cheers to that. But wait. Gage said that to you? Or another guy?"

"Gage. Just the other day."

She's horrified. "I taught him better than that. Seriously, we need an intervention before he screws this up with you. I like you too much for that to happen."

"I'll bring the violence list," Kristen offers, very seriously, and honestly, I'm 79% sure she's not kidding.

Olivia gets a wicked glint in her eye. "We don't need a list for Gage. All we have to do is pull out the board games."

Kristen cackles. "True."

I blink. "Gage doesn't like board games?"

"Hates them," Olivia says. "Though he always ends up having a good time. So, if he pisses you off, just pull one out and tell him you wanna play."

I nod, filing that away like I've just been given nuclear codes. "Good to know. Passive-Aggressive Monopoly is now my version of couples therapy."

Laughter explodes around me just as Gage walks into the room, eyebrows raised at what he's walking into.

"Do I even want to know?" he asks.

"Throw pillows, Gage." Olivia gives him a press of her lips and a shake of her head. "Every bed needs them."

His eyes come to me. "Not mine. I'm not there for the fucking pillows."

His family joins us, and the conversation shifts from throw pillows to Ethan and Maddie's honeymoon. Which is great timing, since Gage has a *Round Two, Princess* look in his eyes, and I was three seconds away from sexually malfunctioning in public.

We spend another hour with his family and while everyone's getting ready to leave, Olivia scrolls her phone and murmurs, "Shit." Then, looking up at Gage, she hands him her phone and says, "This was just posted."

His expression reveals nothing while he reads and still offers nothing when he shows it to Bradford. Neither look as fazed by whatever they're reading as Olivia.

She glances between them. "Are you going to do anything about it?"

Gage eyes his brother. "If you want me to, I will. But as far as I'm concerned, I don't give a fuck about it."

"It shouldn't affect me," Bradford says. "I'll run it by the team."

Gage nods, and it seems, that's that.

And then we're all saying goodbye, and I get swept up in that. Then, once Gage gets me back to his place, I get swept up in him. So, it's not until my brother texts me later that night that I remember the suspense of what Gage had said he didn't give a fuck about.

We're getting ready for bed, and I've just walked into Gage's bathroom to show him a photo on my phone of our girls that I snapped during the week at school pickup when Tim's texts come through. I rest my hip against the counter to read them while Gage alternates between brushing his teeth and eye-fucking my boobs.

TIM:

YOU'VE BEEN HOLDING OUT ON US.

He sends a link to an Instagram post.

TIM:

Amelia. Amelia. Amelia.

TIM:

You forgot to tell us your new boyfriend is a full-blown sex overlord.

TIM:

He owns five sex clubs. FIVE!

TIM:

That's not a red flag. That's a goddamn parade and I am WAVING.

TIM:

Okay, but real talk. Gage gives "has a custom-built throne in the VIP dungeon" vibes.

TIM:

Leather. Shadow lighting. Only answers to "Sir."

TIM:

Or maybe he's more "I wear suits while I spank you and quote business stats" energy.

TIM:

I swear if one of those clubs doesn't have a themed night called "Submit & Sip", I'm starting a petition.

TIM:

And please confirm or deny if there's a loyalty card because I WILL become a platinum member. Ten orgasms and the eleventh one's free.

TIM:

You've been walking around with a sex-club-grade dick and didn't even tell your favorite sibling? MA'AM.

TIM:

I provide love. Emotional support memes. Actual childcare. And you're out here being the First Lady of the kink economy without even a whisper?

TIM:

This is a betrayal I may never recover from.

TIM:

Also, please advise which club is best for crashing. I will NOT behave. I might get us banned.

My head snaps up and I look at Gage as he flicks the faucet off. "You're a sex overlord?" *Shit.* My brother will pay for that. "I mean, you own sex clubs?"

His lips twitch. "A sex overlord?"

"Ignore that. Tim said that. Not me."

I tap the link Tim sent and am taken to an Instagram post.

@THETEA_GASP

BESTIE. Sit the eff down. @gageblack's secret life just hit the TL and we are NOT okay. Apparently Mr. BSE™ isn't just serving CEO energy. He's also serving sex club owner energy. Plural, bestie. FIVE. Count them. FIVE. Did ya'll know? Because we sure as hell did not. Turns out our fave Mr. I Could Fix Him But I Don't Want To billionaire owns a string of elite invite-only sex clubs in NYC and LA, and no, you can't get in, don't ask. And while we're not judging (we stan a Filth Facilitator king), this could have major implications for another Black brother. You know, the one giving President? Let's just say, the tea is HOT and the optics are SALACIOUS. Gage out here collecting safe words while his brother collects votes. Is this gonna tank @bradfordblack's rep? Or is it giving "cool brother with a morally grey portfolio" energy? Jury's out. #staytuned

"Amelia. Stop reading."

I look at him again. "I've already read it all."

"And?"

"And what? I'm just over here waiting for confirmation."

He just watches me for a moment. Carefully. Like he's trying to get a read on me. Then, he nods. "Yes, I own clubs."

I blink.

Sex clubs.

Not bars. Not gyms. Not private member lounges where rich men drink $900 whiskey and pretend they have depth. *Sex clubs*. Plural.

Oh god.

I stare at him like I've never seen him before, even though he's right there, shirtless, towel in hand, casually getting ready for bed in his low-hung grey sweatpants like he didn't just drop the kind of information you should only tell a woman after she's had at least five stiff drinks, not mid-boob ogle in the bathroom.

My brain tries to compute this. Fails.

Because *what even is* a sex club owner? Like, what

does that mean in real life? Am I supposed to know all the ways a person can be tied up? Or how an orgy even works? Because I do not. I can't even perform a good striptease. I once got tangled in my own bra straps mid-strip and almost dislocated a shoulder. Also, is there a code word for "I've made a terrible mistake and need to leave immediately", or do you just scream and hope for the best?

And what kind of sex do you have to enjoy to even start one, let alone five?

It's at this point that my panic sets in.

Because I know the kind of sex I have. Have had. Pre-Gage. It was fine. Solidly three-and-a-half-stars on a good night. A little spanking if the moon was in the right phase. Definitely not the kind of sex that inspires someone to open an entire franchise around it.

Am I vanilla?

Oh god, I'm vanilla.

He's out here collecting safe words and my idea of wild is letting someone see me from behind with the lights on.

My face is burning now. I feel like my brain is filing a missing person's report on my dignity. I try to play it cool, but I'm positive my internal scream is leaking through my pores.

This man has probably got a Red Room somewhere. I've got a pink drawer with two vibrators, and one is dead.

And I have *so many questions*.

What does he like? What does he want? *What does he think I can give him?*

I am not built for elite-level-kink. I'm built for Target

lingerie and internally panicking mid-blowjob over whether I left the oven on.

"Okay." I swallow, trying to shove my panic back down where it belongs. "So, real sex clubs? Like, where there's dungeons and contracts and orgies, and someone hands you lube and a waiver at the welcome desk?"

He's a mixture of amused and still watching me carefully.

"My clubs are the kind of place you go when you want to be watched, but not necessarily touched. We create a sensory atmosphere and curated experiences, not wild buffets of kink. It's invite-only with an application process and background checks. NDAs required. No phones allowed. Full privacy. High-end luxury."

"So, no kink?"

"Oh, there's kink. But I think you're picturing an underground horror show where someone hands you a whip and says, 'Good luck.' That's not what this is."

And yep. That's exactly what I was picturing. A concrete basement with red lights, chains on the walls, and a trapdoor escape hatch. Maybe some yelling. Definitely emotional damage.

"Okay."

I'm trying to find more words, but I think they've abandoned me in favor of processing the fact that this man, the one who touches me like I matter, holds space for every part of me, and might be ruining me for all other men, is into a whole other world of sex I never imagined for myself.

He built clubs. Branded the kink. Curated the orgasms. And then he looked at me, *me*, and decided *I'm* the perfect match for all that?

Gage moves in close and grips my waist. "Amelia. Talk to me. Ask me questions."

I look up at him, and *goodness*, the care he's looking at me with is exactly what I need right now. It reminds me that every step of the way, Gage has met me where I am. He's given me what I've needed to feel safe opening up to this relationship. To *him*.

Wanting the physical connection, I curve my hand over his forearm. "You're into kink?"

His shoulders drop the slightest bit. Like my touch, or maybe just that I asked a question, told him I'm not running.

"I wouldn't say I'm *into kink* the way most people mean it. I don't walk into a bedroom with a checklist or a lifestyle label. What I am is curious. I like to learn what makes someone tick. What lights them up. What makes them feel wanted. Safe. Unhinged, if that's what they need." His thumb brushes against my waist, slow, absent, like he's not even thinking about it. Like touching me is just instinct now.

"If a woman needs control taken from her, I'll take it. If she wants to be worshipped, I'll make her feel it. If she likes pain, I'm not her guy. That's a hard limit for me. I won't hurt someone to turn them on. But if you ask me what does it for *me*? It's watching. That's always been my thing. Watching someone unravel because of what I'm doing to them, or what they're doing for me. Knowing I've read them right, figured them out, or that I'm the only one who sees them that way . . . that's the part that fucks with my head, in the best way."

"Okay. So, you've explored. A lot."

"Yes."

"And been with a lot of women."

"Yes."

"Sometimes more than one at a time."

He nods.

"And you do that at your clubs?"

"I have. Not so much anymore, though."

"Why not?"

"I guess . . . I didn't want that kind of sex anymore. The kind with no emotional connection. Which was all I wanted after my divorce. I just wanted the pleasure, and I found that at the clubs. But it's the emotional connection that's my biggest turn on, so I stopped chasing something that wasn't doing it for me anymore." He pauses. "I stopped going to the clubs about four months ago. And I hadn't had sex for three months before you."

The space behind my ribs hushes, my breath folding in as my body tries to rearrange itself around everything he just gave me. It's not just the words. It's how he offered me the softest thing he owns. How he decided I should have this part of him.

My hand finds his and I move into him. Because when a man gives you the kind of truth most people keep locked away, you reach for him. You show him it's safe.

"Thank you for telling me all that," I say softly.

His eyes search mine, his arm now around me. "I don't need anything but what you're giving me."

"Okay." I want to leave it there. I really do. But I think even Gage knows by now that I don't have that setting. "So, you *don't* want to take me to one of your clubs?"

An amused smile ghosts over his face. "Now's the time to say all the things on your mind, Princess. Do *you* want to go to one of my clubs? I've made it clear where I stand."

"Well, no, you haven't. Not really."

"Really, I did." I think that smile is turning into a smirk. "I just told you I'm a happy man fucking you the way I have been. I don't think a guy can be any clearer than that."

Okay. Now I'm internally rolling my eyes at his smug little "I'm right and you know it" attitude.

This man.

I'm not telling him he's right.

"Just so we're on the same page, my sex club overlord, when I had to stand on a stage as a teen and sing for people, my soul exited the building. Having crowds of people watch me do something is my idea of hell on earth. So, I'm not convinced hanging at a sex club is my scene. Not if it involves people watching me. However, if you were to build me my own private room at one of your clubs, and deck it out with all the kink you wanna explore with me, I'd be up for that."

Because I can already see his filthy mind calculating just how fast he could build that room, I press myself really hard into him, get a little grindy, and say against his ear, "And I am absolutely going to want the recordings from that room too. I'm building myself my very own *Private Gageflix Collection* and I think we could call those reels *The Smutcut*."

His hand immediately grips the back of my neck, which I've started calling "The Submission Switch." Trademark pending. Dignity not included. And heaven help me, but when he does it like he is now, his hand not even bothering to slide under my hair, just grabbing it all like it belongs to him? Yeah, I'm ferally invested.

"Consider us on the same page," he growls, all filth and dominance, and just like that, I've got a brand-new fetish. "And we're getting started on your highlight reels tonight. You wanna rub yourself all over me like that, you're getting face-down, ass-up, and I'm fucking the brat right out of you."

CHAPTER 24

AMELIA

"Do they do this every year?" I ask Kristen as I watch Gage and his brothers in his living room immersed in what might be the world's longest tailgate party. A week ago, I knew nothing about football. Now, I'm more across the NFL than I really think is necessary for someone who still thinks RedZone sounds like a subscription service for serial killers.

"Every year," Kristen confirms. "We call it the Draft-pocalypse."

"Yep," Olivia says. "Welcome to seventy-two hours of testosterone, trash talk, and draft picks." She grins and takes a swig of her beer. "I love it."

"Liv!" Callan calls out. "Get your ass in here, woman. We've got a rep to protect here."

"I'm gathering snacks," she calls back. "Surely, you can survive without me for five minutes."

"Hurry, Liv, or he'll choose another third-string tight end," Gage calls out, and while I can't see his face, I feel the smirk radiating from him.

"Fuck off," Callan says.

"Okay," I say to Kristen and Maddie after Olivia gathers snacks and leaves us. "Have I got this right that these grown men are all pretending that they're NFL GMs building fantasy teams? They're watching this draft, scouting picks, and acting like they'll be making million-dollar calls? And each of them runs his own fantasy team? And Callan and Olivia have been co-managing theirs together for years?"

Maddie grins and nods. "Yes, to all of that, and yeah, Liv's his co-GM. This weekend, she's his Draft Day Ride or Die. I'm pretty sure she's the only reason these guys ever let a woman into their war room."

"Yeah, I'd agree with that," Kristen says. "She might be gathering snacks for them because they'd just grab beer if they were in charge, but she's the MVP. She knows her shit."

"Right." I process. "So, basically this is Dungeons & Dragons, but make it sports-bro edition with touchdowns and tight-ends instead of sword fights and dragons."

Maddie laughs. "You've never been into football?"

"No. One of my brothers is, but not like this." I gesture toward the living room. "*This* seems like a lot."

Maddie keeps smiling. "The Black brothers are *insane* about it. Like, they prep for Fantasy Draft weekend the way most people prep for a wedding. There are spreadsheets. Mock drafts. Group texts that start at 6 a.m. from March on. They take it *very* seriously."

Olivia joins us again, listening in on our conversation. "No lies. Gage has Lucy put his pick times in his calendar. And he color-codes his spreadsheet."

My wide eyes are my only response. I can't imagine Gage color-coding anything.

Olivia laughs. "Green for top targets, yellow is backup options, orange for risky picks, red for the 'Do Not Draft List', blue for sleeper steals, and purple for Hayden's favorites."

I frown. "Why is he tracking Hayden's favorites?"

"Strategic warfare." Olivia grins. "He wants to screw Hayden over."

"Hayden's the best," Kristen says. "He's won three out of the last five seasons. Gage would rather lose than let Hayden win."

"Wow." I'm suddenly seeing my man in a whole new way.

"Yep," Olivia agrees. "Gage doesn't just watch football. He prays at the altar of it."

"Let's be real," Kristen says. "All the Black men treat it like their religion."

"Okay," Maddie says. "Enough about football. I want to plan a shopping trip. I need a hospital robe. Something special that you all help me choose."

"I feel like this should just be you girls," I say, sensing this is a special occasion for Madeline. "You only met me two weeks ago."

"No." Maddie smiles at me. "We met you at my wedding. And well, we all knew who you were before that."

My brows pull together. "Huh?"

Maddie's eyes are sparkling like she's been holding onto a secret. "I saw the way Gage watched you at Luna's birthday party last year. You were already on your way to being one of us back then."

"I second that," Olivia says.

I'm staring at them in shock when Gage walks into the kitchen, his hand gliding casually across my hips as he passes. He doesn't stop, just keeps on walking to the fridge, but that one beat of contact, warm and easy, is all kinds of domestic.

He grabs beers from the fridge, popping one open and tucking the others under his arm. On his way back through the kitchen, he catches my eye. Doesn't say a word. Just holds my gaze long enough to make my stomach flip before disappearing into the living room.

The girls catch all of it, shoot me matching knowing looks, and dive straight back into planning our shopping date for next month, like they didn't just leave me here, rethinking every moment I've had with Gage since that party.

I join in, adding the shopping trip to my calendar, along with a book club night with them two weeks from now.

These women have let me in without question. No proving myself. No careful dance. Just open smiles and soft welcomes. Which isn't something I've ever experienced. Not even in school. I've never fit anywhere easily like this, and *god*, I love it.

Over the course of the last two weeks since I saw them at Gage's parents' home, they've added me to the Black brothers' group chat. When I gave Olivia my number, I thought she was adding me to the girls' text thread. I got the surprise of my life when I started receiving texts from everyone. And I honestly wondered what Gage would make of it. Whether he'd think it too soon in our relationship for this level of family connection. He gave zero fucks about it. In fact, when I mentioned removing myself, he emphatically told me not to. It seems my man enjoys the fact I'm bonding with his family.

Being with Gage is easy. The hardest part is juggling our daughters and trying to find alone time. Our free nights don't always align, so Gage is spending a lot of nights tucking Luna into bed, leaving her with his nanny, and coming over for a few hours with me. Except, of course, if I've got Sarah, because I still want to keep our relationship away from the girls. Gage appears ready to be done with that but hasn't bossed me into his way of thinking yet.

He also hasn't said a word about James and his ongoing bullshit, though I see it in his eyes and the tightness in his jaw that he has feelings, and not good ones. I haven't told my ex I'm dating Gage, but he's aware. Of course he is. Social media is practically treating Gage's love life like breaking news.

Since the day I made it clear I was done with his manipulation, James has shifted to other ways of fucking with me. He'll "accidentally" forget which nights he has Sarah, drop last-minute schedule changes on me, and conveniently "lose" important forms for school, forcing me to chase him for signatures. He's started popping up at Sarah's activities, too, all smiles and Dad of the Year energy, but I'm no fool. I see what he's doing. And so does Gage. My only hope is that Gage doesn't lose his shit and get into it with him on my behalf.

The same goes for work. He's ready to go scorched earth for me there, too. Whenever Sofia's name comes up, or I'm mentioned in a bad light on social media, he's visibly unimpressed. Still, he's kept his distance and let me handle my own business, which is something I appreciate more than I've said out loud.

Work is steady, even if nothing looks like I thought it would five weeks ago. My lawyer is handling the copyright infringement claim Sofia filed, compiling all the supporting evidence to shut this down with facts. I'm trying not to let it consume me, especially since the bad press has mostly eased thanks to Marin's PR skills. Well, that or my association with Gage and all the social media girlies who seem to adore him. I'll take either.

I've wrapped up work on the short indie film and have just started work scoring a small-but-promising documentary series. It's not my first preference, but the director is collaborative and it's keeping me focused, which is exactly what I need while the rest of my career hangs in the air.

For now, I'm just trying to keep all the threads of my life from tangling. Family, work, PR updates, childcare coordination, dating. It's a lot. Nights like tonight, surrounded by Gage's family and wrapped in the warmth of the girls' easy friendship are exactly what I need sprinkled in.

Later, when the penthouse is quiet, and it's just me and Gage, we're in his bathroom brushing our teeth, wrapped in towels after our shower. There's an easy ritual to this now. The casual back and forth about what our plans are for tomorrow, the handoff of the toothpaste, the way he wipes the steam off the mirror with his forearm, water still dripping from his hair, his towel riding low on his hips. It's nothing. It's everything. It's the intimate kind of ordinary I cherish. The kind that sneaks up on you when you're not paying attention and makes your chest ache in the best possible way. The kind I've never had.

I move into him when we're done, resting my hand on his hip. "So, it seems I got lucky that I started dating you in March rather than in, say, July."

He looks down at me, already amused, fully aware I'm taking this somewhere. Gently tucking a loose wisp of hair behind my ear, he says, "How do you figure that?"

"I've calculated there are probably only two months out of every year when you're not obsessing over football the way a teen girl goes full feral over Taylor Swift. February and March."

"Full feral." He says that like he can't believe a smart woman like me uttered those words together. Then he dips his face and steals a rough kiss before bringing his heated eyes back to mine. "The only thing I'm going full feral over is you." His hand slides over my ass, and the way he's gripping me says he's thinking about doing that right now.

"I think I may need that in writing if what I've learned about you tonight is true."

He scoops me into his arms and it's very clear he's already moved on from this conversation. I can't be sure, but I think I need to use the words "full feral" with him more often. I think they encourage his filthy ways.

After he throws me on the bed, and *yes*, it was a throw, he strips the towels from us, moves on top of me, and settles between my thighs. His hands find my body. His mouth finds mine. And there's nothing gentle about the way he kisses me. It's hungry and dark. A kiss meant to say *you asked for feral, now hold on*.

He does his absolute best to ruin me with his lips

and then tears his mouth from mine like it physically pains him to stop, breath ragged, eyes wrecked with need.

I'm breathless. Lips swollen. Heart racing like he's already fucked me instead of just kissing me.

"I'm serious," I say, trying to catch my thoughts while watching him move down my body. "Just how much of your time will I be losing to football?"

He doesn't answer me because he's too busy getting his hands and mouth on my breasts in a very impolite way. He drives me wild with how he dedicates himself to my nipples, licking and sucking like this is the only thing he ever wants to do again. When he's finally had his fill there, his eyes meet mine, blazing with the kind of lust that sends a girl right to the edge. "You really think football's going to come before you?" He grazes his teeth over my nipple the way he knows I *really* like. "You have no idea if you think that, Amelia."

Holy gravelly voices.

I grip his biceps and arch into him without even meaning to.

That voice? Saying my name like that?

I won't survive this night if he keeps talking to me like that.

"You want feral?" he demands, his mouth hot against my skin. "You want me ruined for anything but you?" His voice is a growl now, his hips grinding slow and hard against me. "I'll fucking show you feral."

He flips me over. Really, it's more of a toss. Like he's in a fucking hurry and doesn't have time to wait for me to do it myself. Hands to my hips, he hauls me up until I'm on my knees, breath caught in my throat. "I'd cancel the whole fucking world to be with you." He palms my ass, possessive and rough. "To bury myself in you."

Then his mouth is right against my ear. "Tell me exactly how you want it. You want me to hold back?" His fingers slip between my thighs, teasing, denying. "Or do you want me to lose my goddamn mind and fuck you so deep you forget what gentle feels like?"

I'm a panting mess, so damn wet, losing *my* mind with the desperate need for him to just get inside me already.

"Don't go shy on me, Princess. You said feral. So tell me what you want. Use that pretty mouth and tell me how to break you."

I fist the sheets. "I want you to fuck me like you can't control yourself. Like you'll go insane if you don't fill my pussy all up with your cum."

His groan is guttural.

"Jesus fucking Christ, Amelia."

Then he snaps.

He grips my hips and lines himself up, hard and hot, and in one rough thrust, he drives in.

I cry out, the sound sending him further over the edge.

"You want the truth?" he grits, his pace turning indecent, his need crossing all the way into obsessed territory. "I'd spend every goddamn night making a mess out of you if you'd let me." His grip is bruising. "Make you drip down my fucking chin."

My orgasm slams into me. Hard, sudden, and all-consuming. It tears a sound from me that sounds half scream, half curse. A noise I didn't even know I was capable of. And then I'm gone. Zoning the fuck out, lost in the pleasure, and only barely aware that Gage is still fucking me and chasing his own release.

By the time he comes, he's made a mess out of both of us. Skin, breath, hearts. Nothing untouched. He stays inside me for a long moment, arm tight around me like he's not ready to let go.

Then, finally, he drops a kiss to my shoulder and pulls out. He disappears into the bathroom and comes back with a warm washcloth to clean me up. Quiet, focused, like I'm something he wants to take care of.

Gage fucks like a savage but handles me like I'm precious gold.

When he brings me in close to go to sleep, I look up and grasp his face, pulling him down for a kiss. It's unhurried. Soft. No feral in sight.

I find his eyes when I let him go. "I really liked seeing you with your brothers today. And even though I said all that stuff about football, I like that you guys have that. It's special."

He watches me silently and I think what I said touched him. His voice is gruff with emotion when he says, "It's never mattered what shit we're going through, we've always been there for each other."

Gage has told me about his childhood. About how his parents' marriage was loveless for a long time, about how his father cheated on his mother, about how that affected the boys. But also, about their journey since then to a place where they love each other. The brothers have always been close. But now, they're growing close with their parents too. Old wounds are being healed, and I can see just what that means to Gage.

I snuggle into his arms, resting my head on his chest.

We're silent for a long beat, and then I casually say, "I want you to install cameras in my bedroom."

Gage goes still. And then his arm tightens around me, and he growls, "Jesus fucking Christ."

Though he can't see it, I smile.

Then, I glance up at him, finding his dark eyes already focused intently on me. "You know, so you can watch me anytime you want."

"I fucking caught that," he says, and I'm 99.999% sure he wants to put me over his knee right now and spank the brat out of me.

I smile sweetly and say very innocently, "I just wanted to make sure."

I've got my head back on his chest and am slowly drifting off to sleep when he kisses the top of my head and mutters, "You'll be the fucking death of me."

CHAPTER 25
AMELIA

THERE ARE three kinds of Saturdays.

The first is the mom-frazzled one. Birthday parties, music lessons, school projects, back-to-back logistics with barely enough time to reheat coffee, let alone drink it. You're basically a PA for a very small, very demanding boss with glitter glue in her hair.

The second is slower, but not easier. Laundry, grocery runs, life admin, maybe some quiet reading time if the universe is feeling generous. You spend it trying to catch up on everything you didn't do during the week while pretending that counts as rest.

And then there's the rare third kind.

The unicorn kind.

Where your daughter's at her dad's, you're wearing a red silk dress, and a billionaire with control issues is sending a car to pick you up at nine.

Which, for the record, is practically midnight in mom time. But it's the first Saturday in weeks that neither of us has our girls, and Gage made it very clear we were going to make the most of it. His words, not mine. Mine were something more like "where are we going?" and "can I wear flats?" To which he replied, "You'll want heels. And the whole night."

So, naturally, I'm now standing in my elevator with red silk clinging to my body, my hair falling in soft waves, heels too high, and *absolutely no idea where I'm going*.

He's been evasive. All smooth control and just enough silence to make me nervous.

So I've decided to punish him the only way I know how.

With this dress.

A slip dress.

Red. Dangerous. Slit to the heavens.

It clings like it's trying to become one with my body and is made of the kind of fabric that assumes you haven't eaten carbs since the invention of Instagram. The neckline dips low, the back dips lower. It's the kind of dress you wear when you've lost your mind just enough to think you can handle what comes next.

The elevator opens to the lobby and my doorman does a double take when I walk through. Which, fair, because I *never* dress like this. His expression is a little "do I need to alert security or just offer a high five?"

Gage's car is waiting at the curb. His Mercedes-Maybach. Sleek, black, purring like money. It's not flashy, but it is deliberate. Impossible to ignore. Just like the man who sent it.

Sean, his driver, is standing there in a suit, calm as ever, opening the rear door with a polite nod. He's driven me before. Usually on one of the occasions Gage and I manage time alone. And at other times, when my schedule gets hectic, Gage quietly assigns him to me. Like I'm too important to be flagging down taxis or walking anywhere. It's thoughtful. Helpful, even. It's also peak over-functioning billionaire behavior. I say no. He acts like I'm cute for thinking I have a choice.

I live my life with the mantra "I've got this."

He lives his with "I've got you."

And somewhere in the middle, we brush up against the same need—me, trying to prove I'm fine. Him, proving I don't have to be.

I slip into the car and settle into one of the back seats, if you can even call them seats. They're more like leather thrones. Two of them, divided by a center console housing more chrome and tech than I know what to do with.

The interior is dim, quiet, and smells like Gage. That spicy cologne of his that drives me wild. I sit back, cross my legs, and spot the bottle of champagne chilling in its own compartment. A Gage luxury.

I pour a glass and let the bubbles work their magic. I'm not nervous. I'm just existing in that weird limbo where I don't know where we're going, haven't had a second to overthink it—and oops, I've accidentally poured myself a second glass.

Twenty minutes later, we slow in front of a building in SoHo.

No signage.

No line.

No crowd.

No hint of what lies behind the door.

Sean gets out, circles the car. Opens my door and says, "Ms. Sinclair."

My heels hit the pavement, and my hand goes to my stomach. I smooth my dress. And then I see him.

Gage.

He's dressed in a black suit I've not seen before. New. Definitely. And that black shirt he's paired it with? Lethal. Because hot damn, my man does not like doing up all his buttons or wearing ties, and he knows this is my brand of kryptonite.

He looks like money, danger, and quiet obsession wrapped in control.

And he's not smiling.

He's just looking at me like I'm the only thing in his world that matters.

"You look beautiful," he says, his voice all possessive in that unholy, good-luck-walking-after-this kind of way.

Oh boy.

Holy walking sin.

My core has hijacked the situation like she's living her best life. I, meanwhile, am not coping with this suit, this man, or that scent of his that may be the actual death of me.

"Jesus." I throw out. "You're not even touching me and I'm dissolving into particles."

He doesn't laugh. He just watches me. Amused, yes, but it's the kind of look that promises sinful things later. "Careful, Princess. I haven't even started yet."

He barely gives me time to recover from that promise before his arm slides around me, his hand settling at the small of my back as he steers me toward the building.

I stop him. I'm not ready. Not yet. I need a second to gather myself.

I glance up at the building. It blends in the way only

the expensive ones do. Restored red brick. Tall iron-framed windows. Discreet uplighting that washes the façade in soft gold.

Somewhere inside, the bass hums low. Not loud. Just enough to feel it in my chest. Like the building has a pulse.

There are two doors.

The first is sleek steel, framed in black, with a small brass plaque etched with a symbol I don't recognize. A couple walks out as I'm looking at it, flushed and laughing, on their way to the black SUV idling nearby.

The second door is different.

Matte-black steel, flush with the wall.

No plaque. No handle. No visible lock.

This has to be one of Gage's clubs.

I've barely processed that thought when he leads me to the second door.

As we approach, a narrow strip of amber light flares to life around the frame. Gage presses his hand to the center, and a digital scanner blooms beneath his fingers.

No clicks. No beeps.

The door unlocks like it knows him.

And then I see it.

Just above the scanner.

A single letter, engraved into the steel in elegant script.

A.

The door opens without a sound.

A hush. A breath. An invitation.

I look at Gage. "What is this place?"

He meets my gaze *and his eyes* . . . they don't answer the question; they promise the unraveling. "Yours."

My chest pulls tight, and suddenly, I'm feeling everything all at once. The mystery. The anticipation. The weight of that single letter on the door. And the way he says "yours" like he's placing a precious gift in my hands.

And then he steps inside, holding the door open for me, inviting me into this part of his life.

We walk down a hallway cloaked in shadow and intention. Black walls, lit by a candle-warm glow, and a hush so complete it feels like the air itself is holding its breath. And the scent? It's *mine*. My favorite perfume, diffused so delicately it doesn't announce itself, just *exists* here. Like it's always lived here.

An elevator is at the end of the hallway. The doors are sleek brushed steel. No buttons. Just a small screen that lights up for Gage. It recognizes him. And then we're stepping inside.

The lights are low and warm. The walls, mirrored. *And holy shit.* The music playing is a piano piece I composed a few weeks ago. Quiet, aching, never meant for anything but my own therapy.

Gage doesn't say a word. But he's watching me. And for once, I don't have any rambled words for him. Not when my brain is working faster than it ever has to take all of this in.

We reach our destination, and his hand comes to my back again. Gentle but guiding, and we walk out of the elevator into a room.

I feel it before I've even taken my first step.

The change in temperature.

The sensory explosion of color, scent, touch, sound.

The depth of the gift.

I walk further in. The air is warm, like this room

expects you to take your clothes off and stay awhile. My perfume is here too. Familiar and personal. It weaves around me, tells my deeper parts that this is my space. Because, of course, what my perfume clings to is mine.

The music in this room isn't something I composed. But it feels like it could be. Low, intimate, layered in strings and seduction and heat.

And then there's the red.

Not lipstick red. Not lingerie red. This is deeper. Darker. Richer. A crimson you don't wear; you sink into. It's in the velvet of the blanket on the chaise. In the low-lit corners. In the faintest tint of light cast across the mirrors' edges. It doesn't scream. It hums.

The amber lighting continues into this room. A soft spotlight highlights the chaise. Candles flicker. Shadows dance. My skin glows under it like it's been waiting for this specific hue all its life.

Amber says *you're safe here.*

Red says *you won't leave the same.*

And together, they say *this room was built to worship.*

I trail my hand along surfaces as I walk through the room, fingertips skimming over velvet, silk, cool leather, steel. Over the hanging velvet robe that has my initials embroidered in silver on the pocket. Over furniture that looks functional. Very much not the kind you'd find in a living room.

There's a bench that's low and padded, with shaped curves and straps that make my brain spin. A tall chair that's less about sitting and more about watching—luxurious, oversized, the kind of throne a man like Gage would sit in while turning me inside out with just his eyes.

Mirrors are everywhere. A tall one behind the throne, which means if I'm watching him touch himself, I can see both him *and* me watching. A low angled mirror near the chaise for a voyeuristic perspective from below. Panels of mirrored shelving reflecting the sensual toys. Horizontal mirrors positioned near furniture for viewing pleasure. And a mirror stretched across the ceiling above the chaise—the room centerpiece—its edges kissed with that same deep crimson light.

But tucked between the kink and the luxury, the Gage of it all?

There's me.

Photos. Not blown up and framed like a trophy. No. He's scattered framed photos of me on the walls, tucked between shelves and candles and mirrors like pages from a secret journal. Three in this corner. Two over there. Single photos every now and then. Photos he's taken when I wasn't aware or have simply forgotten. He's caught me mid-laugh, hair wild, happiness all over my face. Shots taken from behind while I'm playing the piano. The tiny moments in life where I'm just being me, all seen through his eyes.

Then, leaning in close, I see the thin brass strip, mounted to the wall. A single bar of music etched into it. It's mine. One of my favorite progressions, one I never finished, but he must have heard me play a dozen times.

Near that, I spot pages of my sheet music. My handwriting scribbled all over, splattered with coffee stains, corners curled. Discarded drafts. Things I threw out because they weren't perfect. Gage saved them.

I move to the last shadowed alcove and still.

A black velvet box hangs on the wall, lit by soft light. Inside it, resting with care, is a single ivory piano key.

I turn into Gage, who is still just watching me without a word. "You did all this?"

It's not even a question I need answered. I know he did. But I ask anyway. Because I'm standing in a room that feels like a sanctuary where nothing is random and everything means something, *and I am not okay.*

He nods. "You said you wanted a room."

I stare at him.

Blink.

Forget how to breathe.

I'm over here in sensory and emotional overload, thoughts in a tangle, emotions in whatever is more than a tangle, and he's just over there saying, "You said you wanted a room," like he just shrugged at my request and thought to himself, *okay, I'll take a crack at it, see what I can build.*

"Okay," I blurt as I fling an arm at the room, "*this* isn't a room. This is so much more than a room, Gage. This is" —I struggle to find the words as I glance around— "chaises, and mirrors, and leather, and silk, and velvet, and candles, and mood lighting, and color, and my music that I don't even know how you got, and my perfume." I stop to catch my breath, finding his eyes again, and slowing all the way down at what I see there. At the look that I don't feel ready to name yet, but, *oh god*, I feel it too. All of it.

"This is," I continue, but the words get caught in my throat.

This could have just been a kink room. Just a fantasy space.

But it's not.

It's personal.

Every detail tells me he's been paying attention.

He didn't just build a space to fuck me in.

He built a space for *me to find out what I want.*

To explore.

To experience.

To feel safe in.

To come undone *with* him, not just *for* him.

"This is a love letter," I whisper.

He moves into me, one hand sliding into my hair, the other skimming my jaw with a touch that says, *I see you. I built this for you. I'd build more.*

"This room's yours," he says, gravel-rough and tightly leashed. "Every chair, every inch of velvet, every goddamn camera. I'll fuck you in it any way you want, but first, I want to watch you forget the world exists. Forget the rules you've been living by. And figure out what *you* want, when the only thing that matters is what sets you on fire."

He doesn't move.

Doesn't crowd me.

Doesn't push.

This isn't the Gage who backs me into walls or kisses like he's starving.

This is the Gage who builds temples and waits at the altar.

And God help me; I think this version might ruin me even faster.

His thumb grazes along my jaw. "There's an app for your phone. It controls the cameras. It's yours. You're the only one who sees what's filmed in here unless you choose to share it. You decide when we hit record. You keep the key." A beat. A breath. "You don't have to set foot in the club unless you want to. The private entrance is yours now. I'll add your hand to the scanner." His eyes hold mine, fierce and steady as a vow. "I might take your body apart in this room, Amelia, but you own every second of it."

My fingers fist into his shirt like it might tether me to reality, but nothing can ground me now. Not with *this* man saying things like *that* in a room he built to worship me in.

He's cracked me wide open.

I am bare skin and heartbeat and surrender.

And I need his lips on mine right now more than I need oxygen.

My hand is around his neck before I've even taken another breath.

Our mouths collide, passion sparking so intensely my body is fire.

Gone is the Gage who was able to restrain himself. Now, he's devouring me.

Hands gripping, tongues tangling, control unraveling with every breath.

His jacket hits the floor. Then his shirt.

Heat rolls off him like this isn't just about sex. It's about me. About us. About everything that hasn't been said out loud yet.

His hands find the skin beneath the slit in my dress, possessive, and just shy of indecent. And then I'm in his arms, legs wrapping around him. I grab his mouth again like I'll fall apart without it, my fingers gripping his face hard, claiming him as mine.

Somehow, he gets us to the chaise without breaking the kiss, without loosening his hold on me, without letting go of that raw, hungry need that's been thrumming between us since I stepped out of his car.

He lowers me slowly to the ground, carefully, like my body's sacred.

And then he pulls back, just a little, his breath heavy against my mouth. The look in his eyes tells me he's holding himself in check by sheer will alone.

"Fuck," he rasps. "I'm trying to be gentle, but you make me lose my fucking mind."

"I don't need gentle."

"I know you don't. But tonight, I want to take my fucking time."

His fight for control is *everything*.

It says I make it nearly impossible for him to keep his hands to himself, his mouth to himself, his body to himself.

It says I have *that* kind of power over him.

And while I never want power over Gage, knowing I have it, knowing he would fall to his knees for me? It's the most devastating kind of intimacy I've ever felt.

He turns and walks to a smooth panel in the wall, so discreet I wouldn't have known it was anything, and presses his thumb to it. A hidden drawer opens, revealing a slim black jewelry box he lifts with care.

By the time he comes back to me, something's shifted in him. His eyes are locked on me, molten and focused, and the look on his face? It's not just heat. It's hunger wrapped in intention.

My breath catches. My pulse stumbles.

Holy hell.

I'm going to need a minute.

But Gage isn't giving me a minute.

No, this man is on a mission to completely wreck me tonight.

He opens the box, revealing a necklace.

It's solid. A sleek, unbroken circle of polished silver. Minimal and modern. There's no clasp. No chain. No visible hinge. I can't even see how someone's supposed to open it.

Nestled in the center of the box is a small silver pendant that's circular, diamond-set, and obscenely elegant. The channel-set stones catch the light, and the rounded bale is designed to slide perfectly onto the necklace.

It's understated luxury. And while it's unlike anything I've ever worn, I'd wear this in a heartbeat. Not because it's stunning and different, but because my heart already wants it. How could it not, when Gage is the one who chose it?

I lift my gaze to him, overwhelmed and a little undone, and suddenly unsure how to put any of it into words. "It's stunning."

Gage is watching me with silent intensity. When he speaks, his voice is rough. "Do you know what it is?"

I look down at the box again, searching for what I've missed because *holy heck* that intensity vibrating from him tells me it's something important. "A necklace?"

"No." His voice is quiet. Weighted in the way a man's voice is when he's handing you his soul. "It's an eternity collar." He lets that hang there, thick with meaning. "It doesn't come off unless I unlock it."

My mouth parts, but no words come out.

Because *this*?

This is not a casual offer.

This is Gage Black handing me the keys to the kingdom of his obsession and saying, *here, wear it around your neck where everyone can see who you belong to.*

A rational woman might blink at saying yes to this after two months. Might think this is too much, too soon. But I am not that woman. Not with him.

I feel this man in my veins.

And if I've learned anything since the moment he first backed me into a wall and claimed me, it's that time knows nothing about connection.

I've felt the way he's handled my body like it's a gift, and my heart like it's breakable.

I've seen the way he listens when I don't even know I'm speaking, and the way he knows what I need before I do.

And when the world came for me, he didn't flinch.

So, no, this might not look rational from the outside. But love rarely does.

And if this collar means what I think it means?

I want it.

God, I want it.

I lift my chin just enough.

Find his eyes.

"Put it on me."

The moment I say it, his eyes flare.

It's not desire.

It's not possession.

It's devotion.

He lifts the collar from the box slowly, like it's precious. Sacred. Then he steps behind me, his body close. One of his hands moves my hair aside, careful not to rush. Then he fits the collar gently around my throat, cool silver meeting warm skin.

I shiver. Not from the cold. From everything this means.

"You sure?" he murmurs, and even though he's asking, I feel every ounce of his need for me to say yes.

I touch the collar. "Yes," I whisper.

He doesn't speak again. Just fastens the collar with the tiny tool. And when it's secured, he kisses the back of my neck, his lips taking their time with my skin.

I feel everything that kiss says.

You're mine, and I'll spend the rest of my life proving I deserve you.

He turns me to him, eyes scanning my face like he's never going to forget this exact version of me.

Then, his gaze drops to the collar. He trails a finger over it, slow and reverent. Lingers there. "The diamonds are for special occasions unless you want to wear them every day."

His thumb grazes the edge again, and I swear my man's going to have trouble taking his eyes off it. "I didn't think you'd want diamonds every day though."

"Gage," I breathe, stepping into him, desperate for the proximity.

His eyes meet mine. My hand finds his jaw. And then my mouth finds his, and I'm kissing him like I need it to live. Like I'm coming out of my skin just to get closer.

This man.

This beautiful, intense, passionate, loving man.

He has stolen my heart clean out of my chest, and I never want it back.

CHAPTER 26
GAGE

"SHE FUCKING WHAT?" I ask Jason, my fixer. The guy who handles shit for me before it ever reaches my desk.

"She's mentioned LA a few times now in those Instagram lives she does, but that's all I have so far. I'll do some digging to see what else I can find, but I wanted to keep you up to date on this in case she's given you any reason to suspect it. And Amelia's fine. We dropped some more distraction content, and the team's been working the comment threads hard. Social's leaned back in her favor. We've tied shit up with Sofia Raye. She's dropped the case, and Amelia will never hear from her again. I'll still keep an eye on this situation, but it feels done now."

Thank fuck.

Watching Amelia get dragged through shit the last few months has burned me raw. Sofia negotiated a ridiculous settlement, but the truth is I would've paid ten times that to make it stop.

To take the weight off Amelia.

To let her breathe again.

To see her smile without bracing for the next hit.

Whatever it cost, I'd have paid it.

Jason and I go over a few work things and before we wrap, his tone shifts. "There's one more thing I want to circle back to. Your bad press."

The whispers about me online that started after the post about my clubs. The slow, steady drip of posts that don't say anything outright, but still make me look like a man with something to hide. One who operates in shadows. Fixes things behind the scenes. The kind of man people suspect of crossing lines I don't fucking touch.

We've been tracking it for weeks but there's nothing there. No name attached. No clear agenda. Just smoke. And I don't waste time on smoke.

"What about it?"

"The noise has gotten louder this week. It's not just fringe threads or gossip posts anymore. There's a pattern forming."

I stay quiet, waiting.

"We're across it all, but whoever's behind it is smart. They're feeding it slow. Anonymous leaks, comment swarms, burner phones. Clean hands, dirty trail. They're building suspicion not scandal. But don't be surprised if this escalates."

"Keep digging. Find me something."

We wrap up, and I immediately call Shayla. When she doesn't answer, I leave her a voicemail. "Call me back as soon as you get this."

Fuck.

I clench my jaw and drag a hand down my face.

I've had a gut feeling since Shayla got engaged to Michael that she'd try to relocate to Los Angeles and take

Luna with her. The kind of gut feeling I've learned not to ignore.

Shayla never loved LA. Now? She's there multiple times a month. And Michael? He's one of those self-proclaimed New York purists who talks a good game about "protecting the craft" and not selling out to LA. But for all his speeches about integrity, his last three movies were big-budget action flicks funded by the LA studios he claims he'd never sell out to.

I asked Jason to keep an eye on things after they were engaged. Nothing's pinged as a red flag until now. And my gut's telling me not to wait.

I call Blair. She picks up straight away.

"Gage. What's up?"

Her snark's dialed down these days. Just barely. But when it counts, she knows how to flip the switch and be professional. She's done good work for me with Luna. And I've adjusted my opinion of her because of it.

I give her a rundown on my concerns and the reasons for them.

"There's nothing concrete yet," I finish. "But my gut's kicking up, and I'd rather be ahead of this than reacting too late."

"You think she's planning to relocate?"

"I think she's laying the groundwork."

"Okay. I'll pull the custody order and go over all the clauses to see if anything in there gives her room to move. Don't do anything until you hear back from me. I want to be clear on where she could argue ambiguity before we escalate."

"I don't need careful, Blair. I need ready."

"Then let me do my job, and you'll have both."

We end the call, and I stretch my neck side to side before releasing a breath. There's nothing in that order that gives Shayla the right to move Luna across the country without going through me. But that doesn't mean she won't try. And if this turns into a fight, it's not me or Shayla who takes the hit. It's Luna.

I shove my chair back and walk out of my office, catching the pale shimmer of Manhattan waking up beyond the glass. I've been up for hours, clearing a backlog of work I never used to have. First time in my life I've fallen behind, and I have the world's most beautiful distraction to thank for it.

On my way down the hall to my bedroom, Luna launches herself at me, still hyped from the sleepover she and Sarah had last night. Amelia and I don't do this all the time, stay together with the girls. We try to keep our usual routine. But sometimes, we give them the fun of a family night in and a school-night sleepover.

"Dad!" She blocks my path, eyes wide and sparkling. Her version of a strategic ambush. It's the look I can't say no to even when I try. "We wanna go to the symphony. Like you and me did last year. But this time with Sarah and Amelia." She pauses for impact. "You know Amelia would love it."

Luna adores Amelia. And ever since I told Amelia I was done sneaking around like a teenager a month ago— the night I gave her the collar—my daughter thinks all her dreams have come true. She's already planning matching bedrooms for when her stepsister moves in.

She knows I'd take her to the symphony anytime she asks. But she's been tying Amelia into everything—every plan, every moment—as if she's trying to glue us together before anything can fall apart. I think she's worried that if she doesn't keep us close, we'll end up like I did with her mother.

The weight of that lands in my chest harder than I want to admit. She's just a kid, and she's already trying to patch cracks that aren't even there yet. And fuck if I'm going to let her carry that kind of fear. Not in this house. Not on my watch.

I ruffle her hair. "I know you would love it, baby girl. Of course, I'll take you."

"Yeah," she says slowly, "but Sarah and Amelia can come too, right?"

"Yes, Luna, everyone can come."

She beams, twirling once like her entire world just aligned. When she starts to take off down the hall, I catch her hand and gently tug her back.

"Amelia and I are good, Luna," I say, keeping my voice quiet.

She nods, eyes wide, looking like she's not quite sure where I'm taking this.

"No one's going anywhere."

She nods slowly, processing, and then gives me a small smile.

I let her go and she darts off, racing all the way to the other end of the hall where Sarah's waiting for her in her bedroom. The girls' excited chatter echoes behind me, fading the further I walk until I can't hear it anymore at the edge of my bedroom door.

Amelia's in the bathroom, phone wedged between her ear and shoulder, listening to someone talk while applying makeup.

Her eyes meet mine in the reflection when I rest my

hip against the counter. She flashes a smile, then drops her gaze to my rolled-up sleeves that are ready for the humidity of the day. She lingers there. And then she gives me a look that belongs in the bedroom—full heat, full drama, silently asking, *do we really need those rolled-up sleeves this early in the day?*

I arch a brow and glance at that dress she's wearing.

When I bring my gaze back, she just shoots me a sexy smile and goes back to perfecting her makeup.

I eye the dress again. It's cream silk with soft pink blooms scattered like a brush painted them on. Sheer in places. Ruffled sleeves sitting just off her shoulders. Legs on full fucking display. A dip at her chest giving more than a hint of cleavage.

And right there above it, sitting at her throat like it belongs there?

Her collar.

The declaration that every inch of her is spoken for.

My eyes fix on it like they always do now. Like they always will.

That collar speaks for her, but every time I see it, it roars in my head—*mine*.

Doesn't matter how many times I see it. That reaction? Automatic.

Amelia finishes her call and pulls back from the mirror, eyes lit. "Guess what?"

"What?"

She wraps both arms around me, and says, "Sofia's dropped her case against me. That was my lawyer on the phone. It's all over."

I bring a hand up to settle at the nape of her neck.

"That's great fucking news." I don't let on I'm already aware. That's between me and Jason.

Her smile is electric, and I can see the weight that's already lifted. "You're taking me out tonight to celebrate."

"Am I?" I say, like I'm not already halfway to planning the whole damn night around her.

Her smile shifts into the kind of sexy look that means my ruin is imminent. "Well, I mean, I hope so, because I don't really have the time to go out and find another man to celebrate with."

"Fuck," I growl, because *just the thought of that* makes me lose my mind.

My hand tightens at her neck, and I bring my mouth to her ear. "Another man touches you, I bury him. You wanna celebrate? I'll start with my mouth, end with my cock, and remind you why it's my fucking collar around your neck."

"Jesus, Gage," she says breathlessly as I pull my head back and ease my grip on her neck. Her arms unwrap from me, and she drops a hand to the counter to steady herself. "I'm not built to withstand you like that at seven on a Tuesday morning."

I bend my face and steal a rough, hungry kiss that's nowhere near long enough. When I'm done, I spend a moment just looking, taking her in, catching my breath. No one's ever affected me the way she does, and sometimes I need the pause to get my head straight, to pull the heat back, to ground myself in her.

I give her neck one last squeeze, her lips one last kiss, and let her go. Then, I change the conversation to give both of us a break from the need that's always right there.

"Luna's in planning mode again. She asked for all of us to attend the symphony."

"She mentioned it to me." She pauses, collecting her thoughts while her expression shifts into that quiet worry she wears when something matters to her. "I'm concerned about her, Gage. I don't know her like you do, but it feels like she's scared of things changing. Of things breaking. It feels like she's trying to keep us all close now that we're together."

"Yeah, I've caught that. I had a quick word with her this morning, but I need to spend more time with her. Dig into it properly." My guilt flares again. "I think she's trying to hold everything together because she's afraid you and I will go the way I did with Shayla. I'll talk to her and fix it."

"That makes sense." She releases a breath. "God, I hate how our trauma affects our kids. I had Sarah so young. I didn't even know what my real wounds were back then, let alone know to heal them so I didn't pass them on."

I watch her as I listen to every word she says—this woman who holds both softness and steel. She's not just smart. She's self-aware. She doesn't hide from her past; she works through it. Quietly. Relentlessly. For herself. For her daughter. And now without even realizing it, for Luna too.

I don't know how I got this lucky. But I'll do whatever it takes not to fuck this up. To keep Amelia by my side.

"We do the best we can in the minute," I say, then pause, because she deserves more than that. "But not everyone does what you're doing, Amelia. Not everyone looks their shit in the eye and chooses better. Sarah's lucky to have you." I let that sit. Let it land. "So is Luna. And so am I."

She stills, and I catch the flicker of disbelief, the instinct to downplay it.

I don't let her.

"You might not see yourself that way," I say. "But I do. Let yourself hear it."

She doesn't respond, and I think she's trying to decide what to do with my words. Then, she says, "Thank you for saying that." Her voice might be soft, but I hear the weight in it that says she heard me.

I give her a second to let it all settle, my gaze drifting down the length of her dress while I do that. "What's the occasion today?" At her confusion, I elaborate, "The dress."

"Oh, I'm having lunch with the girls. We're taking Maddie out for her first outing since she got home from the hospital. And yes, there will be baby snuggles. Annalise is the main event."

Fuck, I like seeing Amelia with my family.

The way she's won my brothers over with her nerdy realness.

The way she's right there with the girls, all in their business, laughing like she's known them forever, and enjoying the kind of friendship I know is new to her.

And the way both my parents have welcomed her with open arms.

I've never gone looking for easy. I don't trust it. Good things come hard and cost something. That's what I've always believed.

But being with Amelia?

Hell if she doesn't make everything feel easy. Not simple. Not shallow. But like maybe this is what it feels like when something fits without needing to be forced.

"That's a sexy-as-hell dress for lunch with the girls," I say.

She catches the heat in my eyes and her hands immediately find my shirt, grasping it. A signature Amelia move; one I'm not sure she even knows she does. But I know. I feel it every damn time. It's the kind of instinct that wrecks me, because it's not calculated or conscious. It's need. Quiet, everyday need. And every time, it reminds me that she's here. In my space. Grabbing my shirt because I'm hers.

"It's really not," she says.

"It really fucking is."

"You think every dress is sexy."

Both our phones light up with a text that's just hit the family group chat. Amelia checks the message while I try like fuck to remove my eyes from her tits.

She groans. "Kristen is still hounding me about that gala."

It's a gala Kristen's hosting to raise money for arts for children. She wants Amelia to perform before giving a speech. The very thing that would make my woman's soul exit the building.

She looks at me like she just had a genius idea. "We need to strategize over this."

"Over what?"

"You, me, dinner, and a strategy session. Teach me your ways of getting out of things."

"I don't need a strategy for that, Amelia. I'd just fucking say no."

She pulls a face. "Ugh. We can't all be like you."

Then, her expression changes, and I just know she's about to hit me with something that'll shoot my focus to shit.

"That's okay," she says sweetly, lips curving into trouble. "If I can't practice *with* you, I'll practice *on* you." Her eyes run down my body, voice turning low and lethal. "I'll sit on your throne. Naked. Just my collar. And I'll touch myself. Edge myself for hours while you watch. And every time you try to touch me, I'll say no." She pauses, let's that hang. "I'd probably need a lot of practice." Her smile is fucking wicked. "Days. Weeks. Maybe months."

Christ.

My palm is straight to her hip, rough and greedy, and I'm yanking her closer until there's no air between us. "You say that shit to me when our daughters are here, and I can't fucking do anything about it?"

She bites her lip. Doesn't say a word.

Fuck.

"Princess, you keep running your mouth like that, I'm going to spend the entire day hard and homicidal."

Still not a word, just that sweet and innocent act that she *knows* fucks with my control.

I kick the bathroom door shut and reach out to lock it, not giving Amelia even an inch.

Then, I lean in close. "Say one more thing like that, and you'll sit on that fucking throne, tied and dripping, and I'll use your body to remind you exactly who you belong to." My hand grips her ass. "You wanna edge me with words? Turn me into something I can't cage?" My fingers dig the hell in. "Then you better be ready for what that gets you."

She's hot and needy from my words alone, and it takes every-fucking-thing in me not to bend her over the vanity and fuck her so deep she won't speak in complete sentences for days.

"I'll kneel between your legs, tongue on your pussy, fingers in it, until you're shaking and begging and soaking wet down your thighs."

She's fucking panting.

"I won't touch my cock. I won't fuck you. Not until I see you fall apart so many times you forget why you were even playing this game."

I grip her chin. "You think you can outlast me, Princess? I'll ruin you with patience. I'll edge you until you're screaming, and when I finally fuck you"—my hand slides between us, claiming her pussy through the thin fabric of her dress—"you'll thank me for every second I made you wait."

She moans, and *goddamn*, I'm losing my fucking mind over this woman.

"Gage . . ." She fists my shirt, turned on as hell with no release in sight.

I dip my head, voice dropping to a growl. "You wanna learn how to say no?" My lips brush hers. "Let me show you what it takes to survive."

She grips my face and absolutely fucking slays me with a reckless kiss that will stay with me all day. When she's had her fill, she keeps hold of my jaw and says so fucking breathlessly that I have to call on every scrap of control I have not to just give her my cock, "The only place I want you to take me tonight is to your throne. And there *will* be cameras on, so bring your A-game for me."

"Christ. You're fucking killing me, Amelia." I let her go, needing a minute to get my shit together.

My hands go straight to my hips, and I drag in a breath through my nose. My body's on fire, cock rock hard, pulse still hammering like I'm about to bend her the fuck over.

I press a hand to the wall. Not for balance. Just to ground myself.

Amelia watches me, chest rising and falling, her face flushed, and yeah, she looks as taken to the edge as I feel. "In my next life," she says, "I'm not having children. I just want a sex overlord and twenty-four-seven options."

"Dad!" Luna's voice comes from the other side of the bathroom door. "We need your help."

"Give me a minute, sweetheart." My eyes are still on Amelia, my body still sorting itself the fuck out.

"Okay, but be quick!"

"I'll go," Amelia says, and with one last quick brush of her lips over mine, and one last grasp of my shirt, she unlocks the door and leaves to help the girls.

I give myself a minute.

A long fucking minute.

And once I've got myself under control, I go and see if they need me. Which they don't, so I head into the kitchen and make coffee for the drive to work. I've just finished when Shayla calls.

"Thanks for calling me back."

"I was out running," she says, slightly breathless. "What's so urgent?"

"Are you planning to move to LA with Michael?"

I'm met with silence, which only stirs my gut feeling more.

Then, "Why?"

"I heard you've been talking about it on Instagram."

"Jesus, Gage. Are you stalking my socials now?"

"No, I'm not stalking you. But I keep tabs. You're the mother of my daughter, Shayla. I have every right to know if you're planning to move Luna across the country."

"Wow. There it is. The controlling tone I know so well."

"It's not controlling to want to know your plans that involve our daughter. You're in LA a lot these days. Michael works there almost full time. Don't insult my intelligence."

"You're reading way too much into this. Even if I was thinking about moving, it's not like I'd just take Luna without talking to you."

"You're damn right about that. We have a custody agreement, and you can't do anything without going through me first."

"And there's the Gage we know and love. The man who has to know everything, read into everything, and manage every situation."

I ignore her shit. "If you're planning something that changes Luna's life, I deserve to know. And not through Instagram stories. You want to move, you bring it to me first."

She laughs, but there's no light in it. "Let me guess, you've already talked to your lawyer."

"Don't test me on this, Shayla," I snap, my patience fraying.

"Wow. There he is. You really haven't changed, have you? Tell me, how's your new girlfriend coping? Let her know if she needs any tips, I'm her girl."

I rub the back of my neck, fighting like fuck to keep my voice level. "You want to uproot our daughter for your boyfriend? Fine. Just know if you try to take her out of the city permanently, I *will* fight it. Every step of the way."

I end the call, my thumb hitting the screen harder than necessary. For a second, I just stand there. Breathing hard. Jaw tight. Shoulders like stone.

That wasn't how I wanted to handle it. Pushing her like that wasn't in my plan.

I meant every word, but the delivery was off. My tone too sharp.

Fuck.

I roll my shoulders, trying to shake it off. But this isn't going to shake off easily. There's too much at stake here and I just threw gasoline on the fire.

I turn to walk back into the bedroom and immediately stop, every muscle in my body tensing when I see Amelia standing there looking at me like she's just seen or heard something that she needs to tread carefully with.

"Was that Shayla?" she asks quietly, her eyes cautious.

"Yeah." I feel that sick pull low in my gut that tells me I just fucked something up that matters. Because I know what her fears were coming into this relationship. I know she's worried I'll hurt her, and I sure as hell know the kind of man she never wants to be with again. And *fuck.* What she just heard had to sound bad.

She's slow to speak again.

"Are you okay?"

"I think she's planning to move to LA, but she won't talk to me about it."

She swallows. "You sounded intense."

I nod, my regret crashing into me again. "I didn't handle it well. Blair told me not to speak to Shayla, to let her do her job. I fucked up." I breathe out hard, but it doesn't help. Not with the pressure of everything I'm carrying. "I know the custody order would hold. If it came down to it, I could stop her from taking Luna. But Jesus, Amelia . . . what kind of father drags his daughter through a war just to say he won? I don't want to fight Shayla in court. I don't want Luna stuck in the middle. But I also can't let her go. I can't lose her."

Amelia doesn't speak straight away. She just watches me—really watches me—like she's stripping me bare with those sharp eyes of hers. Assessing the damage. Reading all the parts I try to keep hidden.

Trying to understand me.

And then, like a tide turning, I see her caution dissolving. Her jaw softens and her shoulders drop with a slow exhale.

She crosses the room to me.

Not tentative.

Not afraid.

Certain.

Her hand finds mine, fingers lacing tight. "You didn't fuck anything up, Gage. You did what you always do. You carried the weight alone so no one else would bleed."

Then she reaches for my face—one palm framing my jaw—and leans in pressing a kiss to my lips. Not passionate. Just *sure*. A tether and a promise and a fucking reckoning.

When she pulls back, she doesn't let go. "You're not alone in this. Not even a little bit."

And goddamn, I feel it in my bones.

She's still here.

We're still here.

CHAPTER 27

BESTIE, say sike rn! Breaking news is that our favorite morally grey zaddy is headline bait and it's giving Joe Goldberg in couture. Like, we always knew @gageblack had "I'll ruin you for anyone else" energy. He's the Black brother with the stare that makes grown women forget why they ever thought red flags were a problem, the vibe that says "I could run a company or a criminal empire", and the mouth that probably says *things we can't print without getting banned.* And we were here for it. Obsessed. Unwell. Spiritually on our knees. But now? He's serving "I'll track your location, install cameras, and monologue about how it's for your safety" energy. Rumors are flying that Gage's little PR "situation" is getting darker. Like, sex club owner + obsession kink + potentially dangerous levels of possessive darker. And girl. THE COLLAR. Ya'll saw it, right???

The sleek silver one @ameliasinclair's been wearing? Bestie, that is NOT from Tiffany's. That is a "you belong to me" collar, and WE KNOW IT. Which . . . hot. BUT. Also . . . help??? Because now people are whispering. About the clubs. About control. About what Gage might be like behind closed doors. So yeah. We're not saying Amelia should be worried . . . But we are saying we're downloading Citizen and watching this like it's *You: Billionaire Edition*. Would we still crawl back to Gage Black and call it feminism? Absolutely. Are we concerned that his idea of foreplay might include blackmail. Also yes. #CollarWatch #AmeliaBlinkTwice #StockholmSyndromSoftLaunch?

CHAPTER 28
GAGE

I READ over the reports my CFO sent through overnight and lean back in my chair and scrub a hand down my face. The numbers aren't catastrophic. Not yet. But the pattern is there. Subtle. Steady. Sliding in the wrong direction. A handful of high-tier clients have quietly withdrawn over the last month. More are asking questions. And that's something I've never seen in my company and don't plan to accept now.

I started building this company after finishing my degree. My father thought I was slumming it. He wanted me to be like Bradford and join the family's textile empire. I couldn't think of anything more soul-destroying. I knew I was building the only future that wouldn't bore me to death.

I did a few years working for a top intelligence firm, saw the holes in how they operated, built a black-book contact list, and used seed money from my trust fund. I started small but carved a niche by being the guy who could make problems disappear.

Now, we're a global intelligence firm trusted by corporations, billionaires, and governments. We locate threats. Track assets. Gather intel. Offer protection and retaliation services. Corporate and political cleanup. We're the kind of firm people whisper about in boardrooms and war rooms. The kind you call when something goes wrong that can't be leaked, fixed, or forgiven.

And yet here I am. Falling behind on work for the first time in my life and watching numbers trend the wrong way. I've built an empire by never missing a threat. And I've let one grow right under my fucking nose.

Looking at the numbers now, and knowing the hours, the blood, the obsession it took to build this up from the ground? Yeah. This burns.

The fucking bad press needs to be stopped.

And I need to get my eye back on the fucking ball.

I spend the next few hours in back-to-back calls. Department heads. PR leads. My top operatives. I've built this company to run without me micromanaging every detail, but when it matters? They answer to me. And right now, seeing the numbers, I know I haven't been checking in the way I usually do.

Just after lunch, Lucy buzzes me.

"Ah, Gage, I think you have a situation out here. One that needs gentle hands. Not your usual."

"The fuck?" I check my watch. I've got three minutes until I go into another meeting with my CFO to drill down deeper into the numbers. "Whatever it is, you handle it."

"Yeah, see, that's not going to work this time. It's Amelia, and the way those tears are streaming down her cheeks screams *I need my man right now*. Just sayin'."

Fuck.

My chair's shoved back and I'm out the door, and *fuck me*, I've never seen Amelia like this. She's sitting in one of the visitors chairs across from Lucy's desk, crying—shoulders tight, hands clenching in her lap like she's bracing for impact. The kind of posture that says the fear of God isn't just in her eyes, it's crawling through her entire body.

She stands the second she spots me, and we meet in the middle.

"What the fuck's happened and who the fuck do I need to kill?" My chest is squeezing with anger, the fucking ropable kind, at the thought of someone hurting Amelia.

Her hands grab my hips like they're the only anchor she has. "It's James," she starts, but her tears get the better of her and she can't get another word out. All she can do is hold me like I'm the only thing keeping her upright. Her expression says this situation is DEFCON 1 level, and yeah, I caught that already.

That fucking motherfucker.

I swear to *Christ* I will end him.

I tell Lucy to cancel my meeting and take Amelia into my office.

Once I settle her on the couch, I rein it all in—the fury, the instincts, the need to fix—and give her what she needs instead. Gentle hands, like Lucy said. And fuck, it nearly kills me to stay calm when every part of me is ready to burn the world down.

"What did he do?"

She works her way through some sobs that get caught in her throat before taking a deep breath. "He came to my place," she chokes out. "He just . . . he just walked in like he owned it. Lied to the doorman to get through."

My jaw fucking locks.

"I didn't even know he was there until he was walking into my studio," she goes on, her words tumbling out now, frantic and broken. "He started saying awful stuff about you. About how dangerous you are. About the collar. He said I'm obviously just letting you use my body however you want. Then he said I was putting Sarah in danger, and that I've lost all good sense of judgment by letting you anywhere near us."

I see fucking red.

"I told him to leave. I told him he was out of line. But he just laughed." Her whole body trembles. "He said he's documenting everything. That if I won't protect Sarah, he will. He said I look pathetic. That I'm just letting you control me. That I'm making it easy for him to prove I'm unfit."

A fucking *growl* builds in my throat, but I force it down. Search for the calm she needs from me right now. Not that anything of what I'm feeling could be confused with calm, but for Amelia, I keep my voice as controlled as possible when I ask, "Did he touch you?"

Every muscle in my body tenses waiting for her answer.

"No." A ragged breath catches in her throat. "God . . . I let him get in my head. I couldn't stop it." A sob tears from her. "He always gets in my head. Even now. Even when I know better." Her voice cracks, like she hates that part of herself the most.

I drop to my knees in front of her even though I don't kneel for anyone.

For *Amelia*? I'll kneel every damn time.

Today, she's been stripped raw by a man who made her doubt her own worth, and I need her to know I will never tower over her. I will not be another man who makes her shrink.

I gently take her hands into mine, even as I feel the rage coiling tighter and tighter inside me. A storm waiting to break.

"Amelia, listen to me," I say, voice rough. "You didn't do a single fucking thing wrong. That man is a coward, a liar, and a manipulative prick who only knows how to control through fear. He doesn't get to use your daughter against you. He doesn't get to touch your peace. And he sure as fuck doesn't get to touch your mind."

She nods, eyes glued to mine, still panicked. But I see the breaths she's now taking, the full fight-or-flight after-shock starting to ease.

"I've got you, Princess. You're safe. He's not gonna win this because I won't fucking let him."

Once her panic's not choking her anymore, and she's okay, I shift my focus to what needs to happen next. I get her home and stay for as long as she lets me. Which is no more than an hour because she's worried she's inter-rupted my work. But I dedicate every second of that hour to ensuring she's grounded, safe, and not carrying this alone. That she knows she's not irrational. That she knows she's not overreacting.

Because fuck that.

I saw her face when she walked into my office. I saw what that asshole did to her.

And I need her to know I'm with her. And I'm not going anywhere.

After she forces me to leave, I get in my car and slam my door harder than necessary. My jaw's clenched so tight it aches. My neck feels like fucking steel cable. I've been holding my shit together for two hours—steady voice, calm hands, keeping my fury on a leash so Amelia would feel safe.

But now?

Now that she's out of my sight, safe in her home?

I can't hold it back a second fucking longer.

I yank my phone from my pocket and call Jason.

"Forget everything else. I want your full attention on finding out who the *fuck* is behind the shit being posted about me online," I grind out. "You said clean hands, dirty trail. I want the fucking trail. Mapped. Memorized. Burned into your brain. And I want the bastard at the end of it gift-fucking-wrapped with a bow."

I've hit my fuck-this-line-in-the-sand point, and I don't care how deep this goes—I want every digital fingerprint, every breadcrumb, every goddamn meta-phoric drop of piss they left behind. And I want to burn them with it.

"Trail's still dirty," Jason says. "The bastard's clean."

"Then we scrub until we hit blood," I growl. "Start digging."

Fuck.

"And Jason? I don't give a fuck what it costs. Pull your whole team in. Work around the clock. Bring in outside help if you have to. Just get this shit done, and get it done fast."

I end the call and stare out the window of the car, breath tight in my chest, pulse a fucking war drum in my ears. I didn't take the bad press seriously enough. Thought it was just noise. Nothing that could touch me.

That was my first mistake.

Because now it's fucked with my company.

But more than that—it touched Amelia.

It was used to shake her, to make her question herself.

That's the line in the sand. The last fucking line.

And whoever crossed it is about to learn what I do to people who aim for what's mine.

My second mistake?

Not making sure James Kensington stayed the fuck away after the first time I saw Amelia flinch at his name.

I swipe open the secure folder on my phone. The one I built the day I realized he might become a problem worth solving.

Photos. Documents. Financials. Quiet witnesses. The kind of rot you only find if you know where to look.

I've held back. Waited. Given him chances he didn't deserve.

For her.

But today, he made it war.

And I don't lose wars.

CHAPTER 29
AMELIA

I WAKE up in Gage's arms the morning after James ripped my soul apart and try to remember what steady feels like, but everything inside me still feels scrambled. My body is here, safe and warm against his, but the rest of me is somewhere else. My thoughts won't settle. My heart keeps kicking like it's waiting for another blow. And no matter how tightly Gage holds me, I can't seem to shake the feeling that something inside me cracked wide open yesterday and hasn't closed yet.

I've untangled most of the bullshit he tried to spin—the gaslighting, the insults, the way he made me feel small on purpose. I see it for what it was now. But what's still crawling under my skin is the threat he left behind. The quiet, calculated promise that he'll take Sarah if I don't prove I'm a good enough mother. That's the part I can't shake. Not because I believe him about being a bad mother, but because I know what a man like James is capable of when he wants control—and because I've seen the courts get it wrong before.

The girls aren't here this morning, which is good. It gives me the space to breathe and think before the meetings I have for work today.

Gage reaches for my hand when I try to leave the bed. He pulls me back to him, into his arms, and takes a moment looking at me.

"If you're determining damage, I'm okay," I say.

"Determining damage?" He's amused. "Where do you get these words from?"

"It's what you do."

The amusement fades from his eyes, and he turns serious. "I handle threats, Amelia. Manage situations. Lock shit down when it gets ugly." His hand slides to my jaw. "But this? This isn't damage control. This is me checking on my woman."

I nod, offering him a faint smile I'm not sure quite reaches. I *want* to sink into this—into him—but there's too much noise in my head. Too much leftover static from yesterday.

I push gently against his chest. "I'm good. But I've got a big day, so I need to get up." It's not a lie, but it's not the whole truth either. I'm not pulling away from Gage. I just need to find myself again before I reach for him.

As I walk into the bathroom, I can feel his gaze follow me—heavy, protective, laced with the kind of quiet intensity that says he won't rest until I'm steady again. And god, I wish I could give him more. I wish I had it in me this morning. But I don't.

When I return from my shower, he's gone from the bedroom. I dress, pull my hair up, apply a little makeup, and make my way to the kitchen.

Gage is at the breakfast bar, coffee and laptop in front

of him. He doesn't say anything. Doesn't crowd me. Just gives me the space he knows I need. Because if there's one thing this man is exceptional at, it's reading people. And not just seeing what they need but giving it. Quietly. Consistently. Like it's instinct.

And even though I can't soften into that right now, I feel it. I see it. And part of me is already aching for the moment I can meet him there again.

I take my coffee and slide onto the stool next to him instead of retreating to the dining table. It's not much, but it feels like something. A choice not to pull away entirely. A way to say I'm still here, even if I don't have much to give right now.

"Did you sleep?" I ask because he's been fighting insomnia.

"A little," he says, without looking up from his screen.

I wrap both hands around my mug, focus on it and the warmth seeping into my palms as I ask, "Have you got a busy day today?"

His fingers still on the keyboard, but he doesn't answer right away.

Then he says, "Princess."

It's just one word. But the way he says it cuts through all the noise in my head. His tone is softer, lower, slower, and it feels like he's speaking to the part of me I've been trying to hold together. It reminds me that he sees straight through me.

I glance over, and he's watching me now, focused but not intense. Calm. Anchoring.

"We don't have to play the polite game. I'm here. However you need. If that's space, take it. If it's quiet, I'll give it to you. But don't pretend. Not with me."

I release a breath.

"Thank you." I reach across and curve my hand gently over his forearm, leaving it there for a moment while I just watch him.

Then, I let him go, and he turns his attention back to his computer. What he's really doing though is giving me space without letting me feel alone.

We stay together at the breakfast bar for half an hour. Gage works on his computer, and I do some admin work on my phone, replying to emails. My first meeting isn't until ten, but I need to run some errands first, so when it's eight, I stand to go into the bedroom and collect my purse.

Stepping close to Gage, I place my hand on his back, gliding it across a little, suddenly needing that contact. His scent, too. It's been here all this time, but now, it's what I need. "I'm sorry I'm not myself this morning," I murmur.

His arm circles around me. Immediately. And his eyes come to mine. "You never have to say sorry to me. Not for taking what you need."

I bring a hand to his jaw and rest it there for a moment before nodding and saying, "I'm just gonna grab my purse, and then I have to go."

"Do you need the car?"

"No. I'm going to brave that humidity you hate so much." Thinking about just how much Gage complains about it, I smile. "Honestly, how are you into so much outdoor sport when you barely survive walking around Manhattan in summer?"

"You try wearing a fucking suit in the humidity, see how much you like it," he grumbles.

"Maybe you should ditch the clothes. I don't think you'd get too many complaints."

"Fuck," he growls before reaching out and dragging me in close, one arm tight around me, one hand to my jaw, eyes burning with heat. "I know you need space today, but I need one kiss before you go."

The second he says that I feel the intense pull to him I always feel.

It's not just physical. It's so much more than that, but god, the need for physical connection we both feel is stronger than anything I've ever known.

We haven't had sex this morning. Haven't even really touched. It's the first time in three months that we've woken up together and not torn each other apart before breakfast.

And now he's asking for one kiss.

Not taking.

Not demanding.

Just asking.

My body instinctually presses into him as I bring a hand to his face and kiss him. It's slow. And I feel Gage trying to keep it that way. It's in the way his arm tightens just a little bit more around me, the way his fingers tighten a fraction on my jaw, and the way his mouth moves with mine, letting me take the lead. It feels like he's kissing me soft when his whole body's begging him not to.

I deepen the kiss without meaning to—just a shift of my mouth, a tilt of my head—but it changes everything. Heat licks at the edges. The kind we never seem to escape.

His hand fists in the back of my shirt, and for a

second, I think he's going to say fuck it to every promise of space and take me right here on the hardwood.

But then he breaks the kiss with a low groan and presses his forehead to mine.

"We're gonna burn if we keep doing that," he mutters.

"I know," I whisper, still catching my breath. "But I needed it."

His thumb grazes my lip. "Me too."

Then he lets me go and I head into his bedroom to retrieve my purse. A text comes through from Kristen while I'm in there, so I take a second to reply.

KRISTEN:

> Amelia! I am on my knees begging you to reconsider the gala. The pianist I lined up has pulled out at the last minute. I'm not even asking for a speech anymore. Just play one piece.

ME:

> OMG I have someone for you! She's a pianist looking for more exposure, and she's brilliant. I'll send through her details.

ME:

> I'm sorry I'm letting you down, but honestly, you'll thank me for it because performing on stage gives me stress rashes, and no one wants to see that.

KRISTEN:

> No, don't apologize! I shouldn't have begged you again. Not when I know how you feel about performing on stage. Thank you for finding me someone else xx

I'm about to send through the details I promised when a text from James arrives, and God help me, I want to ignore it, but I can't. Not since he's the father of my daughter and this could actually just be something about her.

JAMES:

Let me guess, you ran to him after I came over yesterday. Probably had to get on your knees and suck his cock before he'd wipe your tears.

I freeze.

James has never sent me something like this. It feels unhinged.

With shaking hands, I tap out a reply.

ME:

Don't ever send me filth like that again.

JAMES:

Sweetheart, we all know what kind of filth you like now. And it's the kind that's going to make you lose custody of Sarah. You should have thought of that before you decided to fuck him.

Ice cold fear slides down my spine, just like it did yesterday when he came to my home uninvited. My fingers go numb around my phone, the screen blurring slightly as my chest squeezes. It's not just that those words came from him. Something in him has snapped, and I can't predict what he'll do next.

I try to calm my breathing, but it turns shallow and uneven. My stomach churns. I haven't really slept. Barely eaten. I'm running on adrenaline and frayed nerves from yesterday, and these messages send a jolt of fresh panic through my system.

I fight the rising urge to cry, or scream, to throw my phone across the room. But mostly, I fight the spiral. Because I know how fast it comes. How fast fear becomes worst-case scenarios. How fast anxiety becomes certainty.

Dragging in a shaky breath, I force my feet to move. I need fresh air, and I need to ignore these texts.

I press a hand to my stomach as I walk, trying to think about anything but James.

As I near the kitchen, I hear a woman's voice, and then Gage's.

Shayla.

And whatever they're discussing, it doesn't sound good.

Her voice is sharp. Elevated.

Gage's is low and clipped. But rising.

When I round the corner into the kitchen, I walk into a standoff.

Gage is facing Shayla, but he's angled just enough that when I enter, his eyes flick to me. Only for a second. It's like he registers me, but the fury is louder than everything else.

His posture is locked tight, shoulders coiled, every inch of him readying for impact. The edge in his voice is the same one I heard last week when he fought with her on the phone. Sharp. Controlled. But barely.

Shayla's gaze catches mine briefly, but she goes right back to Gage.

"I'm just saying I need us to go over our agreement and make some changes."

"Because you're going to be in LA more," he grates. "Have I got that right?"

"Maybe," Shayla says.

"Jesus Christ, Shayla. Maybe? You either are or you aren't. Which one is it?"

Shayla pushes her shoulders back defiantly. "Don't snap at me, Gage."

Gage plants his hands on his hips and inhales hard. "I'm trying not to snap, but you're not actually saying anything. You came in and started on about your work and needing to be in LA for it. Then you said something about needing to be there to support Michael. Then you said you need to be here for Luna." He takes another centering breath, drops his hands to his sides. "I'm just wondering how the hell you can be in two places at once. Give me something useful to work with here."

"I know I can't be in two places at once. I'm not stupid. I just . . . I just need to figure this all out. How we can make it work with Luna, and how I can make it work with Michael."

"And packing Luna up and moving her to LA is the answer, right?" he bites out.

Shayla's chin wobbles for half a second before she swallows it down. "I don't know, Gage." Her face twists with confusion. "Maybe." Then, her voice cracks when she says, "I think so."

That admission tips Gage over the edge. His entire body goes rigid and the air in the room turns flammable as he says, "Right. So you *are* moving to LA." He pauses and it feels like he's only seconds away from detonation. "And you lied to me about that last week."

Shayla stands so still I wonder if she's even drawing

breath. And god, I know that posture. I've lived it. It's not fear of harm—it's the bracing for what he'll say next, knowing it won't hit skin, but heart.

A flush crawls up her neck and I watch as she slaps her armor on and goes to battle for herself.

Eyes like polished steel, she tilts her chin at him. "I didn't lie, but sure, go ahead, twist my words." Her tone is diamond-sharp.

"You told me I was reading too much into things," he says, angrily. "A person doesn't just decide in one week to make a life-changing decision, so yeah, you didn't give me the truth."

"Have you ever thought that maybe not everyone's like you, Gage? That maybe some of us *can* make a decision in a week?"

"*Fuck.*" He rubs the back of his neck. "Can we just have a productive conversation, Shayla? For fucking once."

"Yes, because you just need facts so you can manage a situation," she spits. "Like humans are situations, which we *aren't*. But you never listened to me whenever I told you that, so I doubt you'll listen now." She stares at him with bitterness. "At least Michael doesn't tally up every flaw like a fucking scorecard." Her voice breaks slightly when she adds, "He doesn't treat me like something broken he regrets choosing."

Her words hang there, heavy and split open.

But Gage doesn't respond to them. He just steamrolls right past them, like they were noise, not meaning.

He reaches for the back of the chair he's standing near, gripping it hard. His knuckles go pale, arm locked like he's holding back from throwing the whole damn thing. "Luna's not moving to LA." He slams that down between them like a verdict, each word clipped and final, and I feel it hit my body like a whipcrack.

Shayla jolts. So do I.

"You are *not* uprooting our daughter on a whim just so you can chase your boyfriend to another city."

"On a *whim*?" she practically screeches. "You are such a fucking asshole. I tried so hard to be everything for you. But I was never good enough." She stops hurling her hurt for a second to catch her breath. "I'm not chasing my *boyfriend*. I'm following the man I'm marrying."

Gage doesn't flinch. Doesn't blink.

"You are not taking Luna with you," he says, so low, so lethal his words feel like a blade.

I recoil at his tone.

It's the tone I used to hear in another man's voice. The one that always meant: this is not a decision you're having any say in.

Shayla draws her entire body up like it's a fortress. "I'm her mother, Gage. And in case you forgot, courts like mothers. Especially when the father works too much to spend the kind of time with them that's in their best interest. I work from home. I'll have a husband to provide Luna a family. Let's see who they choose."

Gage's jaw grinds so hard it looks like he's chewing gravel. His eyes don't darken. They flatline. Cold. Razor-sharp. No mercy. His spine straightens tight. One hand clenches at his side. And his chest expands like he's about to roar, but what comes out is quieter. And far more dangerous.

"You think a court will choose you over me? Try me. I've got lawyers, the money, and the fucking proof that you haven't honored our agreement." His voice doesn't rise, it cuts. "Let's see how far your new husband's willing to go when I drag this through the court. Because I promise you, Shayla, I won't stop until I win."

My heart slams against my ribs.

My nervous system doesn't know whether to run or shut down, so it just *holds*, every cell locked in limbo.

My breath stops like I've swallowed glass.

Every hair on my arms stands to attention as my body reacts to a threat I can't see but can *definitely feel*.

Because I've heard that before, felt this exact pressure.

Not from Gage.

From James.

The weapon that's wielded beneath the words. The one that says the courtroom's already his, the system favors him, that he's got the power and I'm just lucky to speak.

And the voice that didn't raise to yell but sank to something worse. The one that made decisions for me and told me they were facts. That left no room for argument.

You don't get a say.

That's what it always meant.

And standing here now, listening to Gage say *I won't stop until I win*, something inside me buckles.

I blink fast. Swallow hard. Try to ground myself in the facts I know.

Gage isn't James.

He's not.

He's never made me feel small.

He's never used my past against me.

He holds me. He lets me *be*.

But god, this?

This tone. This moment.

The threat of power. Of money. Of *winning at all costs*.

It sends panic shooting through my veins.

My hand trembles slightly as I grip my purse. I step back, just half a pace, but it feels like a mile.

Because I don't know who this man is right now.

And I can't un-hear what he just said.

Shayla's storming out when I find my way back to the fallout. Gage doesn't move. His body's still locked in the same battle stance, his chest rising and falling hard.

The room holds its breath. Even the shadows seem to shrink back. And while silence blankets us, the air is loaded, thick with static that crackles in your bones.

Then, slowly, Gage turns. Stiffly. Like his body hasn't registered the fight is over. His eyes land on me and shock flares in them. Because, yeah, his fury burned so hot he forgot I was even here to see it.

Neither of us speak straight away. I think we're both still reeling from the blast.

Then, I say quietly, "I didn't think you wanted to fight Shayla in court."

His whole body tenses again. "Fuck." He drags his hand through his hair roughly. "I don't. But she made it pretty fucking clear that's what she wants."

I shake my head. "No. I don't think that's what she wants."

He snaps his gaze to mine. Hard. "She just told me to see who the courts choose, Amelia. How the fuck else am I meant to take that?"

"She was fighting for herself, Gage. Because you weren't listening."

His jaw flexes. "I heard every goddamn word she just said." He takes a step closer. Not aggressively. Defensively. Fierce. "And yeah, you're right. She *was* fighting for herself. Not Luna. She wants her life in LA, her man, her image. She doesn't give a fuck what that does to her daughter."

The heat in his voice isn't aimed at Shayla anymore.

It's aimed at me.

And it hits like a slap.

"Yes, you heard, but you didn't listen," I say, the sting still blooming under my skin. "There's a difference between hearing and listening. I saw a woman trying to hold it together in front of a man who stopped listening the second she didn't say what he wanted to hear."

"I didn't stop listening. I stopped trying to translate the bullshit into something that made sense."

My heart pounds hard against my ribs, too fast and uneven, trying to outrun the tension in a room that feels too small for both our truths.

Everything in me is on edge.

My nervous system screams *go*, but I don't.

I've been here before.

Trying to reach someone who only hears what they've already decided is true. Trying to speak a language a man refuses to learn. And I'm done swallowing the damage just because he doesn't know the words.

I'm tired of women being the ones who bend, who explain, who shrink their truth to make it easier to digest.

"You heard a woman trying to manipulate you. I saw one trying to protect herself the only way she knew how. And yeah, I don't think she went about it the right way, but we all act out our wounds differently, Gage." I pause.

"She said she was never enough for you. That she felt more like a crisis to manage than a person to love. And maybe you didn't mean to make her feel that small, but that doesn't mean she was wrong to feel it."

I take a step back.

Then another.

And even though this is my choice, I feel the ache of it unfold between us.

Gage registers both steps like a hit to the chest.

"You're leaving?" he asks, voice lower now. Strained.

"I have a meeting."

"Fuck." He drags a hand down his face, regret already chasing his temper away. "I don't want to leave it like this."

"I have to go."

"Amelia."

He tries to reach for me, but I shift just out of range, my body already closing in on itself.

"No." My voice is soft. Final. "I need a minute, Gage."

"What kind of minute?" His eyes are searching now. Less fury, more fear.

I hold his gaze for a beat that hurts more than it should. "I don't know. I just need some space."

And then I'm gone.

CHAPTER 30
AMELIA

AFTER A DAY I wish never existed, I collapse into bed just after eleven. My bed. Alone. But I eye the cameras I had Gage install months ago and know he would have received the motion alert.

He tried to call a few times today. I'm not proud that I didn't take those calls. That I ignored a man I know is hurting. But I had to put myself first. Protect my heart that's spent the entire day beating too erratically.

They say our nervous system reacts before our brain does, so we're basically out here making life choices based on vibes and trauma responses. So now, I'm ignoring a man I'm in love with because my nervous system saw a red flag that might've just been a trauma-colored shadow.

But as much as I've tried to logic my way past it today, I can't.

It's too real.

Too fresh.

Not even forty-eight hours have passed since James

came to my door and threatened everything I love. Since he tore through my boundaries and said words that slipped under my skin and made themselves at home in places I thought I'd fortified.

And now? Gage's voice—*that voice*—won't stop replaying in my head.

Not because I think he's James.

But because my body doesn't know the difference.

That whole "I decide what happens here" energy goes straight to the part of me that learned the hard way what a danger warning sounds like. And no matter how much my heart wants to trust him, my fear is louder today.

He calls five minutes after my head hits the pillow and this time I answer.

"Hey," I say softly. "I'm sorry I didn't answer your calls. I just . . . couldn't."

"I don't want your apology, Princess. I want to see you."

I close my eyes.

Why does love have to be so hard? So painful at times?

"I'm tired, Gage."

"And I'm not a man who goes to bed on a fight, so we've got a problem here."

"It's late."

"I don't care."

"So, because *you* don't care, I'm not allowed to?"

"Fuck," he curses softly. "That came out wrong."

"Yeah. It did. I think we should both get some sleep and talk tomorrow."

"I'm not leaving this, Amelia. And I do care that you need your sleep, that you're tired, that you're still feeling the burn of this, but I heard you today. I heard how you looked at me like I could hurt you. I listened. And I hated that I did that to you. Because I never want to be a man you flinch from. Let me come over so we can talk."

"See, this is it, Gage. You're not listening to me now. I'm telling you I need a minute and you're not giving it to me."

He turns silent for a long moment, and I hear the clink of ice that tells me he's drinking whiskey.

When he finally speaks, his voice is rough, like I'm dragging him through hell. "Okay."

That's all he says, but he doesn't disconnect the call.

He stays on the line.

And so do I.

Because this ache is too hard to handle alone.

My tears begin a minute into the silence.

I try to keep them quiet, to myself, but fail.

Gage curses softly but doesn't say anything else. And I just know that's killing him. And yet, I can't bring myself to say *please come over and make this all better and fix my nervous system while you're at it.*

I cry for a good five minutes. Not sobs, just gentle tears. I think they're years-deep and have never had the space to release. But also, there are new tears too. The ones I'm crying over not being able to move past my fears.

I love Gage.

I just don't know if love is enough when a person's still learning how to feel safe.

And maybe that's what hurts the most. This isn't about him failing me. It's about me still repairing what someone else broke.

It's about the part of me that hears raised voices and cold tones and checks for sharp edges.

Maybe I needed more time before diving into something this intense.

Maybe I should have waited until my body could tell the difference between a man raising his voice and a man raising a red flag.

I don't want to lose him. God, I *don't*.

But I think I need to find my own center before I can meet him at his.

I stay on the line for another ten minutes, and then I whisper through my tears, "I'll come to you in the morning."

"Whatever you need, Amelia. I'll do it."

CHAPTER 31
GAGE

LOVE IS the sharpest blade I've ever known. And right now, it's pressed hard to my throat. I've survived high-stakes deals, blackmail, and betrayal. But one sleepless night without Amelia? I'm on my fucking knees.

I haven't moved from my goddamn couch all night. The whiskey bottle's half-empty. And all I can fucking hear are those tears of hers.

Amelia's not like anyone I've ever known. She doesn't speak louder to be heard. She pulls away. She retreats when it gets too loud in her head. Slips into that quiet space where she can breathe again, where no one's asking her to explain the storm. And yeah, she spirals. Over-thinks. Needs space. But she also fights to stay open, even when it fucking hurts. I've seen her fall apart and still show up the next day like she isn't carrying the weight of the world. She's scared of needing anyone, but she's letting herself need *me*. And I'm the asshole who fucked it all up.

I've spent the night thinking about everything she

said to me yesterday. The truths she landed at my feet about Shayla. I wasn't in the frame of mind to listen to her yesterday. Not after that fight with Shayla. But fuck, I've had hours to turn it all over now, and I can't help thinking I missed shit in my marriage.

Which is a mindfuck all on its own because it's my job to see everything, to read people, to anticipate their next move. But I don't think I saw Shayla. Not if she thinks she wasn't enough for me. That she was just a crisis to be managed.

Fuck

Shayla and I were young when we met and had three years together before Luna came along. Shit was great until the pregnancy. Something changed between us I could never quite put my finger on. And then, after Luna was born, it only got worse.

I worked long hours. Shayla struggled with a baby. I tried like fuck to be there, and I was. But we fought over everything. Nothing I did was right. All I heard was I worked too much, I stopped wanting to take her on dates, I didn't look at her like I used to. And fuck, I tried. I tried to fix it all. But I see it now—every time I tried to solve a problem, to take her pain away instead of sitting in it with her, I probably made her feel like she was a crisis I had to manage.

Looking back, yeah, I stopped listening to her. Fuck, I did. Because everything she said made me feel like a goddamn failure. And now, here we are, in a fucking shit-show of misunderstandings and a co-parenting relationship that's hanging on by a fucking thread.

And Amelia saw it before I did. Not just the way I treat Shayla, but the way I default to control when I feel helpless. And in doing that with Shayla, I didn't give her the space to speak. Or the space to be listened to.

I shower and dress at six. Am in my office at home by seven. Trying to focus on work but only able to focus on Amelia.

Hayden provides me with a distraction when he calls at seven thirty.

"Everything okay?" he asks. "You and Amelia didn't show for family dinner last night. Liv said you didn't text."

I lean back in my chair and reach for the back of my neck. "We had a fight. One of those ones where you don't know if it's over, but it sure as hell feels like something cracked."

He's quiet for a second. "You want to sit in it or pull it apart?"

"She watched me go toe-to-toe with Shayla and didn't like what she saw."

"Did you like what you saw?"

"No."

"Then you've still got a shot."

"Yeah, I fucking hope so." I exhale a breath. "Were you just calling about dinner?"

"No. I wanted to run something by you that I've just discovered at work."

"Shoot."

"Shit started feeling off a few weeks back. A handful of my clients got hit out of nowhere with random scandals, online takedowns, internal leaks. And then right after the damage? They were approached by a crisis capital firm offering strategic investment. To help them recover, rebuild, get back on their feet. At first, I didn't question it. Looked standard. The firm presented clean. But then it kept happening to more clients. And the timing was too convenient.

"I dug into the contracts. Same language across the board. Same holding company that was legit on paper. In reality, a front. So, I put my guy on it. Had him trace the shell layers. Took a bit, but he followed the trail. It led to Ryan Wakefield."

Recognition flickers. I've heard that name before. "Remind me who he is."

"Priscilla's husband."

Fuck. The woman Hayden crashed and burned over in his twenties. And from what I know, Hayden and Ryan had a falling out last year. "So, we're talking crisis capital firm, dark money version."

The kind that doesn't just *buy* into crisis—they build it. Engineer the fall so they can own and rebuild.

"Exactly. I got hold of Ryan's files. The ones that show who hired him to fuck people over. Client records, financials, emails. And guess who shows up on his client list around the time Amelia's smear campaign kicked off? Her ex-husband."

My jaw locks so hard it feels like something might snap.

Her fucking ex.

Of course it was him. The smug, controlling bastard who's been circling like a goddamn vulture.

My hands clench into fists.

He hasn't just been gaslighting her. He hired someone to drag her name through the dirt. To manipulate the narrative. To humiliate her.

To make her look unfit. Unworthy.

My vision flashes white at the edges.

"He used Ryan's firm to light the match," Hayden continues. "Media manipulation, false tips to journalists, influencer targeting. In exchange, Ryan got legal representation. James is handling his legal affairs now." He pauses. "And Ryan didn't stop there. He came after you too."

My blood runs cold.

"Why the fuck would he come after me? To hurt Amelia?"

"That played into it, yeah. For James. But mostly, I think he targeted you because of me." He lets out a slow, sharp breath, and I feel his anger behind it, like his control is hanging by a thread. "I'm fucking sorry you got caught up in this. Ryan's been gunning for me since he found out Priscilla and I had a thing. His jealousy runs deep. I think he knows we slept together last year after she left him."

Jesus.

"You think he came after me to hurt you?"

"Yeah. There's evidence in the emails that points to that. His team was instructed to seed shit about you and Bradford."

James.

Ryan.

Both of them playing their games, thinking they're untouchable.

They didn't just come for her.

They came for me.

For my company.

For my name.

For my brothers.

And it circled. It breathed.

Because I didn't know who I was hunting.

But now?

Now I have the fucking name.

And everything inside me goes still.

Not cold. Not quiet. *Deadly*.

I don't see red. I see the finish line.

"Put everything you have in the Drive. I want eyes on it today." Our secure, private drive. Just me and my brothers. Encrypted, untraceable, and locked behind three layers of hell.

"You drop that list, and sure, Ryan goes down. But so do people who trusted you to protect them. You could set your own company on fire."

"Then I burn it."

I don't care who gets hit.

Not anymore.

This isn't about damage control. This isn't about strategy.

This is about ending James. Ending Ryan.

Making sure nothing like this ever touches Amelia again.

I'd raze every one of their empires to the ground if it meant keeping her safe.

And I'll burn my own damn world down in the process.

Without a second fucking thought.

Every contract. Every alliance. Every inch of reputation I've built.

None of it means shit if she's not safe.

This isn't about business anymore.

This is about *her*.

Her music. Her name. Her quiet strength that they tried to shatter.

I will tear this world down and build her a kingdom from the fucking ashes.

They hurt the wrong woman.

They made her bleed. I'll make them disappear.

AMELIA ARRIVES JUST after eight thirty. And when my eyes land on her, I suck in a breath. Her eyes look like they've held a thousand sleepless thoughts. Red-rimmed, hollowed out by tears she didn't bother hiding.

I still.

Not the kind of stillness that comes from peace. The kind that comes before disaster.

The second I see her face, I know.

She's not here to rage. She's not here to cry.

She's already done that.

She's come here to do something that will split her in half.

So, I take her in.

Every detail. Every line I already know by heart. Carving her into my memory.

The tiny freckle beneath her right brow, the one she covers with makeup most days but missed today.

The faint line beside her mouth—*left* side, just there —that only shows when she's holding something in.

Her hair that's down, but not like she usually wears it. No gloss. No effortless shine.

And her hands—tight around the strap of her purse like she's holding herself together with it.

I'm nowhere near fucking ready to let her go, but if this is goodbye, I want to remember her like this.

Raw and real and fucking magnificent.

I want to pull her into my arms.

Tell her I'll fix this.

But I don't move.

Because this moment isn't about what I want.

It's about what she needs to say.

And I won't take that from her.

"Say what you need to say, Princess. I won't stop you."

A broken sound chokes out of her, and the way her eyes hold mine says it all. This isn't what she wants, it what she needs.

I close the distance between us in two strides and pull her into my arms. She comes without hesitation, her arms wrapping tightly around me.

And fuck me, I've never felt so raw.

So fucking desperate to hold her together while she breaks.

So goddamn terrified this is the last time I'll get to hold her.

I smooth my hand down her hair while she sobs against my chest. I give her all the time she needs. Hell, I'd stand here forever with her like this if she needed me to.

When she finally lets me go, I meet her gaze and wait.

She swallows hard. "I love you, Gage, but I need to heal myself before I can love you the way you deserve."

Her words knock the breath from my lungs.

"You love like no person I have ever known," she says as tears stain her beautiful face. "You love like you've already decided I'm worth every storm. You respect. You handle with care. You pay attention. You *see* me. And you never make me feel like I'm too much, even when I don't know how to hold myself. Love isn't casual to you. It's something you *show up* for. Every single day. And I want to meet you in that kind of love. I do. But first I need to become someone who can stay when it gets loud. Because you deserve someone who never makes you question that she's staying."

I don't speak. I can't.

My chest's a warzone. My throat's dust.

But I bring my hand to her face and brush away one of her tears.

My thumb lingers there, memorizing skin I already know in my bones.

Then I nod. Once.

Because this isn't mine to stop.

And because she just handed me the most honest, gutting, loving truth I've ever been given.

"You come back when you're ready," I say quietly. "I'll be standing right here."

Her breath hitches.

Not sharp. Not dramatic. It's just caught.

And the look in her eyes says she wasn't prepared for how gently I'd let her go.

Her eyes go glassy again, and for a second, she presses her lips together like she's trying to keep every emotion in.

But one tear falls.

She doesn't wipe it.

Just lets it slide down her face.

And watching the woman I love—with every part of

me I've never given anyone else—stand there tearing herself apart for me, fucking guts me.

And then, she says the one thing I wasn't fucking prepared for.

"I want you to take my collar off."

Her words slam into me like a blow to the ribs, and I can't fucking breathe around it.

My lungs seize.

Breath crawls up my throat and dies there.

"This isn't the end for me," she says, eyes locked on mine. "I'm asking you to take it off because I know what it means. And I want to come back when I'm ready to wear it the way you deserve."

In the space between heartbeats, I splinter inside.

That collar was never about control.

It wasn't about claiming her.

It was about choosing her.

About her choosing me.

Every goddamn day. In every goddamn way.

It was a vow she didn't have to speak. A trust I didn't take lightly.

That collar meant she let me in to see the parts that were sacred to her. The parts she gave to no one else to cherish.

Asking me to unfasten it is like asking me to stop breathing.

But I'll do it.

Because Amelia was never something I was meant to hold so tight she couldn't breathe.

She's something I make space for.

And that's not distance.

That's devotion.

It's staying right here, waiting, while she finds her way through the dark.

It's holding the shape of her in my world, even while she steps out of it.

It's not letting go.

It's loving her enough to know she'll come back when she's ready.

My hand goes to the chain around my neck—where the key has lived since the night I locked that collar around her throat. Where it's stayed. Close enough to feel her, even when she's not with me.

I curl my fingers around it, but I don't move to unscrew it.

Not yet.

Because unclasping this isn't just removing metal from skin.

It's surrendering the one promise I never planned to take back.

She turns.

Quiet. Certain.

And lifts her hair without a word.

That simple gesture fucking ends me.

Not because she's walking away.

But because she's still giving me this—this moment of trust.

My hand is steady when it touches her neck.

But everything inside me is not.

I unlock the collar and gently remove it.

It's just metal.

But it feels like I'm removing a part of myself.

She turns back.

Eyes shining.

And when she steps in, there's no hesitation.

Her hand rises, curling around the back of my neck like it belongs there.

She presses her lips to mine. Soft. Warm. Full of everything she didn't say.

And fuck me, this is the reason why I sliced my heart from my chest months ago and handed it to this woman to love and keep safe.

Amelia is wrecked and still, she's giving herself to me. Making sure I know she's choosing herself without rejecting me.

She's saying *this hurts, but I want you to feel loved as I go.*

I want to remember your mouth, your breath, your stillness.

This isn't the end of us. It's the beginning of me.

Maybe space was the thing I never knew how to give before.

But I'm giving it now.

Every fucking inch of it.

And if that's the thing that brings her back?

Then I'll hold it until my lungs give out.

When she ends the kiss, I keep hold of her jaw.

"I love you. And I'm not going anywhere."

And then she's gone, and I don't know how I'm still standing when it feels like my chest is nothing but blood.

～

LATE THAT NIGHT, after I've gone over every single file Hayden loaded to the Drive, I call Jason.

Throwing the rest of the whiskey in my glass down my throat, I say, "Unleash it."

"All of it?" he asks. He already knows what I mean.

"Everything we've got on Ryan. Every dirty client. Every engineered takedown."

"And James?"

I grit my teeth.

"Most of it. The career killers. The stuff that'll fuck him six ways to Sunday. The hypocrisy. The sex club memberships he tried to bury." The same shit he tried to use against Amelia. Turns out Daddy of the Year has his own file full of filth.

Jason's silent. Waiting.

"Keep the nuclear shit back. I want him crawling before I crush him. I want him to taste what slow ruin feels like. And some of it, we keep for the day he needs a reminder of who I am."

CHAPTER 32

@THETEA_GASP

BESTIE, breathe right through it. The TL is a mess and so are we. Quick rundown: @ameliasinclair got her Velocity Reign contract back (girl left no crumbs); @sofiaraye? PAID to lie (girl the ick is loud); @jameskensington? Softboi turned slimeball – rumors of sex club memberships + unethical everything. MFW I ever thought he was a safe bet. BUT THIS ISN'T ABOUT THEM. This is about *him*. @gageblack Our BSE king. The Main Character of our hearts. And he is not ok rn. The. Collar. Is. Gone. AND SO IS OUR SANITY. Bestie, Gage Black has entered his Sad Zaddy Soft Era and the streets are NOT WELL. It's giving grief beard. It's giving sleepless in Manhattan. It's giving emotional damage in a three-piece suit. And honestly? We'd still risk it. Because that man could stare at us in silence for six seconds and we'd fold like a lawn chair.

His rizz? Still undefeated. But the pain? It's visceral. Rumors say he's taken a financial hit too but idk bestie, the real loss is spiritual. And us?? We're crying in the group chat. We're watching videos like "do you see the way he *looked* at her?" We're lighting candles for the collar. We stan a man in ruins. We stan a man who *feels*. We stan a man who left his soul on the pavement. #MainCharacterMeltdown #DoItForThePlotAmelia-ComeBack #ZaddyInShambles #JusticeForGage

CHAPTER 33

AMELIA

TIM:

Just saw a pic of Gage at an event.
Unshaven. Black suit. That wristwatch.
MFW I remembered you LET THAT GO.

*SENDS GIF OF SOMEONE SCREAMING
INTO THE VOID*

COLIN:

Are we doing this again? It's been three
months.

TIM:

And??? Jesus was dead three days.
Amelia gave up a zaddy with BSE. I am
not healed.

ME:

Please seek help.

TIM:

I DID. His name was Gage Black and YOU let him spiral into the sad billionaire multiverse. He's got BMS, PTSD, and probably three unopened texts from me. He's giving "owns five sex clubs but sleeps alone" rn. You really watched him whisper, "Princess" and said "nah, I'm good."

COLIN:

Tim.

TIM:

NO.

TIM:

She let a man with obsession rizz walk out of her life. And now she's out here pretending she's doing great like I didn't see her watch that interview clip where he said "no comment" with TEARS IN HER EYES. MFW I remember the collar's gone *cries*

COLIN:

Okay, but jokes aside, sis. How's therapy going?

ME:

Good. I mean, it's like digging through a closet where I shoved feelings in shoeboxes labeled "totally fine" and now I have to open them one by one without setting the house on fire.

TIM:

So are you still spiraling every morning like clockwork or are we calling this your calm era?

ME:

I haven't spiraled into a stress-cleaning episode in two weeks, so we're calling that regulated, right?

TIM:

Sis. No. You alphabetized your entire bookshelf by heartbreak level at 2am while crying to a Bon Iver remix. You're not fooling anyone with this "regulated" talk. You ARE the spiral.

ME:

And yet somehow still the healthiest one in this chat.

COLIN:

Low bar.

COLIN:

Speaking of the Sinclair emotional health scale, how are you and Mom going?

TIM:

OH YES. You know, after she learned that James was only "clean" because he hid the bodies. Update on him BTW: Still shady. Recently seen with a 26-year-old yoga instructor named Sky who calls him "Jimmy" in public. He wears loafers in public now. It's bleak.

ME:

Mom's in her "maybe Gage wasn't bad" era. Like ma'am. You once told me I couldn't do better than James. And now you're sending me articles titled "How To Reconnect With The Love of Your Life."

COLIN:

Wait so she's now Team Gage?

ME:

Apparently. She sent me a link to a couples retreat and said "you could heal together." Like I haven't spent years healing from HER.

TIM:

WAIT.

ME:

What now?

TIM:

Your tone is suspiciously grounded. You're engaging. There's no chaotic energy. I know this vibe.

TIM:

You're talking to him again, aren't you? IS THIS A SOFT-LAUNCH ZADDY REDEMPTION ARC?? BLINK TWICE FOR YES.

ME:

I literally haven't said anything to make you think that.

TIM:

EXACTLY. Too calm. Too quiet. This is Amelia, post-reunion hug and probably pre-sexual tension dinner.

COLIN:

You have an actual problem.

TIM:

My problem is I believe in love. And also that I stalk Gage's face like it owes me rent. She's going back. I feel it in my third eye.

I'VE LITERALLY JUST PUT my phone down from their texts when Marin texts. We're not even working together anymore and she. still. texts.

> **MARIN:**
>
> Babes. Not to alarm you but I did a three-card pull this morning and got The Tower, The Lovers, and a sad playlist.

> **MARIN:**
>
> IS HE OKAY?

> **MARIN:**
>
> IS THE COLLAR OKAY?

> **MARIN:**
>
> ARE YOU OKAY?

> **MARIN:**
>
> Like spiritually? Energetically? Cosmically?

> **MARIN:**
>
> His latest vibe is "I unalived my soul for her and now I wear black and speak in poetry."

> **MARIN:**
>
> It's giving Scorpio rising in silent heartbreak.

> **MARIN:**
>
> I know you're doing healing work and I love that for you. But also? Have you astrally projected yourself into his penthouse to check on his vibe?

MARIN:

Babes. Check in. Did he shave? Did he
look at you like he's trying not to beg?
Has his Scorpio moon made eye contact
with your nervous system lately?

MARIN:

Be honest babes. Is there a re-collaring-
in-retrograde or do I need to prepare for
a plot twist?

Seriously, how I get anything done in my life with
these three is beyond me. They form an emotional task
force the second I blink weird. I take one deep breath and
my brothers are planning the Gage Reunion Tour;
Marin's pulling tarot cards like it's a live crime scene,
going through the cards like she's dusting for finger-
prints, trying to solve the mystery of "is Gage Black in the
picture or not"; and everyone's acting like I'm one silence
away from spontaneously re-collaring myself in public.

Which, rude.

Because I'm not.

I'm very private about my self-destruction.

Three months.

That's how long it's been since I asked Gage to take off
the collar.

Three months of therapy, of digging through
emotional rubble with shaking hands. Of sitting in a
room with my therapist who asks me how I feel and
trying not to answer with jokes or polished sentences. Of
figuring out all the ways I was molded by expectations
and unlearning that.

I've made progress.

I don't freeze every time I feel fear in my body. I don't

hear James's voice in my head anymore. I don't spiral the same way I used to.

James no longer finds his way in under my skin. In fact, I rarely see him. Even when we're collecting or dropping Sarah off to each other, we have a system in place where I don't have to see him. My idea. And one I've stuck to my guns on. Let's just say that his downfall did wonders for my peace of mind. And I'm pretty sure I have Gage to thank for that.

God, *Gage*.

Missing him isn't sharp anymore. It's heavy. Constant and woven into my bones. It's like carrying a song in your chest that never finishes playing. Never resolves. Just lingers. Painful in an intimate, quiet, unbearable way.

I still see him. At drop-offs. Pick-ups. Our daughters weaving through chaos with their matching backpacks while I stand on one side of the crowd and he stands on the other.

Sometimes, our eyes meet.

And it takes everything in me not to walk across and throw my arms around him like the last three months were just a very bad dream.

But I don't.

Because I said I needed to heal.

Because he deserves the version of me that won't run when everything gets too loud in my head and my body.

The noise in my mind that spins worst-case scenarios until I can't hear reason.

And the noise in my body that mistakes safety for danger and tells me to run, even when I'm being loved.

I'm learning to live with that noise.

That's why I needed space. To understand that the

danger isn't always external. Sometimes it's memory. Sometimes it's *me*.

And Gage? He gave me that space.

Not the kind that people talk about giving while secretly waiting for you to break first.

Real space.

The kind that holds you from a distance without pulling.

The kind that trusts you to come back when you're ready.

Gage didn't just give me space. He held it.

Without pressure. Without punishment. Without making it about him.

He didn't chase or demand or try to fix the silence.

He just stood there steady, present, waiting.

And I don't think I've ever been loved like that before.

Not with that kind of patience.

Not with that kind of faith.

And tonight, my brothers and Marin might just get what they've been hounding me for.

Tonight, I'm going to show Gage Black he was never waiting in vain.

"OH MY GOD, AMELIA," Kristen says when she spots me walking into the backstage area of the gala she's hosting. "You came! You actually came."

I smile and accept her arms that she throws around me. Kristen's not generally a big hugger, but I'm picking up on her panic that I wouldn't show tonight. Which, fair. I went from a friend who refused point blank to get up on her stage months ago, and then last week, begged for the chance to get up there.

Her eyes light up as she pulls out of our embrace. "I swear I haven't told Gage you're coming tonight. Just like you asked." She bites her lip. "But I may have told Bradford, who may have accidentally let it slip to Hayden. And Maddie may have stolen my phone and saw our texts, and she may have told Liv."

I laugh. "So basically, the entire Black family knows I'm here."

"Except for Gage." The look on her face screams *see I am a good girl.*

"Okay," she says, switching into gala planner mode. "We need you over here." She gestures to where she wants me. "Bron is going to get you prepped."

I cast a glance in the direction she motioned and smile at Bron. Then, I turn back to Kristen. "Thank you for letting me do this."

She narrows her eyes at me. "Honestly, on a scale of one to ten, where are you at with those 'my soul will exit the building and I wanna vomit' vibes right now?"

"If ten is the highest, I'm there." I smile, remembering the reason I'm willing to see if I dissolve into particles on the stage tonight. "But I'm exactly where I should be."

"Good talk. Don't die. It'll cause me a headache of epic proportions if I have to deal with a death tonight."

With that, she's off and taking care of other things, and I'm heading over to see Bron.

Once Bron tells me everything I need to know, I wait.

And try not to pass out.

Because I'm nervous. Not the panic kind. The holy-shit-I'm-about-to-propose kind.

My hands are steady, but my heart is chaos. A little fear. A lot of hope. The wild, fizzy energy that comes with knowing exactly what you want and being brave enough to say it out loud.

This isn't performance adrenalin. It's not stage fright.

It's the feeling you get when you're about to hand your whole heart back to the man who never dropped it.

The night unfolds around me in a glittery blur. Dresses and speeches and applause. I stay behind the scenes, tucked away in a quiet corner near the stage entrance, listening. Waiting.

Every time Kristen walks past me, she squeezes my hand. And when we reach the end of the night and it's my turn to close the gala, she takes the mic to introduce me. All I can hope is that Gage didn't grow bored and leave early. But something tells me, his entire family have made sure he hasn't left.

Kristen's voice carries clear and bright, like she's been waiting all night to say these words. "We have one last surprise to end the evening. A performance by someone very dear to me. She's brilliant. She's brave. And she's here for something very special. Please welcome, Amelia Sinclair."

The room goes quiet. Then chatter ripples through the crowd as I step into the light.

I don't look at anyone at first.

Only at the piano.

But as I reach it—fingers grazing the wood, breath slow and steady—I let myself glance up.

And I see him.

He's standing at the back of the ballroom.

Frozen.

Like he's watching the moment he never dared hope for.

I lower myself onto the bench. And I speak into the mic, soft but clear.

"This piece is personal. It's for someone who once gave me silence and made it feel like love. I wrote it when I realized I didn't have to be fixed to choose forever."

Then I place my fingers on the keys.

And I play.

CHAPTER 34
GAGE

I CAN'T FUCKING BREATHE.

Not when she walks on stage.

Not when she says my name without saying it.

And when she sits at the piano and her fingers touch the keys, everything in me surges.

The ache.

The want.

The relief.

The fucking silence I've been choking on for three months.

I haven't heard her voice in weeks. Haven't touched her, haven't looked at her for longer than seconds without someone between us.

And now she's here.

The first few notes hit low. They're slow and deliberate. It's the kind of opening that tells you the song's not here to entertain you. It's here to say something.

She plays like she's not interested in being predictable.

Just when you think you've figured out the rhythm, she shifts it. Lands a note a breath earlier than you expect or holds it a second longer than she should.

It's not chaos. It's control.

She's telling me something with every change in timing.

You don't get to predict me.

You don't get to solve me.

You don't get to own my voice, even if you'd never try.

You just have to feel me. Stay with me. Listen to me.

And fuck, I do.

Every note feels like it's coming from a place I didn't know she'd let me see again.

It's not polite.

It's not careful.

It's *her*.

Raw. Complex. Still standing.

It's not defiance. It's agency.

She's *saying I'm still mine, even when I'm yours.*

And the way she plays—steady but alive, delicate but never small—it's the sound of someone who knows who she is now.

And that's the most beautiful fucking sound I've ever heard.

The final note lingers, just long enough to wreck me.

It's final. The breath before the song ends and everything changes.

She doesn't bow. Doesn't rush off. Doesn't look at anyone but me.

And when she stands, my fucking heart stutters.

Because I know.

She's walking toward me.

With every step she takes, the noise fades, the crowd blurs.

All I can see is her.

Her chin lifted. Her steady hands. Her eyes locked on mine.

And my whole body reacts.

My pulse feels like it's tearing through my skin.

My jaw tightens, trying to contain every goddamn emotion she's unleashing in me.

And my fists? Clenched at my sides, just to keep myself from reaching for her.

Because she's coming to me.

Not broken.

Not unsure.

She's decided.

And I don't know what she's going to say when she gets here, but I already know what my answer is.

Whatever it is, *yes*.

A thousand fucking times—yes.

She stops in front of me. And for the first time since I let her go, the world doesn't move. It waits. Held in the space between her inhale and my restraint.

There's no spotlight, no mic. Everyone might be watching us, but Amelia's only speaking to me when she says, "I hated every second of not being able to look at you."

My chest pulls tight.

"I didn't leave because you hurt me. I left because my body and mind kept reacting like I wasn't safe. Even when I knew I was. Even when you were right in front of me, doing everything right."

She pauses. Breathes. Doesn't look away.

"And I knew I had to work on that. Because if I didn't, I was going to ruin something I never wanted to lose."

Her gaze flickers, then holds.

"I thought that was why I left. I honestly did. But here's the real truth . . . I was scared of how much it felt like home. You. This. Us."

I don't move.

Because if I do, I'll fall apart.

"I wanted to stay."

Her voice cracks.

"And that terrified me."

The room is so fucking quiet I can hear the shift in her breath.

"But I'm not scared anymore."

I'm going to break. I fucking know it.

"You loved me when I couldn't love myself. You saw me when I didn't know how to be seen. You gave me space, and time, and safety, and you asked for nothing I wasn't ready to give."

Her throat bobs. Mine does too.

"You never asked me to choose. But I'm choosing now."

She steps closer.

So close I could touch her. But I don't.

"I know what the collar really means now. I want it back. Not because I'm yours—" She stops. Corrects herself. "Not *just* because I'm yours. But because I finally know how to be mine, too. And I want both."

I don't breathe. I just feel. And *fuck*, I feel everything.

"I'm not asking you to marry me, Gage. I'm telling you that I'm going to marry you." She swallows. "If you still want that. If you still want *me*."

Fuck me.

The woman I love just walked through fire to come back to me.

And I've never wanted anything more in my life than to give her the world, on whatever terms she fucking wants.

I can't wait another fucking second.

Three months was too long

Three *breaths* was too long.

Her face is in my hands before I even register moving.

I don't kiss her. Not yet.

I just hold her. Just look.

And I think—*mine*.

Every shattered, rebuilt, fire-forged part of her.

Mine.

My thumbs sweep her cheeks as her hands come to my shirt, and fuck *me*, I needed that.

"You put my collar back on, Princess, it's never fucking coming off again."

Her eyes search mine and a slow smile fills her face. "Is that a yes to marrying me?"

"Fuck," I growl, and I can't hold back. I claim her lips, rough, hungry, fucking ruined, and I kiss her like the starved fucking man I am. When I finally let her go, I say, "All I heard in that proposal was being bossed into marrying you." I bring my mouth to her ear. "So let me take you home and make you beg for a cock you already fucking own."

EPILOGUE

BREAKING: THE COLLAR IS BACK ON. And no, we're not talking about a fashion accessory. We're talking about *the* collar. @gageblack's collar on @ameliasinclair's neck. In public. At brunch. IN A PHOTO WITH THEIR KIDS. We're not okay. We are UNWELL. Swipe to see the softest, most unhingedly perfect family photo in existence. Amelia radiant and smug in that I-just-got-engaged-to-my-feral-billionaire glow. Gage looking like he would burn down the world for all three of his girls. Luna and Sarah grinning like they've been matchmaking this for MONTHS. And @shaylablack??? Sitting pretty, sipping champagne, *single and unbothered* after reportedly ending things with her movie producer fiancé (sources say she's "refo- cusing on her brand" and "not taking notes from any man who thinks NY Fashion Week is "too commercial" —drag him, queen.) Oh, and about that LA move she talked about? Gage was willing to co-parent coast-to-coast (father of the year energy) but she said plot twist and bought a new condo in NY instead. Luna wins. We all win. We stan healed adults. We're talking blended family excellence here. We stan a co-parenting queen. We bow to a blended family king. Also?? Gage Black's unproblematic zaddy era is in FULL BLOOM. Soft for his daughter. Obsessed with his fiancée. Respectful to his ex. Still terrifyingly hot and possibly dangerous. We love a morally grey menace turned emotionally available alpha. And the power he holds?? Amelia is FERAL-coded and we are living for it. Yes, wedding invites have NOT gone out yet. But one thing's for sure. Mrs. Black is coming. And we are not. emotionally. ready. We have been ruined by Gage Black and are in our "if my man doesn't give me a collar AND a private sex club room just for me, I don't want it" era. Because yes, the streets are talking. And that room? It's real. #gasp #CollarGate2025 #FeralForGage #CollaredAndUnwell #ThatNeckWasMadeForLuxuryRestraints #PowerCoupleButMakeItFerocious #ZaddyInTheStreetsDomInTheSheets

～

Thank you so much for reading Gage & Amelia's story.
I hope you loved it as much as I do!

Want more?
Scan the QR code to download their bonus epilogue!

The next book is...

Forever, Completely Yours

ACKNOWLEDGMENTS

Writing this book was a hard journey.

After possibly the most difficult life of my year, I finally dragged some words kicking and screaming out of me and put them to paper. And they've become my absolute favourite book I've ever written.

I am so damn proud of this book. And not just because of all the blood, sweat, and tears I put into it, or because I think it's a damn good story, but because of this:

It is my love letter to myself, and to the world.

Because it says the things I needed to hear.

Because it dares to imagine a world where love isn't about control.

Where men don't have to crush something beautiful to prove their power.

Where women get to be whole—complicated, messy, brilliant, fierce—and still be chosen. Not in spite of it. Because of it.

It's a story about what it looks like when a man loves a woman enough to see her clearly. To hold space for healing, not hijack it.

It dares to imagine a love that doesn't punish a woman for being powerful.

A love that doesn't require her to shrink or perform or soften her edges just to be worthy.

It's about a man who sees a woman in all her strength and complexity, and chooses to protect her, not possess her.

About a woman who is tired of being told she's too much, and finally decides she'll never be less again.

And honestly?
That shouldn't be revolutionary.

But look at the world right now.

It's giving patriarchy in full-blown panic.
And it's feminism fighting for its life.

This book is my scream into the void, at a world that keeps asking women to be less.

And it's my answer to that world: NO.

I listened to "Stupid Boy" by Keith Urban on repeat while writing Yours Until Forever. If you know this song, you'll know exactly how it shaped the story.

The world right now is giving "Stupid Boy" on repeat.

And still...
Women rise.
Women rebuild.
Women walk the fuck away and find their power anyway.

This book? It's for them.

For every woman who's been underestimated, silenced, controlled, or told she's too much or not enough.

And, it's for the men who are strong enough to love them without trying to shrink them.

Amelia is me.
And I think Amelia is, in many ways, a lot of women.

This is my love letter to us.
N xx

I'm sending big love and massive thanks out into the world to these people:

Jodie: always, my beautiful friend and best team member I have (IYKYK). No one, and I mean NO ONE has ever loved me like you do. You, my friend, taught me how to hold a person in the palm of my hand and cherish them. I couldn't have written either Amelia or Gage without having learned that from you. I am so lucky to call you my absolute best fucking friend of life. Every girl needs a Jodie in their life.

Rose: thank you, thank you, thank you for always putting up with my chaotic deadlines. I am so grateful to work with you.

Letitia: hoo boy this cover. And the next one. Actually, all of them. Holy shit, we've worked together now for TEN WHOLE YEARS. I adore working with you. Thank you.

To my readers: I hope you loved Gage and Amelia and all their wild friends and family as much as I loved writing them. I am spiritually handcuffed to this couple now. I've been writing for over ten years, and have created over thirty alpha heroes and heroines, and Gage & Amelia are hands down my faves. Solidly. Firmly. I'm actually not even sure how I'll come close to Gage ever again. (Side note: pray for me on that 'k?) So, I've written a bonus epilogue for them that is over 7k more words (6 chapters). Trust me. You need it in your life. But more than that, I've already started working on more bonus content for them. My obsession matches Gage's over Amelia. If you're on my email list, you'll get all of it for free. Thank you for reading this book. And if you talk to your friends about it, thank you. I am so grateful for you because you make it possible for me to still be doing what I love eleven years after starting.

To my bloggers, reviewers, influencers: thank you so much for reading and reviewing and sharing my books with the world. You have no idea just how grateful I am for you.

ALSO BY NINA LEVINE

Escape With a Billionaire Series
Ashton Scott
Jack Kingsley
Beckett Pearce
Jameson Fox
Owen North

Only Yours Series
(The Black Brothers Billionaire Romance)
Accidentally, Scandalously Yours
Yours Actually
Recklessly, Wildly Yours
Yours Until Forever

Storm MC Series
Storm (Storm MC #1)
Fierce (Storm MC #2)
Blaze (Storm MC #3)
Revive (Storm MC #4)

Slay (Storm MC #5)
Sassy Christmas (Storm MC #5.5)
Illusive (Storm MC #6)
Command (Storm MC #7)
Havoc (Storm MC #8)
Gunnar (Storm MC #9)
Wilder (Storm MC #10)
Colt (Storm MC #11)

Sydney Storm MC Series
Relent (#1)
Nitro's Torment (#2)
Devil's Vengeance (#3)
Hyde's Absolution (#4)
King's Wrath (#5)
King's Reign (#6)
King: The Epilogue (#7)

Storm MC Reloaded Series
Hurricane Hearts (#1)
War of Hearts (#2)
Christmas Hearts (#3)
Battle Hearts (#4)

The Hardy Family Series
Steal My Breath (single dad romance)

Crave Series
Be The One (rockstar romance)

www.ninalevineromance.com

ABOUT THE AUTHOR

Nina Levine is a *USA Today* and *Wall Street Journal* bestselling author of over thirty books, including the Escape With A Billionaire series and the bestselling Storm MC series. She's known for dominant alphas and heroines who don't hand their hearts over easily.

She lives in Australia and when she isn't creating with words, she's busy trying to be a Pilates goddess, a Peloton Queen, or drinking one too many gins with friends. Often though, she can be found curled up in the sun with coffee and a good book.

www.ninalevineromance.com

www.ingramcontent.com/pod-product-compliance
Lightning Source LLC
Chambersburg PA
CBHW010423170726
48283CB00011B/3035